Beautiful DEVIL

USA TODAY BESTSELLING AUTHOR
RACHEL LEIGH

For Prince Albert.
Thank you.

For Prince Albert.
Thank you.

BLURB

Two sports collide when a feisty sideline cheerleader meets her match in an arrogant hockey player who is more than just his bad boy reputation.

I fell for the wrong Devil...

Hayes Madden was never on my dance card. He's an egotistical jock who plays for the Devil's hockey team —not to mention, he's my boyfriend's biggest rival.

His sculpted abs and charm do nothing for me. Besides, I'm a cheerleader, not a puck bunny.

When a very graphic video of me and my ex is sent to the entire student roster at Rosewood-U, rumors quickly spread and, to my surprise, Hayes is my unlikely knight in shining armor.

Before long, I find myself falling for the hidden side of him he doesn't let anyone else see.

It's time for me to learn if this is all a strategic act of revenge against his nemesis, or if Hayes really is the beautiful devil I've fallen for.

"Sometimes we fall in love with the most unexpected person at the most unexpected time."

PLAYLIST
CLICK HERE TO LISTEN
https://spoti.fi/3TlcnbA

Down Bad by Taylor Swift
Hurtless by Dean Lewis
I Miss the Misery by Halestorm
Stay by Rihanna & Milky Ekko
Fade Into You by Mazzy Star
Trustfall by Miles
Unsteady by X Ambassadors
I Can Do It With A Broken Heart by Taylor Swift
Live Before I'm Dead by From Ashes to New
Homesick by Lexi Jayne
Feels Like I'm Falling In Love by Coldplay
Love Me Like You Do by Ellie Goulding
Circles by Post Malone
Something Just Like This by The Chainsmokers
I Love it When it Rains by Loveless
Hangfire by Wind Walkers
Blinding lights by X Ambassadors
Birds of a Feather by Billie Eilish
Angels Fall by Breaking Benjamin
Hold Me Now by Caskets
Washed Away by Savage Hands

CHECK OUT THE PINTEREST BOARD

PROLOGUE

BROGAN

"Brogan! You just killed five people! What the hell?"

I shrug, raising my hands on either side of me as I look over at my new friend and teammate, Jared. "Whoops."

Staring at the blood pooling under the bodies, I tilt my head. "Isn't that the whole point, though?"

"Not if they were all on your team," Jared deadpans.

I laugh, tossing the controller to the floor as I get out of the large beanbag chair. "I don't think I was made to be a video game girl."

Jared chuckles as he shuts off the console. "Yeah, maybe just stick to cheer."

Lucia comes running into the room looking perfect as ever. "Come on, we're going to be late for the party!"

Glancing in the mirror in Jared's room, I fluff up my hair and adjust my dress. This still doesn't feel real. My nerves begin to get the better of me and there's a small part of me that wants to chicken out. After a grueling week of cheer camp and tryouts, all three of us made the team, so tonight we are going out to celebrate.

"You good?" Jared asks as I continue to stare at my reflection.

I nod, but he must not believe me because the next thing I know, he's handing me a small glass filled with clear liquid.

"To an unforgettable year at Rosewood U."

He and Lucia down their drinks and I follow suit, welcoming the burn of the cheap vodka as it slides down my throat.

An hour and two shots of courage later, we're all looking hot as hell as we stroll up to the Kappa Rho frat house, the notorious party hub on campus. Standing tall at the end of the long tree-lined driveway is a large white colonial house that makes the actual White House look subpar. There are people everywhere. And I mean *everywhere*. I've never attended a party this big, and it's hard not to feel like a small fish in a big pond.

The perk of going somewhere that's littered with this many people is that it's so easy to blend in. At least, that's my hope.

Back home, I lived for parties. I was a social butterfly who enjoyed spreading her wings and meeting new people, but this is a lot to take in, even with my high-ranking social status.

My clothing options were limited since I didn't pack much for cheer camp, but I did bring a sexy little black dress that hugs my curves and exposes my cleavage. It's sleek and slutty and just my style. I'm not actually a slut, but I'm also not the type of girl who hides what God gave me. Some judge me—others praise me for my confidence.

I fluff my long blonde hair again, framing a few strands around my face before taking a calming breath. It's slightly intimidating walking into a party when you don't know anyone except the two people you're showing up with.

Lucia and I stick close to Jared as he offers up high fives to practically every person we walk by. I'm actually surprised he's so well-known, considering he's only coming up on his second year here. He has a magnetic personality, though, so I should have expected it. It's probably why he got picked for the cheer team; his smile and energy are hard to beat.

"Let's get you ladies a drink," Jared says as he leads us into a kitchen packed with even more people. If I had to guess, there are at least two hundred people at this party.

Jared and Lucia are both entering their second year at Rose-wood U, and I actually just met them during cheer camp. We clicked immediately, and now we'll be cheering for the Devils' football team together this fall.

Lucia and I follow behind Jared like two little ducks, passing by so many good-looking men it's hard not to get caught drooling. Freshman year at Rosewood U is already fixing to be a good time and it's still a few months away.

"Damn." My head turns to follow what might be one of the hottest guys I've ever laid eyes on. That was no boy, he's a grown-ass man.

"Wild, right?" Lucia says as she rubs some pink gloss across her bottom lip.

"Totally. But in the best way," I retort as I reach for a cup beside the keg. Another hand reaches at the same time and calloused fingers brush against my soft ones. I look down and see the rugged hands of a man. When my eyes slide up, I find a pair staring right back at me.

Unable to break my gaze, I stand there silently dumb-founded. It's like I've been put under a spell by his mesmerizing stare. I can't even begin to guess what color his eyes are. They're this strange blend of captivating hues. The inner circle is a deep brown, surrounded by emerald green, which fades into ocean blue before ending with a thin ring of black. It's like looking into a kaleidoscope.

I'd like to think that the shock of a new place and new people is what has me staring sheepishly, but I can't help myself. High school boys just do not compare to the man in front of me. Which is why I helplessly drink up every inch of him. It's not just his eyes, but his body too.

Okay. I lied about the last guy my eyes magnetized to. This man right here has to be *the* hottest guy I've ever laid eyes on. Dark hair with frosted tips, sun-kissed skin, and muscles for days. His pouty lips and chiseled jaw are the icing on the cake.

The audible huff that climbs up his throat throws me completely off guard and the next thing I know, the guy is pushing my hand out of the way and snatching the cup from me.

"That was rude," I mumble under my breath.

Obviously annoyed, he snares the keg nozzle. His eyes lift as he fills his cup. "Look, if you wanna undress me with your eyes, you can do it in my bedroom since you're that interested."

Heat rises in my cheeks as an unhumorous laugh escapes me. "You've got to be kidding me right now. Undressing you with my eyes?"

"Are you denying it?" He tosses the keg nozzle at my chest and I grab it before it falls.

I mean, I was, but who even says that? And I would never admit it. Especially now that I know what a complete and utter asshole he is.

"In your dreams," I snarl.

"Unfortunately for you, my dreams aren't filled with women who like to waste my time."

All right, forget everything I just said. He's not the hottest guy I've ever laid eyes on. His appeal was lost when he opened his mouth to speak.

"Your ego is far too big for your head." I aggressively begin filling my own cup, cutting off eye contact so that I'm no longer tempted to look at the godlike body in front of me that holds the personality of a rotten potato.

He must not give a shit that I'm choosing to ignore him, though, because Mr. Asshole here has the audacity to press two fingers to my cup, tilting it slightly to the left. "Such an amateur," he tsks. "Less foam if you hold your cup like that."

He walks away with his shoulders taut as he sips on his beer.

"Don't take it personal," Jared says as he comes up behind me. "Hayes doesn't like anyone."

"That's blatantly obvious. What a fucking jerk." My eyes roll to find, who I take to be, Hayes, pushing his way aggressively through the crowd.

Hayes flashes a quick glance at me over his shoulder and I

hate the way my heart flutters. That right there is the kind of asshole I usually fall for. There's something flattering about being the only one to get the sweet side of a bitter man. Something in my gut tells me there is nothing more to Hayes than what he just showed me. An egotistical guy who knows he's good-looking and uses it to his advantage.

I can tell by the scathing glare he's pegging me with right now as he stands with his back against the wall and his foot kicked up behind him—he's ruthless, and there isn't an ounce of shame in his veins.

"What's his story?" I ask Jared, feeling curious for reasons unbeknownst to myself.

Jared hesitates a moment before saying, "Just another asshole who treats people like shit and gets away with it. Heed my warning," Jared continues. "Hayes Madden is a player. He cares about no one and nothing but himself."

"Sounds like you know him pretty well?"

"I know enough, and he isn't worth another thought." Jared looks toward the wall, watching Hayes with anger burning in his eyes. It's not a look I'm used to seeing on Jared, and it makes me even more wary than I was before. "Hayes has a reputation at Rosewood U. Just stay out of his way and you'll be fine."

"Stay out of his way and I'll be fine?" I laugh. "I'm not scared of Hayes, if that's what you think."

Jared shrugs, taking a long pull of his beer like he's trying to distract himself. "Like I said, he's not worth another thought."

"I'm not thinking about him." I grin mischievously, scanning my eyes over all the other perfectly good eye candy in the room.

I feel his gaze scrutinizing me, looking for any hint that I might be lying.

I smack him playfully on the arm. "I'm not! There are plenty of other guys here to captivate my thoughts."

"I believe you," he says with a sarcastic bite. Jared tosses an arm around my shoulders and leads me out of the kitchen. "Now, where'd our girl run off to?"

I look around the crowded space in search of Lucia, but she's nowhere in sight. "I'm not sure. Should we try and find her?"

"Nah." He shakes his head before downing the rest of his beer. "She'll appear at some point or another."

The sound of chanting rings in my ears and I move closer to the noise, taking Jared along with me. "Is that…" My words trail off as I approach a closed door. Leaning into it, I push my ear to the hard surface. I shoot a thumb to my right. "Do they have the Lions game on down there?"

Jared's shoulders rise then fall. "Maybe."

Without a second thought, I turn the handle on the door and pull it open. "I'll be down here if you need me." I take the first step but pause and look over my shoulder. "Keep an eye out for Lucia, okay?"

Taking Jared's advice, I don't give Hayes another thought. *And that thought didn't count.*

Three beers and a couple shots later, I'm standing with a group of guys, rooting for the Detroit Lions in front of a big-screen TV in the basement. Seems I'm the only one because the majority of them are hoping the Broncos pull out a win.

I've been a Lions fan since I was a toddler. Some of my favorite memories are of my dad and me watching the game. He lived in Michigan most of his life and was born a Lions fan, and because of that, I was, too.

I'm on the edge of my seat—which says a lot considering I'm standing. The quarterback makes a play action to the receiver. He loads up and… *Oh fuck,* he's faking the pass. Another receiver is streaking down the sideline and he's got it!

Go! Go! Go!

"Fuck yes!" I shout as the receiver catches the pass and walks the ball into the end zone. My hands flail in the air. "That's it. Game over. We win! Talk shit now," I howl to the guys around me, who are pacifying their burnt egos with their heads hung low.

"It's their first win of the season. Pure luck. No skill," a guy beside me says. "If you wanna see real talent, watch a hockey game. That's where the excitement is."

"Keep telling yourself that," I bark back. It's not until I look at him that I realize it's none other than Hayes *fucking* Madden. "Ugh," I groan. "It's you."

"In the flesh," he croons, waving his arms out to the sides as if he's someone exceptional. "What's your deal anyway? A couple hours ago you were imagining me naked, and now you're disgusted by my presence."

"A couple hours ago I didn't know you were a complete asshole. Don't worry, though, you opened your mouth and spoke and the spell shattered before my eyes."

He turns to face me, arms crossed over his tight shirt that exposes the outline of his rigid abs. *Stop it, Brogan.* He's not a midnight snack—he's a cocksure jerk.

"So you admit it?"

"Admit what?" I huff.

He grins, assessing me. "That you were imagining me naked."

Thanks a lot, asshole. Now that he mentioned it, I am imagining him naked. It's like telling someone not to look at the person directly behind you. You *have* to look.

I observe the sleeve of tattoos on his arm and in my imagination, he has more on his pectoral muscles—possibly even his side. My gaze drops to his lower half and I can't help but wonder if he's a shower or a grower because that bulge…

My train of thought is interrupted at the sound of him clearing his throat.

"Damn," he drawls. "You're doing it again, aren't you?"

I might actually think he was joking if it weren't for the lack of humor on his face. Not a single twitch of the lips.

He is *far* too pleased with himself right now.

I narrow my eyes. "How you were gifted a body like that with a shit personality I will never understand."

"Look," he begins, clearly stuck more on the fact that I admitted he was attractive and not that his persona makes my skin crawl. "Let's just call it like it is and get this over with so we can both move on with our lives. You're hot. I'm hot. There's obviously some sexual tension burning between us. So we might as well—"

I hold up a hand. "Please stop before you embarrass yourself further. The only thing between us is animosity. In fact, I don't even know why I'm still talking to you." I take a step back and lift my shoulders. "Have a nice life, Hayes."

"Whoa, whoa, whoa." His hand lands on my shoulder, stopping me. "How do you know my name?"

My gaze remains fixed on the empty wall in front of me. I blink rapidly as responses fumble around in my head.

If I tell him someone told me, he'll think I was asking about him. His already enormous ego might actually cause his head to explode. I tilt my head slightly to the left, not bothering to turn and face him as I respond. "I…I heard someone say it."

"Who?" he quips.

I lift my shoulders. "I dunno. Someone. God, you're so desperate." I take another step toward the staircase, but once again, I'm stopped. This time, with his body right in front of mine.

His eyebrows cave as he examines me, and the longer I look at his skeptical glare, the more heated I get.

"Go. Away!" I grit out. It's moments like this that I hate myself and the pull I have to guys like him. It's like my pussy is screaming *we can fix him* while my brain tells me to run away.

"If you know my name, it's only fair that I know yours, too." He reaches out, taking a strand of my blonde hair and wrapping it around his finger.

A puff of air flares my nostrils. "No, it's not." I smack his hand away, trying to move around him. He steps to the side, blocking me *again*.

"Must be hideous if you're not willing to share."

I roll my eyes and spit out the first name that pops in my head because I don't want this jerk knowing a single thing about me. "Anna."

His tongue clicks on the roof of his mouth. "Anna, huh? You don't look like an Anna."

Popping my hip up, I press my hand firmly to my side. "How so?"

"Anna is such a sweet name. Something tells me you're not a sweet girl."

I give him a piercing stare, resisting the urge to push him out of my way. He's right, though, I'm not a sweet girl. I stand up for myself and Hayes Madden is no exception. "Either tell me what you want or get the hell out of my way."

"You didn't let me finish what I was saying. You just took the compliment I gave you and ran."

"Compliment? When did you compliment me?" I sputter.

"I said you were hot." This time, he rakes his eyes down my body and his intense gaze makes me feel like my dress is no longer on.

"You also said *you* were hot."

He shrugs, stepping closer so that we're hardly an inch apart. "Is self-confidence unattractive to you?"

"No," I stammer. "But arrogance is."

"Anyways, *Anna*." He puts extra emphasis on the fake name I gave him. "I was saying, we need to just get this over with."

I can't help the laugh that rumbles up my throat. "Get this over with? Are you insinuating…no." I stop myself because it's absurd. "I can't even say it because it's *not* happening."

"Does the word fuck make you nervous?" His tone is teasing, but I'm so riled up I could smack him across his cocksure face.

My mouth forms a perfect O. "Wow. You really are something else." Shaking my head, I turn to walk away, *once again*, but I'm halted, *once again*. Only this time, Hayes wraps one of his large hands around my waist and pulls me back into him.

I shouldn't be turned on by his forwardness, but for some fucked-up reason, I am. Why am I attracted to guys like this? And *whyyyy* in God's name is there this sick part of my brain that thinks I can bandage their emotional wounds and fix their broken parts?

All the alcohol I had must be going straight to my head because instead of running forward, I'm moving backward—straight backward until my backside is flush with his chest. Hayes wraps an arm around my shoulder from behind and pinches my chin as he tugs my head back. I peer up at him, a good six inches, I'm guessing, because I'm only five-foot-four and he has to be six-foot tall.

"So, how do you wanna do this?" he whispers with a rasp in his voice.

"If I have to explain it to you, you shouldn't be doing it."

He chuckles, a deep rumble in his chest that has me clenching my thighs. "You've got quite the mouth on you, Legs."

Did he really just peg me with a nickname?

My cheeks flush with heat. Hell, my whole body flushes with heat. "Legs, huh?"

"That's right. Since you won't tell me your real name, I'll just give you one. Because I'm about two seconds away from thrusting myself between those perfect legs."

"Ah. So you do know what you're doing?" I quip.

He tugs my head back farther, this time much more aggressively, and my body is literally burning with desire. "I'll let you be the one to decide that."

I'm lost in his sultry eyes when he suddenly pulls me into a bedroom—a very messy bedroom. There's a small table lamp on a nightstand beside the bed and clothes scattered all over. "Are we allowed to be in here?"

Hayes trails hot, eager kisses down my neck, over my collarbone, and down to my shoulder. With one hand, he unzips the back of my dress, and it falls softly around my ankles. I take two small steps out of it, feeling exposed as his hungry mouth moves lower and lower down my body while he unclasps my bra.

Before this can go any further, I ask the question that's heavy on my mind. "You're clean, right?" I hate being a mood killer and I really don't want to embarrass Hayes, but I know I am, so I need to know he is.

He doesn't even seem fazed as he reaches his hand out, slaps it around on the top of his dresser and brings a paper between us. I take one glance at it, pleased with the results, then I toss it in the air. I assumed we were in a random member's room, but a random person wouldn't have Hayes's test results on their dresser. "So this is your room?" I ask, officially ruining the moment.

"Sure is." He nonchalantly unclasps the button on his worn black jeans, revealing a hint of his black boxer briefs.

So Hayes is a frat boy. I don't know much about fraternities, but from what I've heard, the guys in them don't have the best reputations, especially when it comes to commitment and relationships. Not that I'm looking for that with Hayes. *God no.* I already regret having sex with him and we haven't even done it yet.

I should walk out of this room right now, but I'm a glutton for bad decisions and the second Hayes drops to his knees, I relish in the way his calloused hands feel against my skin.

He grips the waistband of my satin panties and he slowly pulls them down my hips. I lift one foot and then the other as he takes them off. The cool air hits my bare skin and goosebumps erupt on my body.

His lips kiss up my thighs teasingly before he stands. Peeling his shirt off, he tosses it with the rest of the scattered clothes on his floor. I nearly gasp when he removes his pants and briefs confidently. As he should be because holy fuck he is hung like a damn horse and to top it off, he's got a piercing.

Why am I surprised here? Hayes is definitely the kind of man that would pierce his dick. Suddenly, my nerves get the best of me and I look at him with panic in my eyes. I've never seen one of these piercings before and now I'm about to feel it inside me.

"Don't worry, Legs." He presses two fingers to my chin, closing my hung mouth. "We'll make it fit." He winks and my mouth falls right back open.

I don't even care that he knows I'm stunned—or speechless, really. *My God, he is well-endowed. And beautiful.* And I was right, his chest muscles are tattooed. There's a sprawling tree with branches that spread across his flesh. Surrounding the branches are various objects—a hummingbird, a stopwatch, a menacing skull. I bet each one tells its own story, which only adds to the mystery of this arrogant man.

He walks me back until my legs hit the bed. Leaning back, I crawl onto the mattress as he stares down at me. His eyes go up and down my legs with appreciation before he bites his lip. Reaching out, he trails his fingers down my chest to my abdomen before they reach my dripping center.

Should I be embarrassed by how wet his arrogance makes me? *Definitely.* Am I? *Not even a little.*

Spreading my legs for him, he groans before pushing two strong fingers inside me.

I curl my back, forcing pressure against his hand while he remains standing beside the bed. His defined muscles glisten with sweat and the veins in his forearm flex with each thrust of his hand.

His gaze is stuck between my legs while I hungrily drink him in and sink into the pleasure he gives. And my God does it feel good. I savor every second, anxiously awaiting his girthy eight— maybe nine—inch cock to be inside me.

Hayes moves his fingers with precise expertise, finding the spot that has me clenching my walls. I inhale a deep breath, filling my lungs with his intoxicating scent of cedar and bergamot.

The pad of his thumb presses against my clit with just the right amount of pressure and a soft moan slips through my lips. As he continues pumping his fingers deep inside me, my sounds grow louder and more urgent.

A guttural whimper escapes me when he abruptly pulls out his fingers and crawls on top of me.

"Don't worry, Legs. I'm going to fill this pussy up."

Fortunately, I'm on birth control because he forcefully shoves his bare cock inside me.

I grab onto his shoulders, my nails digging into his flesh. A sharp jolt of pleasure shoots through me as I feel the stretch. It burns as much as it feels good, making me press my heels into his ass to encourage him further.

The coolness of his metal piercing presses against my G-spot with each thrust and there's no doubt I can feel his length under my belly button.

This man is not only blessed with a huge cock, turns out he's skilled with it, too.

Sweeping up one of my legs, he leans into me while bringing my knee to my shoulder. He tilts slightly to the left as he pulls out, only to fill me right back up.

I gasp, lifting my eyes to find his beautiful crazy ones staring back at me. For a brief moment, I see something deeper than I think he wants me to see and I reach my palm to cup his cheek. It's like our souls connect and I roll my hips to meet his thrust.

Hayes falters for a second as we connect on a level I don't think he is ready to connect on. Clenching his jaw, he places a hand beside my head before lowering his body over me and breaking our eye contact. His hot breath tickles my neck, before he bites down and I cry out. He pounds into me, almost like a punishment for making him feel something he didn't want to feel.

My mouth falls agape, chest rising and falling against him as he takes me back to the brink of release.

"Oh, God," I cry out.

Every nerve in my body ignites and my arms instinctively wrap around him, nails digging into his back, leaving marks. Our bodies move in sync and the sounds of our pleasure mingle in the air as we both find our climax together.

He pulses inside me, prolonging my release even more. My legs are shaking when he finally stills, my chest heaving.

As I lie there in a daze, Hayes urgently pulls out of me and rolls his naked body off of mine before sinking into the mattress beside me.

My labored breaths slowly return to normal and when I turn my head with a smile, I notice Hayes looking at me with a blank stare. His eyes quickly snap to the ceiling.

"So, umm…" He scratches his head, avoiding any further eye contact. "I've gotta get up early in the morning and I should probably get some shut-eye."

There's a huge party happening right on the other side of the door and he's seriously going to bed?

Then it hits me. *No fucking way.*

My body shoots upright, taking the flat sheet covering my breasts along with me. "Wait. Are you kicking me out before your dick even has time to dry?"

Shame, regret, remorse, anger—every damn emotion I hate shoots through me. *He just played me like a fucking fiddle.* Jared warned me. Told me not to give him a second thought. But what did I do? I climbed right into his bed and for two whole seconds I let him in.

Hayes's expression twists as he strokes the stubble on his chin. "Ya know, when you put it like that it makes me sound like a complete asshole." He pauses for a beat. "But yeah. I guess I am." He makes this annoying clicking sound with his cheek and it's taking everything in me not to lay my fist on said cheek right this very second.

"Oh my. *God!* You truly are an asshole!" I jump off the bed, letting the sheet fall so I can get dressed as quickly as possible and get the hell out of here.

"In my defense, I never denied it." He scoots up and leans his back against the headboard, hands folded behind his head.

"Stop looking at me!" I snap as I kick up random articles of clothing strewn across the bedroom floor, searching desperately for my own. As I lift my foot to take another step, I realize something is caught on my toe. I glance down and see a lacy red thong—that is not mine—dangling from my foot. "Disgusting!" I spit out as I quickly kick it off.

I catch Hayes still looking at me from the corner of my eye and…*fuck it.* I swing my hand back and pinch the flesh of his cheek between my fingers. "I said stop looking at me!"

For the first time ever, he smiles. He actually fucking *smiles.* Which pushes my last button.

When I finally find my bra and dress, I throw it on quickly, not giving a damn that I'm leaving my panties behind.

This must be a pattern with him.

Jared said he was a player and I didn't listen. Except, when he looked down at me with emotion in his eyes, he didn't feel like a player. For a second, I thought maybe this could be more than a one-night stand.

Calmly, I walk to the door and steel my spine. "This actually works out better," I say, turning back to him. "If I had stayed any longer, it would have been a waste of *my* time."

His brows pinch before his face falls just enough that I notice. *Check mate, Hayes Madden. You messed with the wrong girl.*

"Can't have that," he says without any bite.

"Goodbye, Hayes Madden. I truly hope I never see you again."

As soon as I'm out the door, I head for the stairs. Once I'm out of that suffocating basement, I search haphazardly for Jared or Lucia. There's not a chance in hell I'll tell them what just happened, but I need to get out of this damn house.

I'm officially swearing off asshole men. I don't care how attractive their bad boy personas are. The next guy I go for will be one of the good ones.

Still scouring each room for them, my body collides with another when I turn down a hall and my head ricochets off the wall. "Ouch," I shriek as I rub the sore spot.

When I look up, I find a dark-haired, blue-eyed angel of a man staring back at me. He's wearing a Devils football jersey, which leads me to believe he plays ball for Rosewood U.

With his hands on either side of my shoulders, he looks down at me, genuinely concerned. "I'm so sorry. Are you okay?"

I'm shuffled over to a nearby chair as he kneels beside me. "Do you need water or anything?"

Aggressively sweeping away a damp spot under my eyes, I shake my head. "I'm good. At least, I am now."

A minute or so passes of him watching me for any sign of traumatic injury. When in reality, I really am fine. Aside from the weight of regret and shame on my shoulders after having sex with Hayes, I'm physically fine.

The cute guy smiles. "What do you say we get out of here? There's an ice cream shop that stays open late a short walk away. You look like you could use some ice cream."

Now, listen. I swear I'm not a slut. I'm really not, and I have no intention of having sex with this guy, or any other guys for a very long time. But this has to be fate. Seconds ago, I swore off assholes and now Prince Charming is right in front of me.

"Ice cream sounds perfect," I say, and he helps me to my feet.

"Great." He smiles, showing off his perfect white teeth. "Oh, I'm Kamden Donnelly, by the way." He extends his hand to me.

I lay my hand in his palm and literally feel the electricity sizzling between us. "Brogan," I say with a flirtatious grin. "Brogan Astor."

CHAPTER 1

BROGAN

SITTING cross-legged on my twin bed in my cramped dorm room, I prop my phone up with a stack of textbooks and tap the call button, anxious to see my *now* boyfriend before his game this afternoon.

Kamden and I started talking when we met this past spring after cheer camp. It just so happens, he plays for the Devils' football team. After instantaneous sparks flew between us, I knew I had to explore this.

Three weeks ago, we made our relationship official. Things are going...*okay.*

It sounds bad when I put it that way, but things really are just *okay.* So far, our story hasn't been one of epic love. For a while I thought maybe it could be. When we first began talking, it was exciting. I would watch my phone for his call then stay up all night talking to him.

For some reason, once the space between us closed and we could finally be together physically, it was different than I expected. Don't get me wrong, I'm crazy about Kamden. I'm just not sure I'll ever be crazy in love with him. Our priorities don't line up, and he's more of a guys' guy than boyfriend material.

It's possible I'm just too needy, but I'm not so sure that's the problem. Let's just say, Kamden talks the talk, but he doesn't walk the walk. He makes a lot of promises with very little follow-through.

Over these past couple days, he feels further away than he did when we were living on opposite sides of the state. Not to mention, I'm an open book while he is a tightly closed one. Even after the endless phone calls and all the time we spent talking, I still feel like I know nothing about him. He doesn't even talk about his family. All I know is, his parents are still married. His dad is strict as hell and a Rosewood U alumnus who owns Madd Tech, and he has a brother he doesn't talk to, or about. I'm pretty sure he told me all of that in one breath when he was drunk and he hasn't opened up about his personal life any more since.

Kamden's gorgeous face appears on the screen, big blue eyes and a wide smile that mirrors mine. He really is what wet dreams are made of. Not only is he said to be the best receiver Rosewood U has ever seen, he might even take the cake for best-looking. Dark hair, blue eyes, tanned skin, and muscles for days. I can't deny I am heavily—maybe even insanely—attracted to him.

I wish I could put my finger on what's lacking between us because more than anything, I want this to work.

"Hey, baby," he says as he stands in his dorm room. "I was just thinking about you."

My heart swells. Kamden really can be so sweet and it's moments like this I feel guilty for even doubting what we have.

"I've been thinking about you, too," I tell him. "I just wish I could see you in person before the game."

"Me, too." His words come out in short gasps, punctuated by heavy breaths.

Why does he look like he's on the verge of an orgasm, as we speak?

"What are you doing, baby?" I ask with a chuckle, though I suspect I already know what he's doing. His shirt is off and his arm muscles tighten each time he lets out a long breath.

Kamden angles his phone downward, revealing his fist

clenched around his erect cock. Turns out my suspicions are correct.

Wow. Now that is a sight for sore eyes.

He bites the corner of his lip and my insides quiver. "Told you I was thinking about you."

"And what exactly were you imagining when you were thinking about me?" Excitement bubbles in my chest as I wait for his response with bated breath.

He points the phone downward again, showing me as he pumps his cock. "I can't stop thinking about how it would feel to be inside your tight, wet pussy."

I sink into the soft pillows that are propped against my headboard and hastily take off my shorts. My legs bend at the knees so I can join him in this little pregame quickie. "You've got me thinking the same thing."

He growls, "Fuck, baby. Are you touching yourself for me?"

"Mmhmm," I hum. My fingers graze over my stomach before tracing between my slick folds. A wave of need crashes through me. I arch my back and roll my hips, massaging my swollen clit in slow, deliberate circles.

"How's it feel?" Kamden asks.

"Feels good." A soft moan slips through my lips as I increase the pressure. My body tenses and relaxes as a sweet release builds inside me.

"Show me," he demands, his voice raspy and thick. "I wanna watch when you come."

With my phone now in my hand, I stretch my arm out and let him watch as I bring myself to the brink of an orgasm. I stare at his face—the corded veins in his neck flexed and his mouth agape as a grunt slips out of his perfect parted lips.

My fingers move faster, the heat between my thighs intensifying. "Kamden," I moan before pursing my lips and breathing heavily through my nose.

"Fuck, Brogan," he grunts, and the sound of my name rolling out of his mouth sends me over the edge.

Hot lava rushes through my veins. Clenching my thighs, I

buck my hips and let my orgasm take over. "I'm coming," I cry out. The sound of my pleasure echoing in the room around me.

I watch intently as Kamden's body tenses and his release shoots from the tip of his throbbing cock onto a towel on his bed. My body trembles as electricity shoots through my core.

My muscles feel like melted butter as I relax onto the bed and close my eyes, basking in the afterglow of orgasmic bliss.

Kamden lets out a contented sigh. "That was sexy as fuck, baby."

"It sure was." I grin. "I sort of miss this."

Back when there were miles between us, Kamden and I would have video sex at least twice a week. Now, it's few and far between since we have each other at our disposal. Well, for the most part anyway. Lately, Kamden's been busy with football, and I've been busy with cheer. But once the season ends, things will get better. At least, that's what I keep telling myself.

"I gotta go," he says hastily as he shuffles around in his room. "See ya later, 'kay?"

"Of course you will." I blow him a kiss. "Good luck today and I'll see you…"

My words fade when the call drops. I shake my head in annoyance. "…at Piggy's after the game," I mutter to myself.

A second later, a text message from Kamden pops up on my phone and my smile immediately returns. That is until the video he sent finishes loading and I realize he recorded our video chat and just sent it to me.

Me: You recorded us?

Kamden: Sexy as fuck, huh? Save it for a rainy day. Might come in handy ;)

As much as I want to lash out at him, I can't be angry. We do look pretty hot in the video.

My eyes catch the time on my phone and my heart jumps into my throat.

Fuck! I have to be at the stadium in twenty minutes!

CHAPTER 2

BROGAN

We're in the final stretch of the game. I look out at the thousands of fans in the stadium as I cheer. "Let's go Devils. Let's go. Let's go Devils. Let's go." Various shades of blood orange and black paint the crowd as they chant along with us—their voices raw with emotion as they manifest our victory over the Eagles.

A sense of urgency hangs in the air as the timer runs out. Our team is down 21–24, but it's our ball and we're practically in the end zone. There's no doubt we can still snag this win.

With my pom-poms in my hands, I shout our cheer at the top of my lungs. We work the crowd, pumping them up as the play begins, but when it does and the stands fall silent, we cheerleaders do the same.

Catch it, Kamden!

You've got this. Go, baby, go!

Oh, fuck.

My heart splinters. That's the game.

This loss is a tough one.

Cheerleading is its own sport and my focus should be on the fans and not the game, but it's hard when my boyfriend is the one who just missed the winning pass in the end zone. This was their last chance, the final play.

The clock runs out and my eyes stay locked on the dwindling time. When the final buzzer sounds, a collective sigh erupts from the stands, washing over us all like a sharp gust of wind.

It's our first loss of the season and the road to undefeated victory has come to a brutal end. Defeat hangs heavily over us and the look of sheer disappointment on the faces of my teammates mirrors mine.

"We'll get 'em next time," Gabby, our cheer captain, says in an attempt to boost our spirits. She picks up her pom-poms and makes her way to the row of benches in front of the fence. I'm certain Gabby feels that same gut-wrenching agony in the pit of her stomach that I feel.

My boyfriend Kamden is her ex and she's still grossly obsessed with him. My distaste for her aside, I know she cares and the pain in Kamden's eyes was heartbreaking for anyone who witnessed it. Which would be the thousands of people watching the game.

After taking a few pictures with fans, we make our way inside to the locker room. Defeat clouds us all as we change out of our uniforms, preparing to go on with our day. The majority of the team goes to Piggy's Pub after the home games. It's one of the few places in Rosewood where they don't check IDs, so naturally, it's where most of the students hang out. Although half of our crew is old enough to drink, the other half is not—me included.

I change out of my uniform into a jean miniskirt and burnt orange crop top, paired with a pair of black over-the-knee boots. My blonde hair, still damp from sweat after the intense game, somehow held its curls, so I give them a nice fluff, touch up my makeup, and head outside with Lucia and Jared to wait for our ride to Piggy's.

An hour later, I'm sitting in a booth with a half-full glass of blackberry mojito in front of me. My shoe taps relentlessly against the floor underneath the table as I anxiously await Kamden's arrival.

Avery, who is sitting beside me, slaps a hand to my knee. "Would you stop that? He'll be here."

Avery isn't on the cheer team, but when I'm not on the sidelines, we're always together. Two years ago, when my mom uprooted my sisters and I to a new town, I was walking around the corner in the hall at my new high school when I collided with a five-foot-eight bombshell who looked like she just stepped out of a fashion magazine.

Wavy brunette hair that hangs down to her tailbone, soft honey eyes, and cheekbones that nearly touch her eyelids when she smiles. She was a little intimidating at first, but I quickly learned she's the sweetest person ever. After helping me pick up all the papers that fell out of my binder, we realized we were heading to the same class, so we walked together. We've been inseparable ever since.

I rub my lips together, smoothing my sticky gloss. My eyes remain pinned to the door, and when it swings open, they widen with hope. Another group of football players saunter in, Kamden's best friend Jeremiah included. But Kamden has yet to arrive.

"I don't think so, Ave," I say with a sigh. "I know he's beating himself up hard over this one. I bet the last thing he wants is to face all of these people who are wondering how he could have missed the winning pass."

Jeremiah and the four guys he came in with crowd around the round table where the rest of the team is sitting.

I bump my shoulder against Avery's and inch my ass toward her. "Lemme out. I need to talk to Jeremiah."

"Ugh," she grumbles as she slides out of the booth. "You're so impatient."

Avery doesn't understand. She's never competed a day in her life. Unless you count credit card limits. Sure, she was a spectator at the game, but she doesn't realize how much pressure athletes put on themselves to perform well.

To her, sports are just hobbies. Her family is filthy rich, so she doesn't have to work for anything, and she doesn't have an athletic bone in her body. The only reason she's attending Rose-wood U is because her father demanded she get a degree. He doesn't care what she studies as long as she studies something.

"Are you ready for another?" Lucia asks, pointing to my half-full glass from across the table as I slide out.

I shrug my shoulders and grab my glass. "Sure. Why not."

The *only* perk of not having a car at Rosewood U is not having to drive anywhere. I'm well-versed in the bus schedule on campus and an Uber is just a tap away when we're out.

With my drink in hand, I make my way through the crowd that's suddenly gathered. Naturally, the majority of flaunters are women. I swear they sniff out the sweat on these men anytime they're in public.

Jeremiah stands with his back to me, so I approach him from behind, glancing at the girl he's talking to. She's got jet-black hair set in perfect curls and she's twirling a lock around her finger. I've never seen her before, but by the mean mug she's throwing at me, I'd guess I'm interrupting something. None-theless, I tap him on the shoulder, stealing his attention.

His dark chocolate eyes, coated in frustration, snap to mine.

Oh yeah. About Jeremiah—he's a top-notch asshole and doesn't like to be approached unless called upon. I literally can't stand him, but I put up with him. I'm certain he feels the same way. And if his furrowed brow and lack of words aren't telling enough, the audible sound of him breathing through his nostrils is.

"Sorry to interrupt. I was just wondering if Kamden is on his way?"

He looks past me, glowering as if he has better things to do. "You got a phone, don't you? Call him and ask yourself."

I bite my tongue, fighting the urge to lash out. "He's not answering me."

His eyes slowly roll to mine. "Guess he doesn't wanna talk to you then."

Keep your cool, Brogan. He's like this with everyone. It's not personal.

Sure as hell seems like it is, though. He didn't treat me this shitty until Kamden and I made our relationship official. I'd swear he's jealous of the time I spend with Kamden.

"Thanks for your help, Jer," I say with a sarcastic bite to my tone. "Much appreciated."

With a smug grin plastered to his face, he turns back to his fuck toy for the night. I clench my fists, resisting the urge to grab the butter knife on the table beside me so I can plunge it into his back.

Karma will take care of him. May the next pussy he slides himself into be infested with an incurable disease.

I maneuver through the tables and bodies and return to our booth. Reaching across Avery, I grab my phone and sling purse. "I gotta go," I tell them regretfully.

"What? No!" Avery hisses. "We just got here. You haven't even finished your first drink and you've got another waiting."

"Sorry." I shrug. "Kamden isn't answering my calls or texts and I need to make sure he's okay."

Avery sighs with her straw between her lips. "So his pride was temporarily emasculated. He'll get over it."

I fling my bag over my shoulder and open the Uber app on my phone. "Maybe so," I tell her. "But his friends are all jack-asses and I hate the thought of him beating himself up all alone."

"Who says he's alone?" Jenny curls her shoulders forward and the way she rapidly averts her gaze has me wondering if she knows something I don't.

My finger freezes over the order button on the Uber app. "Who else would he be with?" I glance around at his teammates. "Everyone is here."

But not everyone *is* here. Kamden's not, and neither is Gabby.

"You don't think…" I can't even finish that sentence because it's absurd. "No. Kamden can't stand Gabby."

Lucia and Jenny share a look and if one of them doesn't say what they know right now, I will lose my shit.

"What?" I huff eagerly.

Avery shoots them both a glare and on my behalf she asks the question I don't want to know the answer to. "Are they together? Because if they are..." She starts sliding out of her seat, ready to fight a bitch.

"No," Lucia assures her, or at least, attempts to. "At least, not that we know of. It's just odd, right? I mean, where are they?"

With a heavy sigh, I hit the order button on my phone. "I plan to prove you both wrong. Kamden would never cheat on me."

They share another look and I know exactly what they're both thinking. *He cheated once, he'd do it again.*

But I'm not Gabby and our relationship is not the same as the rocky one they had. We're good. Solid. We're fine. There is no way in hell Kamden is with his ex right now.

"You can't just go to his dorm," Avery says with worry in her tone.

I quirk a brow. "Why not?"

"Because." She frowns. "What if he is with her and you walk in on them. You can't unsee that."

"I won't," I stammer. "Because they aren't. This is ridiculous, you guys."

These accusations are really starting to piss me off. I'm so sick of hearing about Kamden and Gabby all the time. So they dated? Who fucking cares. They're over now.

"Then I'll come with you," Avery tells me as she gathers her things, drink still in hand.

"No," I spit out. "Stay and have fun with the girls. I'll be fine. Promise."

The last thing I need is to hear Avery tell me how she was right and I was wrong if by some chance they *are* together. Which they're not.

Much like I don't get along with Kamden's best friend, Kamden doesn't get along with mine either. Avery is certain he's going to break my heart.

Kamden doesn't have the best reputation with girls. He and

Gabby dated for a year and apparently, he cheated on her. I'm not sure why she even wants him back after he broke her heart, but I can only assume it's because Kamden is royalty at Rosewood U. His "usually" stellar skills on the field, paired with the fact that his family owns one of the biggest cyber security companies in the world, make him a magnet for women.

Avery sucks down the rest of her drink then puts her empty glass on the table. She steps closer, her voice a near whisper. "You sure, B?"

B is what she calls me when she's using her serious tone. When she's being playful or joking around, it's usually bitch or slut. We have that sort of friendship, and I treasure it with every fiber of my being.

"Positive," I assure her. "I'll see you back home later." Home being our dorm room at Hallstrom Hall.

"Okay." She pulls me in for a hug. "Don't let what they said get to you. You're probably right. He's just beating himself up right now…alone."

My arms tighten around her before I take a step back. "Thank you," I tell her before heading toward the exit.

Pushing the door open, I step outside and the cool night air smacks against my bare skin, sending a shiver up my spine.

I hug myself with my phone clutched under my armpit, watching impatiently for the red Camry my driver is in even though it's still a ways away.

I brush off any negative thoughts about Kamden and Gabby. Even if for some strange chance they are together, it doesn't mean there is something going on between the two of them. Kamden assured me the flame between them burnt out long before they broke up. He claims he never actually cheated on her because they were on a break, but I honestly don't know what to believe.

I try to call Kamden one more time. My Uber is still six minutes away, so I have time to cancel if he's just running late.

As suspected, it goes to his voicemail, and this time, I decide to leave a message. "Hey, Kam—"

My words are cut off when a strong force pushes me into the building. My back crashes hard and I feel the crunch of my spine against the brick surface. With my breath in my throat and my head in a daze, my phone slips from my hand and goes flying somewhere in the midst of, what appears to be, a fight that broke out.

Still sitting on the sidewalk where I landed with my back pressed against the building, I watch two men who seem to be locked in a violent confrontation. I catch snippets of the verbal assault. Something about someone running over someone's foot and breaking it.

Ouch.

I'm about to push myself off the ground when a fist goes flying through the air, but the guy ducks just in time, missing the blow by a split second.

The guy who almost got hit turns around and my heart jumps into my throat.

Him.

His familiar eyes are the first thing I notice. The second thing I notice is that his hair is darker. The blond tips have grown out and are barely visible now.

Hayes takes steps toward me, walking away from his own fight while the other guy—who's being held back by his friend— hurls insults and threats at him.

The corner of his mouth lifts into an egotistical grin. "Hello again, Legs. I told you we'd see each other again." He extends his hand as if he actually expects me to accept it. I stare grossly at it like it's coated in cyanide.

"Well, come on now. Don't be a stubborn ass. Let me help you up."

My lip curls in disgust as his eyes skim down my body, landing on my legs. Remembering I'm wearing a skirt, I quickly clench my thighs together. "Now who's the one undressing the other with their eyes?"

"Been there. Fucked that."

"God, you're infuriating. I see your ego is still larger than life.

And for what it's worth, having sex with you was the biggest mistake of my life."

His fingers trace along the stubble on his chin. "Ya know, I wish I could say it was the biggest mistake of mine. But I once slept with an older woman who claimed to be a witch and she said she cast a spell on me when I told her I didn't do relationships. She actually fucking cackled on her way out of my room. Talk about regret."

"Why the hell am I even listening to this right now?" I deadpan as I push myself onto my feet. Dusting off the gravel on my leg, I don't even look at him out of fear his gorgeous physique will put *me* under a spell. *No. Never again.*

"Look. I was just trying to help. Not my fault you're such a stubborn ass."

"Why would I let you help me?" I stammer. "Your childish street fight is the reason I'm down here in the first place."

"About that," he begins as he draws his fingers around his mouth, smearing a streak of blood. "I actually saved your life. So a thank-you would be nice. I won't hold my breath, though."

"Please do," I growl. "With any luck, you'll pass out and I can continue on with my night."

The sound of a horn blaring grabs my attention and when I finally see where it's coming from, the vehicle speeds off. Not just any vehicle. My Uber ride.

"Hey!" I throw my hands in the air, shouting, "Don't leave."

It's pointless. He's gone.

"Thanks a lot, jackass. You made me miss my ride home."

He smirks. "There's the thank-you I was looking for. "

My eyes dart to a man coming swiftly toward us. "Look out!" I warn.

In one swift motion, Hayes spins around and lands a powerful punch on the man's jaw. The assailant stumbles backward and Hayes turns back to me, maintaining a calm smile on his face as if punching a guy in front of a bar is the most normal thing ever.

When it comes to Hayes, I'm honestly not even surprised.

"Wish I could say it was good seeing you again, but it wasn't. Have a nice life." My eyes scan the sidewalk for my phone, but with so many people passing through here, going in and out the door and down the strip, I can't find it. I keep looking and with every passing second, the knot in my stomach tightens.

Hayes rubs his bloodied knuckles. "You've got a way with words, Legs. Anyone ever told you that?"

I spin around to face the jackass, hands on my hips. "Why are you following me?"

"Wow. Someone really pissed you off tonight."

"Yeah," I retort. "You."

He shrugs nonchalantly. "Story of my life. Always pissing someone off."

"Yeah, well, maybe it's time you reevaluate the way you treat people." I bend down, trying to look for my phone when I realize Hayes's eyes are glued to my ass.

"Why? I'm perfectly happy with my life."

Rolling my eyes, I try to turn so that he can't see the ass I have worked very hard on because it is a privilege he does not deserve. "Yeah, well, you pushed me, I dropped my phone. So I am *not* happy right now."

His index finger shoots up. "Correction. I saved you."

I laugh dryly. "In the midst of your masculinity battle, you and that jerk pushed me into the building. How the fuck was that saving me?"

His brow lifts. "Masculinity battle?"

"Well, yeah. Isn't that why all guys fight?"

He crosses his arms as if deep in thought, tapping his finger to his chin. "I did run over his foot with my bike, so I don't blame him for coming at me. Doesn't mean I won't defend myself, though."

Ah. So he's the culprit who ran over someone's foot. It's not surprising.

I shake my head in disbelief while making another attempt at walking away from him. "I have to go."

He grabs my arm, not forcefully, but enough that he stops me in my tracks. The way his eyes scan me, it's as if he can feel the spark between us as much as I can. Which is why I pull away from his grip. "Lemme help you find your phone. I'm already late for work, but it's the least I can do."

"Work? At this time of the day?" I look around, wondering what he could possibly do to show up at work this late in the evening.

"Money isn't only made when the sun is up. Some of us have to work at night, too." He casts his eyes down just briefly, as if he's embarrassed. But not even two seconds later, the Hayes I can't stand returns.

I'm sort of surprised. Not that he has a job, but that he's heading to work after fighting outside of a bar. It's a little odd.

Regardless, I don't say anything as I crouch down to get a better look at the sidewalk. If he wants to help me find my phone, I'll let him because I'd really like to find my boyfriend before he cheats on me.

Ugh. Why do I think like this? Why am I always expecting the worst-case scenario?

A group of people come toward me, not paying any attention, and just before they collide with me, someone grabs my arm and pulls me onto my feet and out of the way. I stumble, but quickly regain my balance as strong arms wrap around me from behind.

I lunge forward and out of his hold. "Thank you," I say quietly, because as annoyed as I am right now, I'm still a decent human being.

"Twice," Hayes quips.

My forehead creases as I look at him in confusion. "Huh?"

He steps closer, the heat of him somehow cutting the cold around me. "That's twice I've saved you now."

I take a deep breath. "Whatever."

Minutes pass with no luck when Hayes puts something in front of my face. "You're welcome."

I snatch my phone from his hand, relief flooding my veins.

But when I turn around to really thank him, I catch his backside, walking away.

I'm not sure why I wait, watching him disappear into the mix of people, but it's not until he's out of sight that I swipe my phone open and order a new ride.

After a tiring twenty-minute wait, my ride arrives and I'm exhausted. Like, barely able to keep my eyes open exhausted. So instead of trying to track down Kamden, I put my trust in him and I go back to my room so I can crash.

Freshman year is supposed to be fun. It should be about finding myself and what I really want in life. It should be full of adventure with my friends and nights partying where we go home and laugh about all the crazy shit we did together.

It should not be about fucking playboys and worrying if my football star boyfriend is going to cheat on me with his ex who is my captain. Yet, here I am.

You need to learn to make better choices, Brogan.

CHAPTER 3

BROGAN

THESE EARLY MORNING practices on Sundays are for the birds. I barely slept and my body is aching fiercely. I'm not sure if it's my run-in with the brick building last night or all the movement from the game.

The only good thing about being here is being able to watch Kamden.

Standing on the sideline, my eyes remain fixed on him as he races to the end zone, ready to catch the pass from his teammate.

Most of our practices are held inside the sports arena, but occasionally, when the weather is nice, we practice outdoors. Today, it just so happens Kamden and a few of the other football players stuck around after their morning workout and they're out on the practice field.

I watch intently as the ball flies through the air in a perfect spiral. I swear I can feel the breeze from that throw against my cheek.

I hold my breath, waiting to see if Kamden catches the pass.

Almost there. You've got it...

"Brogan!" The sound of a sharp voice breaks my concentration before the ball even lands in a pair of hands.

I turn to see our head coach, Wendy, her face twisted in frustration. "We're here to practice, not to watch *them* practice."

"Right." My cheeks flush with heat. "What can I say? I love the sport."

"The sport, or Kamden Donnelly?" one of the girls coughs out.

"Football and cheerleading are two different sports," Coach Wendy says. "Right now, I need you to love *our* sport. Now focus."

Laughter erupts beside me and I roll my eyes. I suspect it's mostly the upperclassmen because they're the ones who have been giving me a hard time ever since practices began this past summer. I was the only freshman to join the team this year, and from what I've heard, the new girls get it bad. I believe it now, too. They haven't made it easy on me.

"Pay attention, ladies," Coach Wendy barks, snapping her fingers. "Let's run through the halftime routine one more time before practice ends."

As the remix blares from the speaker, we all march back into formation, clapping our hands in unison before transitioning into our pyramid formation.

"He's gonna break your heart," Gabby says as she comes to my side, ready to lift Jules in the air. I don't even look at Gabby as I push upward with the sole of Jules's shoe in my palm. I grunt as we hoist her up, and my hand shakes as Jules flails her arms trying to balance herself.

I choke on a laugh because this girl will do damn near anything to get under my skin. "No need to worry about me. My heart is fully intact. But thanks for your concern."

"Oh, don't mistake my warning for concern." She giggles annoyingly. "What Kamden and I have doesn't disappear because of one mistake. I can guarantee he's still madly in love with me."

"By mistake, you mean when you cheated on him, right? Or was it when he cheated on you? Sounds like more than one mistake to me."

She grunts as she helps balance Jules and my wrist wobbles a little. "We moved past that."

"Is that so?" I quip, only half focused on the routine now that Gabby is jabbering away.

"Yep. Ask him yourself."

I bite back a smile, sarcasm dripping from my tone. I don't believe her for a second. "If he's the one who's still madly in love with you, then why do you hit him up after every night of drinking? You realize I'm usually with him, right?"

"Usually is the operative word," she snickers. She's trying to get under my skin. That's how girls like Gabby work.

I calm the rage simmering in my chest. I know Kamden is her ex. And no, I didn't break girl code because Gabby is not my friend.

Jules wobbles and shakes and the next thing I know, she's jumping down from the pyramid.

"What the hell, Jules!" Gabby scoffs as she throws her hands in the air. "That's it. She's not cut out for this. I say we put Lucia back on top. It's obvious Jules has the balance of a seesaw."

I'm probably the only one who sees the humiliation on Jules's face—or at least, the only one who cares. She's trying so hard.

"It's okay." I pat her on the back. "You'll get there."

Her silence speaks volumes and I can't help but feel like she's blaming me for almost falling.

"We're not making any changes," Coach Wendy calls out with a sharp tone. "Back into formation and this time…" She pins me with stern eyes that burn into my skin. "No more bickering. We might not all be friends, but we're still a team."

I roll my eyes to Gabby's scathing glare. She bites back a catty smile, pleased with herself.

The next go-around, we nail it. We look fucking beautiful out here. Jules is steady and stable. The rock stuck in the bottom of her shoe is only mildly painful. And Gabby keeps her bitchy mouth shut.

"That's what I like to see," Coach howls. "That was great, ladies. But tomorrow, I expect perfection."

The team scatters, some form a circle and gossip. Likely about me, considering Gabby is at the center of the ring. Jules wanders off and I jog to catch up with her. She crouches down, reaching into her duffle bag. I come to a roaring stop when I'm at her side. "Hey. Is everything okay?"

Her head snaps around, tear-filled eyes peering up at me. "Not really, Brogan. Your little argument with Gabby almost had me face-planting out there."

I let out an airy chuckle. "Don't be silly. We wouldn't have let you fall."

"Really?" She stands, shoulders drawn back. "Because that's not how it felt when I was up there. And because of that, I look like the one who lacks the skills to perform. You know how she is, Brogan. Just ignore her before she destroys this season for you."

"I'm…sorry, Jules. I had no idea."

She scoffs, snatching her bag up and aggressively throwing it over her shoulder. "Of course you didn't."

"Jules." I throw my hands up, but before I can get out so much as a sincere apology, she walks away.

She's definitely pissed. But after some time, she'll cool down. Letting Gabby get to me mid-routine wasn't my finest hour, but if I can prove to these girls I'm serious then maybe it won't be so hard.

I have no idea how I will survive Gabby this season, but I really need to find a way to block her out of my head. She might be captain, but I don't have to acknowledge her or her nasty words about my relationship with Kamden.

Turning around, I watch her and her groupies who are snickering with their gazes dancing from me to each other.

I'm not used to this sort of treatment. Back home, everyone loved me and if they didn't, I didn't care. I've always been nothing short of who I am and if people didn't like it, then fuck them. But this is different. This is my team and the place I was supposed to have a fresh start. So far, my relationship with

Kamden is only costing me things I care about instead of adding to my life.

I grab my duffle bag and sit down on the first row of the bleachers to wait for Kamden to finish up. Aside from a text last night where he said to stick around after practice, we still haven't talked since the game yesterday and I'm anxious to see how he's doing.

Reaching into my backpack, I pull out my sketchbook and shading pencil to kill some time. Drawing has always been my favorite pastime, even if it's not something I share with many people. Now that I think about it, I don't think Kamden even knows I like to draw.

As a kid, I would spend all my free time hunched over my sketchbook meticulously drawing dresses and other articles of clothing. My love for fashion was evident in the piles of *Seventeen* and *Teen Vogue* magazines scattered around my room. My passion for the art is why I'm working toward a degree in fashion merchandising.

One might ask why I chose fashion merchandising instead of fashion design. The truth is, I lack confidence in my abilities. I'm terrified of rejection and even more terrified of failure. This way, I still get to immerse myself in the industry doing something I love, even if I'm not the one creating the designs.

I drag the pencil down the blank page, forming the curves of an evening ball gown. I imagine it in a soft shade of baby blue with delicate crystals garnishing the corset.

Lucia comes jogging up to me after doing a lap around the outdoor track, so I slap my sketchbook closed. She doubles over and presses her hands to her knees. "You hanging around here for a bit?" she asks with heavy breaths and beads of sweat dripping down her face.

"Yeah, Kamden and I still need to talk."

She straightens her back, eyes wide. "Like, *the* talk?"

"No," I chuckle. "I'm not dumping him if that's what you're asking."

She snaps her fingers and clicks her tongue. "Damn."

I just shake my head because I know how much she dislikes him. "Kamden and I are just fine," I tell her as I put my sketchbook and pencil back in my bag. "I can't say the same for his ego, though. I know he blames himself for losing the game."

She lets out a dismissive, "Eh," before adding, "his fragile ego needed a good swift kick if you ask me. He'll get over it."

"Not you too?" I sigh. "Why do all my friends hate my boyfriend?"

"I don't hate him," she reiterates, glancing over at him on the field. "I just think you can do a hell of a lot better. You make Kamden a priority in your life and he doesn't do the same for you."

"He's busy with school and football," I say, feeling my defensive walls come up.

"And you're busy with school and cheerleading." The way she looks at me kind of reminds me of my mother. Her calculating eyes are always telling me to never accept less than what I'm worth. But that's the thing. Here, I am no longer a big fish in a pond I know well. Here, I'm a guppy in a sea of sharks circling their prey. And all I want right now is to have at least one shark on my side who isn't afraid to bite.

I breathe a sigh of relief when Kamden comes walking toward us. "I'll call you later," I tell Lucia, ending our conversation.

"Protect your heart, babe, because you won't let anyone else do it for you."

I dwell on her words for a second. I assume she means I won't listen to her or Avery about their distaste for Kamden. But my mind skids to a halt when Kamden tugs off his practice jersey, revealing the glistening muscles of his chest and arms. He runs the damp fabric over his forehead, wiping up the trickling beads of sweat.

My feet spring out in front of me and I stand up. "Hey," I say, trying to sound chipper despite my sheer exhaustion. "How was practice?"

Not even a hint of a smile forms on his face as he stares at me with a pinched expression. "A lot fucking better than last night."

"Look," I begin as I run my hand down his damp arm. "I know you're beating yourself up over the game, but—"

He takes a long stride back, putting distance between us. "You think this is about the game?"

My hand drops to my side while I rack my brain, trying to figure out why he's so pissed. "What else would you be so upset about? Is it because I went to Piggy's without you?" That's a long shot because we always meet up there after the games and he was the one that didn't show.

"No!" he stammers. "This is about the long-ass voicemail I listened to on my phone when I woke up this morning. Were you hanging out with Hayes fucking Madden?"

"What?" I spit out. "No! Of course not!"

A blazing flush of heat creeps up my neck and spreads across my cheek, my heart thumping against my rib cage. I feel like a child who's been caught red-handed with her hand in the cookie jar, when in reality, I didn't do anything. He just happened to be there.

"You're fucking lying, Brogan. I heard the two of you on the voicemail." His eyes narrow in on me and the anger on his face only intensifies. I've never seen him like this before. I am equal parts scared and pissed off.

"We didn't hang out." I reach out to touch his arm, but he quickly moves back even farther. It's like there's a chasm between us.

"Kam?" I say softly, trying to help him understand. "I saw Hayes, yes. He ran into me, literally, when I was leaving the bar to try and find you. Why didn't you come to Piggy's like we planned?"

"I was at my dorm in bed after that disaster of a fucking game."

My heart hurts knowing he was going through that agony alone. "I'm sorry, Kam. I really wanted to be there for you."

"Sounds like you were otherwise occupied." He glares at me, his eyes cutting like glass.

I notice his fists clenched at his sides, jaw ticking as he grits out, "Did you fuck him?"

His words throw me completely off guard. My chest feels like it's going to cave in. *How does he know?* "I can't believe you're even asking me this?"

He steps closer until I can hear the grind of his teeth. "Answer the fucking question, Brogan. Did you fuck him?"

He knows. There is no way out of this one. I have to be honest.

"It was…before—"

An exasperated huff escapes him as he whips around. "This is just fucking great." Pacing back and forth, his fingers dig into his hair and pull at the roots. "Do you have any idea how much I loathe that guy?" Coming to a sudden halt, his eyes glower at me. "Hayes and I can't stand each other, and *my* girlfriend fucked him!"

"Before you," I finish, my voice cracking with each word. "I didn't even know you when it happened. Hell, I didn't even know him. It was a mistake and I wish more than anything I could go back and…unfuck him." Bad choice of words, but I'm shaken right now. I'm surprised I'm even able to string together coherent sentences.

"Well, that's the thing about spreading your legs for strangers, Brogan. You can't *unfuck* them." He looks at me like I'm a dirty whore, and it makes my heart break in a way I wasn't expecting. If he were to break up with me here and now, it would hurt, but nothing like the way his words are cutting into me right now.

"Wow," I drawl as anger sparks inside me. I can't believe he's acting like this over something that happened before we even met. "I don't have to explain myself to you. It's not like I cheated. Not like I ever would."

"You slept with my enemy!" he snaps. "Do you have any idea how that makes me look?"

Crossing my arms, I stand my ground, refusing to show him how much his words are getting to me. "How it makes *you* look? No, Kamden. I don't. How *does* it make you look?" I ask, my tone condescending to match his.

He's silent for a minute—careful with his words because he knows I'm just as fired up as he is. "It makes me look like I went after his sloppy seconds out of spite."

His words hang in the air, stinging like a slap to my face. I feel my eyebrows scrunch together as I glare at him in disbelief. "That was low, Kam. Even for you." I snatch my bag off the bleacher and throw it over my shoulder as I walk briskly away from the practice field.

A few seconds later, I glance over my shoulder, half expecting him to follow after me. But he's not there. Tears prick the corners of my eyes as I reach into my bag at my side to get my phone.

Once I've got it, I shoot a text to Avery.

Me: Where are you?

Avery: Hallstrom Lounge. Why?

Me: Piggy's in an hour?

Avery: Hells yeahhhh!

CHAPTER 4

BROGAN

AFTER A QUICK SHOWER in the locker room, I threw on a pair of joggers and a cropped white tee paired with white sneakers and got a ride to Piggy's. My hair is still damp as I walk into the dimly lit bar, and my face is makeup-free—thankfully, because I've been in tears ever since my conversation with Kamden. Lucky for me, Piggy's is dead.

Avery is already seated, alone, at a booth in the back. I go straight to her. As I approach the table, I notice she's already got us each a drink—our favorite blackberry mojitos.

"B," she lets out a soft sigh when she notices the tears welling in my eyes. She stands up and wraps her arms around me and I collapse into her embrace. "What's wrong, babe?"

"Kamden and I got into a huge fight." I sniffle as I rub my damp eyes on her fleece hoodie.

She rubs circles on my back. "I'm here for you. Drown your sorrows and tell me all about it."

We sit down and I tell her all about Hayes and how we slept together on the last day of cheer camp in the spring. Then I tell her about my run-in with him last night.

"My phone must have been recording the entire conversation on Kamden's voicemail."

"And you're sure one of you mentioned the time you slept together?"

"I'm pretty sure it came up." I half shrug, knowing Hayes has no filter and I get too worked up around him to remember the exact exchange.

"You know what?" she begins, and I can tell by her tone she will not be in favor of Kamden. Not that she ever is. "Fuck Kamden." *I called that one.* "Everyone has a past. If you knew every girl he fucked, I bet you wouldn't have touched him with a ten-foot pole. He'll get over it."

It's a typical response for Avery. *He'll get over it. She'll get over it. This will pass.* And she's right. Usually he does get over whatever he's fussing about. But this time is different.

"He said Hayes is his biggest enemy. Apparently, they can't stand each other." I roll my eyes. "And it makes him look bad because he had Hayes's sloppy seconds."

"He called you that?" She grabs at her chest as if she were clutching pearls.

"Is it weird that that's what hurt the most?" I glance up at my friend who looks like she might actually go on a murder spree right now.

"B, you're not sloppy seconds. Any man that gets between your legs is blessed with gifts from the gods themselves to have a piece of you. If he called you that, he is forever on my shit list."

I snort because he has already been on her shit list. It started the day we became official and he decided to cancel our plans to have a beer and watch a game with his friends.

"He hasn't messaged you or anything to apologize?"

Checking my phone, I find no missed messages or calls. I flash her the screen, then lay it down on the table as I bow my head.

"Fuck him," Avery practically spits.

I scratch my head, a heavy breath flaring my nostrils. "Yeah," I spit out. "Fuck him. Mr. Judgy Judge can kick rocks if he wants to be pissed about something so stupid." I grab my drink off the table and stick the straw between my lips, sucking down half of the contents.

My phone buzzes on the table and I quickly set my drink down and pick it up.

"It's a text from Kamden," I say with skepticism in my tone.

"So much for *'fuck him'*," she mumbles as I read the message.

> Kamden: First I find out you had sex with a guy I hate, then YOU get pissed at me. That's bullshit, Brogan. I don't want you anywhere near that guy ever again. I mean it. I don't want you talking to him or bumping into him on the streets. I can guarantee he put himself in your way just to get under my skin.

Anger burns in my veins as I slam my phone down on the table. "How dare he think he can control me?"

"Oh, hell no," Avery seethes. "What did he say?"

I push my phone at her and allow her to read for herself. This isn't the first time I've let Avery read my messages. It's probably why she hates Kamden so much. I share all the bad stuff with her and she rarely gets to see the good parts of our relationship. Even if lately they seem few and far between.

Avery's thumbs move at rapid speed across my phone as she types out something to him.

"Don't you dare," I tell her as I reach across the table and try to take it from her before she has a chance to hit send.

I'm too late when she hands it to me, a smile grazing her cheeks.

"For fuck's sake, Ave. What did you do?" I ask as I read *my* response to Kamden.

> Me: Fuck you!

Okay. Not as bad as it could have been. And it's actually what I would have liked to say.

Avery picks up her glass and holds it in the air, so I do the same. A clank rings out and we finish off our drinks.

"Do you remember that time we went to Darell Young's party junior year and we cheered so hard our glasses shattered in our hands?"

"How can I forget?" We both laugh. "It was the same night we were skipping around the pool and bumped into Addison and knocked her in the water."

Avery claps a hand over her mouth, giggling. "I felt so fucking bad for that. The girl was beyond wasted."

"Apparently not bad enough because while you were laughing so hard you peed your pants, I was getting in the pool to help her drunk ass out."

"Ahh," Avery sighs. "The good old days where we had no responsibilities."

"It's only going to get worse from here on out."

Avery holds up her glass again. "At least we have tonight."

I clank mine against hers, softly out of care of repeating history. "I'll cheers to that."

Two hours later, our booth is cluttered with empty glasses. A warm buzz has settled in my stomach as Avery and I enjoy a carefree evening. She threatened me with a shot of tequila every time I mentioned Kamden, so the topic of him has been off the table. The last time I drank tequila I had sex with Hayes. *Ugh.* Just the thought makes me nauseous.

I can't help but wonder if there was any truth to what Kamden said about Hayes purposely inserting himself in my path just to piss Kamden off. Hayes has proven to be a self-centered prick who is only motivated by his own desires, but would he really stoop that low just to piss off someone he doesn't like?

Doesn't matter, I have no plans of ever seeing him again. And it's not because Kamden told me to stay away from him. If it were anyone but Hayes, I might actually do the opposite of what Kamden said. *I'm spiteful like that.*

I still can't believe he had the audacity to tell me who I can't talk to. After my parents' divorce, I swore I'd never let a man control me. My dad is a great dad, don't get me wrong, but he had a way of manipulating my mom into doing what he wanted instead of what *she* wanted.

She was a lawyer who decided to become a stay-at-home mom because my dad thought it was better for us girls growing up. I never saw her smile quite like she did the day she accepted the position as district attorney in Willow Creek. It came with the cost of us moving away from my friends and my dad, but it all worked out the way it was supposed to. Now she's happily married to Grant and I've gained four pain-in-the-ass stepbrothers.

"One more drink?" Avery waggles her brows with her empty glass in the air.

I look down at my phone and see that it's already after nine. We both have a seven-a.m. class in the morning, so I need to make the responsible decision for us. Part of me wants to go talk to Kamden and figure out where we stand at this point. I'm not about the in-between stuff. I've watched season three, episode fifteen of *Friends* more than enough times to know I will never "be on a break" with a guy.

I really shouldn't have a serious conversation with Kamden after I've had this much to drink. I'll undoubtedly say something I regret.

Smacking my dry lips together, I say, "I think we should head back to campus."

With a grunt, Avery sets her glass down. Her red-rimmed eyes look back at me and I'm certain mine are a similar shade of intoxicated. I don't normally go out when I have classes the next day, but I had to do something to refrain from chasing after Kamden and giving him a piece of my mind, or groveling at his feet. *No! I will not do that.* Our relationship is definitely not worth a full-fledged grovel. Besides, it's not in my blood to be a pushover.

Avery sluggishly takes her phone out of her purse and leans

into the table. "I'll order us a ride." Her words slur and I'm confident I made the right choice, for both our sakes.

"Done," she says as she slips her phone back in her purse. "Black Honda CR-V. Five minutes. Head out front and I'll meet ya there. I gotta pee. If he comes, stand in front of the car and don't let him leave without me."

I laugh. "You'll be fine. We've got plenty of time."

She holds up her hand, fingers sprawled. "We've got *five* minutes."

"Five minutes." I chuckle. "Got it."

Avery scoots out of the booth, and her knees knock as she holds on to the back of a chair beside her. "I shall return." She spins on her heel and heads to the bathroom. Clearly, she's had one drink too many.

I'm one to talk because my head feels like a bowling ball when I stand up. I toss a few extra dollars on the table, even though we've tipped our server exponentially after each drink. We don't do tabs. It's too risky since we're drinking underage.

When I step outside, the cool air hits my face and I swear it slightly sobers me up. A row of cars lines the street, so I keep an eye out on the other side to watch for our ride.

A minute later, he pulls up under a flickering lamppost. *That definitely wasn't five minutes.*

I raise my hand to signal our driver as I step between two parked cars and onto the street. It's pretty quiet tonight, and when I look both ways before crossing, there are no headlights in sight.

Suddenly, the screeching sound of rubber on asphalt rings in my ears. The bike swerves to the left, narrowly missing me before coming to a sudden stop next to a parked car. The next thing I know, I'm staring deer faced into a pair of piercing eyes behind a helmet.

I don't even know where he came from. He had to have been going at least ninety miles an hour.

The sound of the engine dies and I watch in shock as he swings his leg over the seat.

"What the fuck!" I hear him holler as he pulls off his helmet.

"You have got to be kidding me," I mutter when I come face to face with the devil himself.

His lip curls at the corner. "You really gotta watch where you're going, Legs." He points in front of where he's standing.

"You almost killed me!" I growl. "Again!"

"Actually," he begins. "I'm pretty sure I saved you...*again*. I could have easily taken you out." Hayes hooks his helmet on the handle and drags his leather-wrapped fingers over the smooth surface of his bike. "Not gonna lie, the thought crossed my mind."

"Saved me?" I laugh dryly. "And let me guess, you expect a thank-you?"

Something about Hayes's rugged appearance sends a rush of heat through my core. His disheveled hair is pushed back off his forehead, stray strands wisping in the wind. He's wearing a shiny black leather jacket, matching boots, and torn denim jeans that expose his kneecaps.

Avery appears out of nowhere, running toward us with her hand in the air. "We're coming," I hear her drunk ass shout as she walks right in front of an oncoming car. Hayes reaches out and grabs her by the arm, jerking her back to safety.

"I take this to be a friend of yours?" He smirks. "Two peas in a pod."

"Oh, screw off," I grumble. "Ya know, this isn't a race strip. You're seriously going to kill someone if you don't learn how to drive that thing. Didn't you run someone's foot over the last time I saw you out here?"

He quirks a curious brow. "Ya know, you seem to be at that bar a lot. Do I smell a drinking problem?"

I look at my invisible wristwatch, sneering. "Aren't you late for work?"

"Actually, due to my extracurricular activities, I had to quit my job."

I plant my hand on my hip and cock my head. "Lemme guess, drug dealer?"

Hayes tsks. "You and that mouth of yours…"

"Whoa now." Avery grins. "Am I interrupting something?" She waves her hand between Hayes and me. "Do you two need a minute because the tension is thick as hell right here."

"No," I spit out, glowering at my new enemy. "Hayes was just leaving and so were we." I grab her by the arm, ready to pull her to our ride, but she digs her heels into the pavement and pulls against me.

"Ahhh," Avery gushes. "So you're the guy she fucked last spring that her boyfriend told her to stay away from?"

"Avery!" I hiss, throwing my hands in the air. "Why?" *She's such a little shit when she drinks.*

Hayes raises a single brow, a sly grin spreading across his face. "Is that so?"

I narrow my eyes. "As if you didn't know."

He shrugs lazily. "No idea what you're talking about, Legs."

"Legs?" Avery giggles. "Ooh, that's sexy. And so cute that you two have nicknames already." She smacks my arm with the back of her hand. "I like him already. Kamden never gave you a nickname."

My chin drops to my chest and I tap my foot impatiently.

Hayes takes a step back. "Did you say Kamden? As in Kamden Donnelly?"

My eyes shoot up. "Oh, shut up," I hiss. "Don't play dumb with me. You know exactly who my boyfriend is."

Hayes barks a laugh. "Wait a damn minute. You're seriously dating Kamden Donnelly?"

Part of me wants to believe he really is messing with me right now, but the shock on his face says differently. He actually looks sort of pale. There is some serious animosity between those two guys and now I'm curious as hell why.

I've never even seen them interact. I guess it's possible Hayes really didn't know Kamden and I are together. That would mean none of our run-ins have been planned. That would also mean fate is a real bitch because the run-ins can stop any day now. I've been seeing far too much of this prick.

"You really didn't know?" I ask suspiciously.

Hayes walks toward his bike, but his skeptical eyes remain glued to me. "Not a single fucking clue. *Wow*," he drawls. "And here I thought you had good taste when you climbed into my bed." His head shakes disappointedly as he snares his helmet from the handle. "Good luck with that relationship." He slides his helmet on and swings his leg over the seat of his bike before bringing the engine to life.

"Oh, B. He is hot!"

Our driver lays on the horn and I grab Avery by the hand, leading her safely across the street. "Don't even give him a second thought," I tell her as we get into the car. Someone once told me that and I wish I'd have listened.

"You should totally fuck him again." I glower at her, and she throws her hands up in surrender. "Okay. Okay. I'm done."

As we drive away, I find myself turning around in the seat to watch Hayes's taillight disappear into the night. And *now,* I'm not giving him a second thought.

CHAPTER 5

HAYES

I'M CROUCHED on the bench, threading the laces of my skates through each eyelet when my teammate, Finch, plops down next to me. "What landed you in Deeter's office this time?" he asks with a smirk.

"He just had to ask me something. No big deal."

Finch claps a hand to my back. "Just remember, I'm here for you, brother." He skates off and I draw in a deep breath of the cool air.

Finch is the closest thing I have to a friend because I don't let many people in, but we're still not at the point where I share too much personal information with him. The truth is, Coach Deeter is on my ass about my grades, *again*.

Same song and dance, different school year. I'm not smart like the majority of my teammates. After spending a year on a tier-three junior league, I did an open tryout for the Devils' team. I was damn sure I was just wasting their time. Then, by guts and glory, I was selected to join their roster.

It's been two years now and I know without a doubt it's purely talent that got me on the team, not brains. If it weren't for me being the best center the Devils have seen in fifteen years— their words, not mine—I'd be out on my ass right now.

I just have to keep my eye on my long-term goal, which is to get drafted into the NHL. Hell, I'll even settle for the WHA. Anything that allows me to do what I love while paying the bills. Lord knows, my shitty off-season jobs don't do that. Fortunately, I saved enough from my paychecks before I quit my job so I could survive the season. It's not much, but it's enough to eat and pay rent.

It's hard as hell for anyone to juggle school, training, and games, let alone a part-time job on top of it. Each year I'm given no choice but to quit whatever shit-paying job I get, then find a new one when the season ends.

Now all I have to focus on is hockey and school.

At the end of my conversation with Deeter, I promised I'd get my GPA where it needs to be and get us that big W in the season opener this Friday. I know I've got other shit going on in my life, but right now, hockey is number one. It's more than just a hobby for me—it's what I hope will be my livelihood; something I need to protect at all costs because it's my refuge from a life of poverty.

I sweep away the negative thoughts infiltrating my mind because the last thing I want is to feel sorry for myself. Even when life threatens to pull me six feet underground, I drag my claws in the dirt and climb back to the top.

"Madden," I hear Lundell, one of our associate coaches, call out from center ice where the team is stretching. "Get your ass down here."

By the time I get my gear on, I've missed warm-ups and I know damn well I'm gonna get shit for it.

I tug on my practice jersey, slip on my gloves and bucket helmet, then join my team in the center of the rink. The sound of my blades cutting through the ice mixes with sticks tapping against pucks.

We begin a round of shooting drills and as I'm slapping the puck back and forth with Finch, my mind wanders to that girl. Pretty sure her name is Brogan. Actually, I know it is because I asked around when I found out she's dating Kamden.

I still can't believe she's with that asshole. I'm not even sure why it bothers me so much. It's not like I have any strings attached to her, and the chick is as annoying as a dripping faucet. The way she looks at me, like I'm worth less than the dirt on the bottom of her shoe, it digs deep at something I don't want to acknowledge.

She is hot as hell, though, so I'll give her that. Curves in all the right places. Long, wavy dark blonde hair that frames her heart-shaped face and electric blue eyes that are damn near blinding. And those fucking legs, they go on for days. The stupid nickname I gave her is fitting as hell because while she might have been undressing me with her eyes the night we met, I was thinking about how good it would feel to spread her gorgeous thighs.

"Who is she?" Finch asks, and I notice his subtle smirk as I smack the puck back to him.

"No idea what you're talking about," I play dumb, but he must've noticed how distracted I was when my brain unwillingly shifted to thoughts of her.

"Oh, come on. I saw you smiling like a schoolboy just now. You were thinking about a girl."

The scuffed puck hurtles toward me, spinning on its side as it slams into the smooth surface of my curved stick. I toss it back and forth a couple times, shifting my weight from one foot to the other.

"You're delusional," I quip as I flick my wrist and send it back to Finch.

He stops the puck against the ice with a satisfying smack. "I call bullshit."

Finch knows damn well I'm not telling him a thing, so he might as well give up. He's like this annoying little brother who likes to pick and pick. He's a good guy, though. A little too emotional for my liking and always wants to talk about the deep stuff, but I don't give him too much shit for it. After a few minutes of trying to crack my hard shell, he finally gives up—as per usual.

We continue our back-and-forth passing drill until Coach blows the whistle. Then we do fifteen minutes of endurance skating—an extra five for me because of my tardiness on the ice. *Fuck you, too, Coach.* I don't say it. Never would. I have the utmost respect for the man, but he sure is a pain in my ass sometimes.

All the while, I can't seem to get Brogan out of my head. And more so, the fact that her friend knew who I was. I wonder if she's been talking about me or ever thinks back to that night. Shit. I can still practically feel her tight pussy clamping down around my shaft as I thrust in and out of her heat.

Coach sounds the whistle again, startling me before signaling us to gather off the ice for a team meeting. Shooting me a stern expression, he makes it clear that there are consequences for our actions—missed practices, tardiness, and poor grades included. I fucking hate when he uses me as an example. He doesn't even have to say it out loud, the entire team knows he's directing his words at me as he lists off what will not be accepted by the precious school we play for.

The meeting comes to an end and we're dismissed with instructions to head home, study, and get a good night's sleep for our home scrimmage tomorrow against our biggest rivals, the Lords. University students are able to attend for free to show their support for the team and it's usually a pretty good turnout.

"Fuck, man," Theo—another teammate, and one of my many housemates—says as we enter the locker room. "You must've really got on his bad side this time."

I roll my neck, cracking my tense muscles. "He'll get over it. Always does."

Truth is, I'm not even slightly worried. Coach Deeter would be a fool to kick me off the team. I'm an asset, and he knows it.

After changing out of my practice gear and putting it in my locker, I catch the bus back to the student center because I'm hungry as fuck. Reaching my hand into the front pocket of my leather jacket, I fish for some cash. When I pull my hand out, I'm happy to see I've got a crisp twenty-dollar bill.

Daddy's eating good tonight.

I walk into the student center, pleased to see that Cluck's Chicken is still open. It's hit or miss this time of night. Lately they've been closing early due to being understaffed, which blows my mind considering there are thousands of students here that could get jobs. Guess they're the lucky ones who don't need it.

"How's it going, Hayes," my favorite Cluck's cashier asks from behind the counter. She's a sweet girl, but not my type. She always blushes when I approach and almost never makes eye contact. She's also the type of sweet that I stay away from because her heart would literally tuck itself into my bed and pull the blankets up the second I made her come. I'd never be able to get rid of her.

I lean into the counter, arms crossed as I narrow my eyes just so I can see the pink of her cheeks. "Going good, Kaley. How's your night been?"

Her gaze darts behind me, as per usual. "We've actually been pretty busy tonight. A bunch of students are watching a game in the student lounge."

"Is that so?" I take a look over my shoulder, peering down the hall at the glass walls of the lounge. "Who's playing?"

She shrugs. "I don't even know. But I think it's a football game."

I nod. "Cool. Cool." I look up at the menu, thinking I might change up my usual, but when I remember I need to stick to lean protein, I go with what I eat every time I stop by here. "I'll have two grilled chicken wraps with avocado, spinach, and tomato."

Kaley snorts. "Already punched it in before you even told me."

I smack my palm to the counter as I straighten my back. "You're on top of it tonight." I slide her my twenty-dollar bill and when she hands me my change, I drop a dollar in the tip jar.

"I'll have it out for you in just a minute."

"Thanks, Kaley."

As I'm waiting, I wander down the hall, curious what game is playing.

The student center's lounge is a hub of activity. There are a few others spread out on campus, but this one is the largest. It's filled with recliners that are often occupied by napping students. A few flat-screen televisions that usually blare sports. More times than not, there's an intense game of ping-pong happening, or a heated game of pool.

As I walk closer, my eyes immediately gravitate to a blonde silhouette. Her back is to me, but I know those legs. A smile creeps across my face. This night just got a whole lot more interesting.

"Hayes," I hear Kaley raise her voice and when I spin around, I practically slam into her. There she is, holding my bag of food with a wide smile on her face. "Here you go." She all but pushes it into my chest and when I take the bag from her, I feel the light brush of her fingers against mine, purposely, no doubt.

"Ugh. Thanks," I tell her. "Enjoy the rest of your night. Don't work too hard."

"You, too, Hayes." For some reason she loves saying my name.

I walk away holding in a chuckle, and when I look over my shoulder, I see her smile widen farther as she waves. I flick my fingers in the air and head straight to the lounge to see how much shit I can get myself into tonight. Brogan is going to be pissed when she sees me. And I can't fucking wait.

I step into the room, immediately engulfed in the sound of hoots and hollers from everyone gathered around the big screen to watch the Bucks and Cougars college football game.

I reach into my bag and pull out my chicken wraps, tossing the empty bag into a nearby trash bin. Navigating through the tightly-packed crowd, I make my way toward Brogan.

Keeping my presence unknown, I stand behind her, watching and listening. To her, not the game.

Her eyes are focused intently on the TV. I notice each quick breath and muttered curse. Every once in a while, she lets out a heavy sigh, or a sudden jolt of excitement that pulses through me.

She's so hung up on the game that she doesn't even realize I'm standing behind her stuffing my face with chicken wraps.

I've never met a girl who loves sports so much. Even if it is the wrong sport. Don't get me wrong, football is great. It's a nice pastime when hockey isn't playing on TV. But there really is no comparison when it comes to feeling that exhilarating rush we all crave.

"Hayes, my man!" I hear the voice come from behind me before a hand smacks firmly against my back. "Long time no see."

Brogan spins around and we come face to face. The jig is up. Not that I was actually hiding. Keep your enemies close, right?

"How ya been?" The guy with his hand on my back says with a crooked smile. He looks at me expectantly, waiting for a response. But the longer I study his face, the more certain I am that I've never met this guy before.

"Brock," he says, noticing my quizzical expression. "We had AP History together last semester."

Rolling the wrappers from my dinner in my hand, I pass them to Brock. "It was good seeing you again, Brock. Can you do me a favor and toss those? Thanks." I give him a swift pat on the back as I step around him.

I lean into Brogan's side and shoot a thumb over my shoulder. "Who the hell is that guy?"

She laughs. "Why are you here, Hayes?"

"What do you mean why am I here? Same reason you are." I point to the big screen. "Came to watch the game."

"Do you even like football?" she asks. "Pretty sure you said you're a hockey fan."

"Ah." I smirk. "You remember?" I clear my throat. "And yes, I do enjoy hockey. But football is all right, too."

"Oh, come on. That was a bullshit call!" Brogan hollers at the screen before returning her attention to me. "So you're saying you prefer to watch barbaric men on ice skates?"

I laugh. "There's more to it than that. But yeah, I guess I do."

"Shhh," she hums.

My eyebrows pinch together. "Did you really just shush me?"

She puts a finger over her mouth, holding it there before grabbing my forearm and digging her fingertips into my skin, her eyes focused intently on the screen. "Gooooo!"

I can't believe she just shushed me. Nobody shushes me.

I look down at her hand bracing my arm, noticing her nails painted in blood orange and black, our school colors. I bet she goes to all the football games.

"Who do you think will win?" I ask, stealing her attention from the game again.

She quickly releases her grip on my arm, her fingers falling away like she didn't realize they were there in the first place. "Oh, the Bucks for sure. Their win is in the bag."

"Hmm." I tap my chin, strategically thinking. The Bucks are down right now. They just got a penalty on the last play. *I think she's wrong.* This could go one of two ways, but I'm willing to take the risk. "Care to bet on it?"

Her eyes snap to mine and she chuckles. "If you really want to bet that the Cougars are going to win, you're a bigger idiot than I thought you were."

I'm slightly offended here. I've been called many names, but idiot is new. I get it, she hates me because I slept with her then basically kicked her out of my room. But in my defense, I never gave her any reason to think it was more than just sex.

"You think I'm an idiot?"

A growly sound rumbles in her chest as she keeps her stare fixed on the screen. "I think you're persistent. And annoying. And a player. And I'm pretty sure I said I never want to see you again. Yet here you are...*again.*"

Ignoring everything she just said, I get back to the bet. "Two minutes left in the game. Are you in, or are you out?"

She turns her body toward mine, arms crossed tightly over her chest. "What's the wager?"

I lift my shoulders. "What do you want?"

"I want you to stay away from me for good, so I can fix my relationship. Kamden hasn't answered any of my calls today and I think it's only right that I blame you for that."

"Me?" I bring my hands to my chest. "What the fuck did I do?"

"I don't know yet, but I'm starting with the fact that you pissed him off in the first place. Then I'll run with the idea that you knew my phone was recording that voicemail and purposely talked about the night we…"

"Fucked." I say it for her since she doesn't have the gall to say the word herself. "We fucked."

Her cheeks tinge pink and it makes my lip curl in response. "Whatever," she grumbles.

"And I didn't purposely record anything. I didn't even know you and Kamden were a thing. As for me pissing him off in the first place, maybe you should ask him why he's so pissed."

"I can't," she raises her voice. "I can't ask him anything if he won't talk to me."

"That's his problem then."

She shakes her head, obviously annoyed. "Anyways, that's what I want *when* I win. Stay the hell away from me."

"Deal," I tell her. Yet, for some reason, regret is gnawing at my insides. There is a good chance she's going to win, and I'm not sure I'll be able to stay away like she wants. I might not like this girl, but I love getting under her skin. It's satisfying in some fucked-up way. I also can't deny that I thought about her a lot after she walked out of my room that night. I've thrown away a few pairs of stray panties in my room over the years, but for some reason, I kept hers. *Also fucked up.*

Brogan curls her fingers at me. "All right, let's have it. What do you want on the very slim chance the Cougars win?"

"The Devils' hockey team has a scrimmage game tomorrow night. Students get in free. If I win, I want you to go."

She snorts, crossing her arms in disbelief. "Are you seriously asking me to go watch a hockey game with you? I don't even like you."

"I don't like you either, but no, I'm not asking you to watch a game with me. In fact, I won't even be watching. I've got plans."

"Lemme guess, a date?" Her eyes narrow, almost like she is trying to guess what I have planned.

I respond with a lazy shrug. I could tell her my plans, but I wanna keep this girl on her toes. Besides, I swear I just saw a flash of jealousy in her eyes.

I continue, "I want you to get a taste for some real excitement because I love saying *I told you so.*"

"You would," she gripes, the creases in her forehead prominent.

I tip my chin proudly, a smug grin playing on my lips. "By the end of tomorrow night, you'll be the Devils' hockey team's biggest fan. When you lose our little bet, I'll make sure there is a rinkside seat waiting just for you." I bop her nose, and she growls before slapping my hand away.

"*If* I lose." She makes her words clear.

"All right, all right. *If* you lose."

Brogan turns her attention back to the game as the play begins. "The Bucks might be down by four points but they only have twenty yards to go with thirty seconds on the clock. It's in the fucking bag," she announces confidently.

I don't even watch the game; I watch her. Every twitch of her lips, the way her cheeks pinken under my stare.

Her chest is rising and falling rapidly as the play unfolds. Then, she goes still, so still I don't even have to look at the screen. I'm pretty sure she's holding her breath.

"Catch the damn ball!" she shouts as her feet leave the ground.

"He fucking fumbled it," I hear someone holler from the crowd gathered around us.

The second Brogan's face drops in her hands, a grin spreads across my face. Her misery is my triumph.

Seconds pass and a heave of heavy sighs fills the room,

telling me all I need to know. When I finally look at the screen, I see that the Cougars won.

I lay a heavy hand on her shoulder and she lifts her head. "I think the Bucks win just fell out of the bag, Legs."

"I hate you," she seethes.

"You can hate me today as long as you don't fall in love with me tomorrow. I don't wanna have to break your little heart."

She scoffs. "I don't think that's gonna be a problem."

"We'll see about that." I drop my hand. "Front row next to the players' benches. Your name will be on the seat. Bring a friend." I give her my back and walk to the door to leave, feeling fucking victorious.

CHAPTER 6

BROGAN

"Remind me again why we're in this freezing arena?" Avery shivers as we shuffle our feet to find our seats. "Oh, right," she continues. "Because you lost a stupid bet."

She's right. It is freezing. My nipples are damn near ready to slice through the three layers of fabric I've got on—bra, tee shirt, and hoodie. A heads-up from Hayes would have been nice, but that would've made him appear to be a good guy.

I look down at the seats that are all full. Hayes said my name would be on mine, but where?

I spot two empty seats, four people down, and I sigh in relief. "Sorry," I squeak as I slip past a few students who are sitting.

When we finally make it, my shoulders slump and I rip the signs off each seat.

"Legs, and Legs's friend." Avery laughs. "He's hilarious."

"He's a moron." I growl as I ball the paper in my hands and stick it in the cupholder on my seat. He wasn't kidding, though, these are amazing seats. I can literally reach out and touch the glass.

"Damn," Avery drawls as she scopes out the Devils' team that's caged inside some plexiglass. "We got front-row seats to all the hotties."

"There ya go," I tell her. "You've never dated a hockey player. Maybe that's where the end of your misery lies."

Avery comes off as a hardass, but the truth is, she wears her heart on her sleeve. She just keeps ending up with punk-ass boys when what she really needs is a man.

The second my ass hits the seat, I pull out my phone, hoping Kamden texted or called.

"Anything?" Avery asks and I shake my head no.

I stick my phone in the front pocket of my hoodie. "I'm done. I'm not texting or calling him anymore. This is getting ridiculous. If he wants to act like a child and throw a tantrum then what we had must not have meant anything to him."

"Good for you," Avery says as she holds her phone out in front of us. I drop my sour face momentarily and force a smile as she snaps a pic of us. "He's showing his true colors, B. I'm glad you're finally seeing them."

She thumbs at her phone for a minute before setting it in her lap. Looking left, then right, she says, "Where is Hayes anyways? And how is he going to sit with us? All the seats are taken."

"Oh, he's not coming," I quip, just another reason to be outrageously annoyed.

Her expression contorts. "Huh?"

"Yeah. Apparently, he's this big hockey fan and he thinks it's the best sport ever to grace the earth, so he wanted me to watch a game so he could say he was right and I was wrong. But he had plans tonight."

Her eyebrows jump. "A date?"

"Hell if I know…or care." My shoulders slump a little, but it has nothing to do with Hayes and everything to do with losing this damn bet.

"Sure you don't." She pulls her phone back out, already bored. Instead of arguing with her, I'll just let her think what she wants.

I really don't care if Hayes is on a date. Actually, I sort of hope he is. I hope he's totally smitten, falls head over heels for the girl, then I hope he's forced to leave his underwear behind when he gets kicked out of her room.

The arena lights flicker before dimming, a sign that something is about to happen. About damn time. I feel like I could fall asleep right now.

A spotlight illuminates the ice as a group of six cheerleaders skate out. They look stunning in their blood orange and black halter tops and skirts—skilled, too. I wish I would have learned how to ice skate. I bet they have so much more fun out there than we do on the sidelines. The one, and only, time I went skating, I fell and busted my ass then vowed never to do it again.

As soon as the team comes onto the ice, the crowd roars, so I clap my hands along with them. Ever the dutiful cheerleader. After ten minutes of just watching them skate and slap around a puck, I let out a big yawn.

I don't know a damn thing about hockey, but I'm baffled over how this is exciting, let alone bet-worthy. *That's it.* Hayes hates me so much, he wanted to bore me to death.

The announcer's voice booms through the speaker, announcing the teams. Devils versus Lords. Oh, I know that team. That's Callan's school—North Ridge University. It's Callan's dream to play on that team someday.

Interest piqued, I straighten my back and watch the players warm up. *Still boring.*

The national anthem begins, so we all stand and I place my hand over my heart. Once it concludes, the players gather in a tight circle at the center of the rink. Their sticks rise before they all skate into line formation.

With my hand in my pocket, I pull my phone out slightly just to steal a glance, only to find that I have no missed calls or messages. Disappointed, I slide it back in my pocket. I meant what I said about chasing after Kamden; he was disrespectful to me and owes me an apology. I just hate this limbo. Are we still together or not? Because it's starting to feel like not and I can't say I'm all that devastated about it. Avery was right, he showed his true colors and if a stupid voice message that he took out of context is going to send him packing then he isn't someone who deserves my time.

Stretching my arms, I lean back and prepare myself for an uneventful couple of hours. Then again, Hayes never said how long I had to stay. Just that I had to come. I don't know anything about hockey, but if they have a halftime, we're dipping.

The referee's whistle blasts through the rink as he drops a puck onto the ice. In a split second, players surge forward with their sticks raised. The sound of bodies colliding echoes in the air as players fight for control of the puck.

A couple hockey players slam right into the glass barrier in front of me. "Holy shit. That was wild." I laugh as my back pins to the seat.

One of the players on the Devils' team turns around and my heart jumps into my throat. I would know those eyes anywhere, that paired with the cheeky grin and wink he sends my way. Holy fucking shit. *Hayes plays for the Devils' hockey team?*

He said he wouldn't be watching tonight because he's *playing* tonight. Why am I stunned speechless as I look at Avery who's pointing her finger at the rink?

"Did you see that?" Avery gushes. "That guy just fucking winked at you, B."

I gulp. "Yeah, I saw." In fact, I still see him because my eyes are traveling everywhere he goes. In the blink of an eye, he skates back to the bench. His helmet comes off and if there was any doubt that it was Hayes, it's quickly squashed. He looks right at me and I shake my head, trying not to smile.

He thinks he's *so* cute.

Well, joke's on him because the next time we make a bet, I'm making him go to a home football game so he can see that we both can have a little mystery in our lives. It's just a shame we have limited home games, and I don't travel to the away ones. Currently, only twelve cheerleaders go to those and it's all upperclassmen. The league is trying to change that rule, but right now, funding and space have limited the opportunity.

Avery nudges me and I snap my eyes away from Hayes

who's going back out on the ice. "I think your one-night stand wants a second."

"Hayes and I hate each other," I tell her in my most reassuring voice.

"Love and hate are two sides of the same coin, B. I think he flipped and it doesn't look like you're far behind."

I sink into the seat, eyes back on the game. "You're insane. I have a boyfriend, in case you've forgotten."

"Actually, I have, and I think your *boyfriend...*" She air quotes. "...has forgotten too. How long has it been since you've talked to him again?"

Hand back in my hoodie pocket, I fumble with my phone, only this time, it's not because I want to check and see if Kamden called. This time, I'm gripping the fuck out of it because she's right.

"I sort of hope you're right. If he forgets, then I can forget, too."

We watch the game—well, I watch the game while Avery scrolls through her social media accounts, and before long, I surprise myself by getting into it.

It's now the end of the third period and there's no doubt I'll be leaving here with more knowledge of the sport than what I came here with.

I can't believe how passionate the fans are over the game. The team doesn't even need cheerleaders because the stands are packed with their own personal squad.

The puck flies in the air and with intense focus, Hayes sprints across the rink and lunges for it. He slaps the puck around with his stick, bringing it closer and closer to the goal.

The crowd erupts in utter chaos and my heart races as my eyes stay locked on Hayes.

You've got this, asshole.

With a powerful swing of his stick, Hayes fires the puck toward the net. The goalie lunges in an attempt to block it, but it's too late. The puck sails into the goal and the Devils score a point.

My eyes stay fixated on him and I won't deny he's a hell of a player.

I jump to my feet, clapping my hands. "Yes!" I shout at the top of my lungs, my voice overpowering the ones around me.

Hayes skates down the rink, stopping momentarily as he looks at me cheering him on. My pounding heart flutters and the feeling throws me off guard. I break my gaze from him and sit back down. I have no idea what that was inside my chest, but I know it can never happen again.

"Someone's a new fan." Avery waggles her brows with her phone still gripped in her hands.

"Nah," I tell her. "Sure, it's fun to watch, but I don't even know anything about hockey."

"I wasn't talking about hockey. I was talking about Hayes Madden."

I let her words stew for a minute before saying, "Hayes Madden can rot in hell."

"Keep telling yourself that, B. Before you know it, you'll be following him straight into the fiery depths.

No. Just no. Hayes played me like a fucking fiddle. And it would have been fine and dandy if he wasn't such an ass about it. He literally kicked me out of his room less than two minutes after he put his dick in me. Even when I had every intention of leaving what happened between us as a one-and-done, he actually took the initiative to tell me to leave. I never felt so used and disrespected in my life.

Every time I think about it, I get angry all over again.

"Let's go, babe," Avery says as she stands up.

I look at her. "Huh?"

"Game's over. Devils win. Yay." She waves her hands in the air unenthusiastically.

I was so lost in my thoughts I didn't even realize the game ended. My traitorous eyes search for Hayes one last time, but he's gone.

Avery and I weave through the stands and make our way to the arena's concourse. Popcorn crunches beneath my shoes as I narrowly avoid body slams and collisions with plastic cups filled with beer.

"Well, that was more fun than I expected," I tell Avery as soon as we step out into the cool night air.

"It was a great time. Let's do it again, oh…never." Sarcasm drips from her tone. Avery has no interest in sports of any kind, unless it involves watching a guy she's simping on. Fortunately, she's a good friend and she allows me to drag her to events such as this one.

Just as I'm pulling my phone out of my pocket to order us a ride, I hear someone holler, "Legs, wait up."

Normally I wouldn't give it a second thought because my name is not Legs, but *someone* seems to think it is.

"We have company," Avery sings. "I'll order the car while you go talk to the guy you hate that you're falling for."

"I am *not* falling for him!" I stammer. But I'm starting to think the player is falling for me. He's been showing up everywhere I am far too much for it to be a coincidence.

With a heavy sigh, I whip around to find Hayes jogging toward me with his phone clutched in his hand. He's still in his bulky gear, aside from his helmet. A layer of sweat coats his hair, making it look darker than usual.

His hands go palms up out in front of him. "What did ya think?"

My lips twitch with a smile as I cross my arms over my chest. "Shouldn't you be showering or something?"

Hayes casually raises his arm and takes a deep breath, nose wrinkled. "You saying I stink?"

"Oh, I'm sure you smell about as good as a bag of rotten potatoes."

He claps a hand over his chest and gives me a mischievous glance. "You're such a sweetheart."

"I try." I bite the inside of my cheek, trying desperately not to let a smile escape. Hayes makes it hard. As arrogant as he is, he's also pretty…real. And much more down-to-earth than I would have guessed after that first night.

He walks closer until we're only an arm's length apart. "I saw you cheering for me out there."

Averting my gaze, I say, "I was cheering for the team."

"Mmmhmm." He presses two fingers to my cheek and forces me to look at him before letting go. Even though his hand has returned to his side, I can still feel the heat of his touch on my face. "You had a good time, didn't you?"

It hurts to say this out loud, but he saw me getting into the game, so he'll see right through the lie if I try. "I'll admit, it wasn't as bad as I expected."

A cheeky grin spreads across his face and just as he opens his mouth to speak—likely something sarcastic or a joke that's meant to be funny but falls short—Avery joins us.

"Thanks for the sweet seats," she tells Hayes. "We had a great time. Didn't we, Legs?"

My lips press into a thin line and I shake my head at my jerk of a best friend. "The best."

Hayes points to Avery. "I like her."

"Why, thank you," she says with a bite of flirtation to her tone. "You'll have to forgive my friend, she's sort of a buzzkill."

"I've noticed." Hayes glances at me with a grin playing on his soft lips.

I hate the way those looks make me feel. It's equal parts elation and nausea.

Avery reaches her hand out to Hayes. "I don't think we've officially met, I'm Avery."

"Hayes," he tells her, returning the gesture. "You two got plans for the rest of the evening?"

"Yes!" I blurt out, while at the say time, Avery pops the P on her "Nope."

Hayes chuckles. "So which is it?"

I grab Avery by the arm, pulling her away from Hayes before she falls under his spell. It's easy to do.

"Homework," I spit out on a whim. "Lots of homework."

"That's a shame," he says, now looking at Avery. "A friend of mine wanted to meet you."

You fucking asshole. I grit my teeth and swallow the words down.

Avery perks right up. "Oh really? A friend on your team?"

Hayes nods and it's taking everything in me not to smack him. "Yep. You caught his eye during the game and I told him I might be able to convince you to come to Legends with us tonight."

She quirks a brow and it's like watching a scene from *Clueless* where Tai is convinced Elton is in love with her. "What's Legends?" she asks, and I listen because I'm curious myself. Not that we're going. *Not a chance in hell.*

"Only the best sports bar around. It's where all the players and fans go after the games."

I hold my fist to my mouth and cough out. "And puck bunnies."

Hayes's gaze snaps to mine. "Someone's been studying the sport."

"Oh yeah." I grimace. "Because puck bunnies have an entire chapter in Hockey 101."

Avery holds up a hand to shut me up and I groan. "So this Legends," she continues. "Can minors get in?" Her hands wave between us. "Because we're only nineteen."

"For sure," Hayes quips. "I've been going since freshman year."

"And that makes you…" Avery asks, as if she's doing me a favor by digging for information on him, from him. I'm not sure what more I have to say to make her believe I'm not interested.

She's insufferable at least.

"Third year, junior."

I'm sort of surprised Hayes is a junior. I assumed since he and Kamden were enemies, they were the same age. But Kamden is only a sophomore. I'm still so curious about what went down with these guys to make them despise each other so much.

"No. Your age." Avery taps her index finger to her lips. "How old are you?"

"Twenty-one."

Pleased with his response, she waggles her shoulders. "Perfect. You're buying us both a drink."

Hayes's sultry eyes skate to mine. "Deal." He curls his fingers at Avery. "Gimme your phone so I can text you the details."

Sure. Go ahead and steal my best friend while you're at it. You already stole my panties.

Hayes finishes up with her phone and gives it back to Avery, then gives me a look. "See you ladies soon?"

I'm not sure if it's a question or not, so I just shake my head and mumble, "Whatever."

"What the fuck!" a loud, deep voice booms from behind me. Hayes's eyes shoot past me and his face twists into a scowl. When I see his fists clench, I immediately spin around and find Kamden stalking toward us.

My heart hammers its way down to the pit of my stomach.

"Is this a fucking joke?" Kamden gnashes as he glowers at me. "I thought I told you to stay the hell away from him and you came to his fucking game!"

"Chill the fuck out, man," Hayes intervenes by stepping up to Kamden.

"It's okay," I whisper, stretching my hand out between the two of them.

"No!" Kamden growls before shooting daggers at Hayes. "It's not okay. I see what the fuck you're doing, Madden."

Steam rolls from Kamden's flared nostrils while Hayes just stands there, not affected in the least. I'm actually surprised, considering Hayes's fight I witnessed in front of Piggy's.

"And what is that?" Hayes asks nonchalantly.

"You're trying to get a rise out of me by homing in on my girl."

My eyes roll because it actually pisses me off that he'd even say that. Kamden has ignored me for days.

"Hayes didn't even know we were together, Kamden. But he's right. You need to chill out. There is nothing going on here.

Avery and I just came to watch the game because there's a guy on the team who caught her eye."

Kamden scoffs. "Of course there is."

"Hey!" Avery snaps at him. "What's that supposed to mean?"

With a deep exhale, he shoots her a scowl. "I think we both know what that means."

I shake my head in disgust at Kamden and change the subject quickly before Avery claws his eyeballs out. "What are you even doing here, Kamden?"

Furious eyes turn toward me as he pulls out his phone and brings up a picture. "One of the hockey cheer girls posted this," he says.

In the picture, Hayes has a guy slammed into the boards and it happened to be right in front of me. I remember that. It was just before Hayes made the winning goal.

And I'm grinning.

Kamden has no idea that the smile is because the guy landed an uppercut to Hayes's chin and it was hilarious to me. But apparently Kamden doesn't care what I have to say or he would have picked up his damn phone, so I just cross my arms instead.

"Damn, Donnelly. You sure do have a way with the ladies." Hayes looks at me and shoots a thumb at Kamden. "You're really dating this tool?"

My eyebrows pinch tightly together as I shake my head at Hayes. "Stop making things worse."

He shrugs. "What? I'm just surprised is all. Especially since I also saw a pic today. Only this one was of him and that snooty girl he was dating. What's her name again?" He snaps his fingers. "Oh, right. It's Gabby."

Kamden's jaw tics as he barrels toward Hayes. I jump in front of him while Hayes laughs, egging him on.

"Oh, was *your girl* not supposed to know about that? My bad."

"What's he talking about?" I ask Kamden as I shove him away to prevent him and Hayes from throwing down out here.

As pissed as I am right now, I'm slightly afraid Hayes would pound his face into the asphalt and I don't want the cheer team to be pissed at me for letting one of our best players get injured.

"He's full of shit," Kamden snarls, trying to reach over me, but I shove him back.

Avery holds her phone up with the screen on Gabby's Flash-Chat page. "There's nothing there."

"Why would you say that?" I ask, turning toward Hayes who is thumbing through his own phone.

"Because it's the truth. In fact, I took a screenshot of it." He holds up the screen, showing me a picture of Gabby with her lips pressed to Kamden's cheek.

"I was chilling on the couch and she just came up behind me and took it. I swear," Kamden says remorsefully. His eyes are pleading and I know it would totally be a Gabby move, but he's ignored me for days so my trust in him is minimal at this point.

My bottom lip quivers so I suck it between my teeth. "Where?"

He doesn't answer, just lowers his head, and in my gut I think I already know. Grabbing Hayes's phone from his hands, I get a good look at the couch in the picture. That's all I need to see. I shove it back into Hayes's chest without even looking at him. I'm seething at Kamden.

"She was in your dorm last night!" My voice rises. "I was calling you over and over again and *she* was with you!"

His hands fly in the air before dropping abruptly to his sides. "She just showed up with Laney. What was I supposed to do, kick them out?"

Laney is Gabby's best friend who is also on the squad. She's had a thing for Kamden's roommate Jeremiah since the start of the semester. Regardless, Kamden could have left, or at the very least, answered my calls and told me she was there.

"Are you seriously turning this around on me?" Kamden huffs. "I just found you in the parking lot with a guy I can't stand who you spread your fucking legs for."

I don't know what to think or say. "I can't believe you just said that to me." My voice is low, shock still racing through my body. I might not be proud of what Hayes and I did, but no one gets to make me feel like a whore.

Shaking my head, I take a step back, then another. Tears well in my eyes, and I hate crying in front of people. It sits next to the discomfort of getting a tooth pulled. "I have to go." My head drops as I walk away from them. A pang hits me in the chest and it's then that I realize, before Kamden showed up, I actually did have a good time tonight.

Avery walks briskly to my side and throws an arm around my shoulders. "I'm sorry, B."

A single tear skates down my cheek, but I sweep it away aggressively. "I'm done with him. So fucking done."

She sighs, and I'm sure it's a sigh of relief. Kamden has been an ass to her since day one and that's one red flag I shouldn't have ignored. Sometimes I think Avery knows what's best for me when I don't even know myself.

Suddenly, the symphony of shouting rings in our ears, followed by the sound of bone on bone. I turn around quickly and immediately run to Hayes and Kamden, who are rolling around on the asphalt. "Stop!" I shout at the top of my lungs. "Someone stop them!"

A group of people passing by stop, and a couple guys pull them apart. Spectators begin crowding around as the guys lash out at each other, vile and hateful words spilling from their mouths.

Avery holds me back with her arms wrapped around me.

"You think that uniform makes you something? It doesn't." Kamden fumes as blood drips from his nose onto the pavement. "You're a scumbag piece of shit, just like you've always been and always will be!"

Hayes brushes a bead of blood from his lip. "And you fucking think Daddy's money makes you something? Guess what? It doesn't. Have fun living in his shadow for the rest of your fucking life."

Tears flow from my eyes and I don't even attempt to hold them back as my heart breaks in two.

I'm just not sure who it's breaking for.

This isn't about me. It goes far beyond me and Hayes or me and Kamden. Something big happened between these two and while I wanted to know before, I don't think I do anymore. "Let's go," I tell Avery.

She nods as she turns me away from the commotion. "I take it we're not going to Legends?"

Avery is pretty damn good at distracting me enough to make the tears subside while we get the hell away from whatever that just was.

A small laugh escapes me as I swipe away the tears on my cheeks. "Not this time, babe."

CHAPTER 7

HAYES

"HERE YOU GO, SWEETIE," the cute waitress says as she hands me a paper towel wrapped ice pack. She insisted no matter how many times I told her I didn't need it. Wearing the evidence of a fight is like a badge of honor for hockey players, and it's even better if we don't get a concussion out of it. Though, there is no way Kamden can actually hit that hard.

He might play football, but his job is to catch the ball, not defend a puck like I'm used to. So this busted lip is nothing to me.

Just to appease the girl, I bring the ice to my mouth, and when the sting subsides, I hold it there.

"You think it's broken?" Finch asks in regard to Kamden's nose.

I blow out an airy breath. "One can only hope." Truth is, when he said those things about Brogan, I just lost it. I might hit 'em and quit 'em, but I don't talk about them like they are a whore. And he's supposed to be her boyfriend. That's fucked up.

"I still can't believe that fucker came at you on your own turf," my buddy, Lenny, says as he slides a freshly opened bottle of beer in front of me. I take a long swig, letting the cool drink soothe this weird ache in my chest. Kamden never should have been outside the rink tonight, but he came at me like he was hunting me.

I don't make a habit of running out of the locker room with all of my gear on. In fact, Coach and everyone else frowns upon it. But I had to talk to her. I knew she would leave the second the game was over, so as soon as I got out of my skates, I ran.

Coach will no doubt have my head about it later, especially because I made a scene in the parking lot. I'm just thankful there were no scouts there to witness it. That, and I paid off a few puck bunnies to make sure that any pictures of the altercation didn't get out. Which is why Finch offered to cover my tab tonight. He knows I'll pay him back, but right now, I think I need to just forget.

The bet with Brogan was supposed to be something fun, something just between us. Leave it to Kamden to ruin that just like he has done with everything else for as long as I can remember.

A few more of our teammates join us and our burly-ass goalie, Tank, throws his hands in the air. "I heard we're kicking someone's ass tonight."

I laugh as I drop the ice pack on the bar table and pick up my beer. "He'll get what's coming to him. No fucking doubt about that."

Kamden Donnelly was spared tonight, but when he least expects it, I have every intention of destroying him.

A few hours later, I'm toasted.

Scratch that, I'm fucking hammered. There was a happy medium at some point in the night. I was celebrating with my boys and feeling good. I had finally forgotten about Brogan and her shitty boyfriend.

Then some chick came into the bar that looked just like her and I started downing shots to get her out of my head. Shit went downhill fast from there.

Now the room is spinning and my head holds the weight of a bowling ball—and that's with me sitting in a chair. The second I stand up, I feel my body weight shift to the left and the next thing I know, I'm crashing into a high-top round table and watching glass shatter at my feet.

I hold my hands up, showing everyone I'm good. "I'm fine. Everything's fine."

Lenny throws an arm around my waist and I look up at him between the creases of my slitted eyes. "A little too close for comfort, big guy."

"That's it," Lenny says as he holds me up. "Let's get you home so you can go to bed."

I pull against him and sputter. "I'm not a fucking toddler. I can go to bed when I wanna go to bed. Now bring me back to campus so I can find that son of a bitch, Kamden. Then I'll put myself to sleep."

Anyone who knows Lenny knows he can physically overpower damn near any student at Rosewood U. He's intimidating at seven feet tall, with arms that could bench press a small car. He's as soft as they come, though. Like a big teddy bear with a heart of gold. We make jokes sometimes that he's like a dad to all of us. And right now, I think the title has gone to his head.

By the time we're outside, I don't even remember making it this far. A car pulls up and Lenny opens the back passenger door. "In you go," he says, practically stuffing me inside the car. He slams it shut before I have to chance to say thank you—*or fuck you.*

"Where ya taking me?" I ask the driver, who I can't see because it's dark as hell.

His growly voice echoes in the small space. "The destination said College Drive."

I shake a finger at him, barely able to keep my head afloat. "Nope. Take me to Hallstrom Hall."

"You'll have to make the change on the app you ordered from."

I pat my pockets in search of my phone, but I don't feel it. "Did you take my phone?"

"No, sir. I didn't take your phone."

I lean forward, bracing myself between the two front seats. "What about your friend?"

"My friend?"

"Yeah," I stammer. "Your friend up there with you."

"I'm alone, sir. There is no one else up here."

I drop back in my seat, dwelling on what he said. I could have sworn there were two of them. *Fuck. I'm wasted.*

In a last-ditch effort to find my phone, so I can change my destination, I dig my hand into the inside pocket of my jacket. "I got it," I shout as I pull it out. "I got my phone. Your friend didn't steal it. He's lucky too. I'd beat his ass."

The driver remains quiet and I'm pretty impressed with his level of patience. He must have kids. Toddlers, even. Toddlers that are in bed because they were told to go to sleep.

But I'm not a toddler and I can do whatever the hell I want.

By the time I open my rideshare app, the car comes to a stop. My eyes shoot to the left out the window. "Hey, this isn't Hallstrom Hall."

"As I said, the destination was not Hallstrom Hall. You can exit now."

I scratch the top of my head, dumbfounded. "But I found my phone."

To my surprise, the back door comes open and it's mind-boggling because the driver is still sitting up front. Must be his friend that was up there with him.

Two hands wrap around my lower waist and I'm pulled out of the car, which actually pisses me off.

"Get your fucking hands off me," I grumble and wriggle in an attempt to break free.

"Calm your ass down, Hayes." The voice is familiar and when I lift my tired eyes, I'm happy to see my good friend, Finch.

"Finchhhh," I howl. "Where the hell did you come from? I thought you were still at the bar."

"Dude. I left the bar two hours ago. Lenny called and woke my ass up and told me to come out here and get you."

"That Lenny's a good guy." I pat Finch on the shoulder, a smile on my face that feels a little off. Or maybe that's just me as I start tilting sideways. Or it's the earth spinning and now that I'm drunk enough I can feel it.

Finch wraps his arm around me and I lean into him. I'm a little fearful I might knock him down because he's built like a hockey stick, but the fucker is fast as hell on the ice.

"You're a good guy, too, Finch. You're all good people. Everyone but me. I'm a fuckup. A broke-ass fuckup."

I'm dropped onto the couch in the living room and once again, I'm not sure how I got here. "You're not a fuckup, man, but you are fucked up. Go to sleep." Finch tosses a blanket over me and I roll onto my side, realizing I still have my phone in my hand.

"I found my phone again," I call out, but I get no response back. "Yeah, fuck you guys, too."

I swipe open the screen on my phone, admiring the wallpaper. It's a shot of me scoring the final goal in our final game last season. *If you want a magical life, you have to make magic.*

My mom told me that before she died. I've been trying ever since.

Pushing away the thoughts of her, because I don't like to think about her, I open up my contacts list and scroll until I see "Legs." Then I tap the message icon.

Me: Your boyfriend is an asshole.

I still can't wrap my head around their relationship. What are the odds that Kamden fucking Donnelly—my biggest rival on campus—ends up dating the girl I slept with last spring. It just doesn't seem real. I can actually understand why he'd think I'm pursuing her, but this time it has nothing to do with him.

Brogan is sarcastic and cavalier, yet she calls me the arrogant one. She always has some snarky comeback for everything I say and doesn't know how to use the expression "thank you" appropriately. Now that I think about it, she's sort of a pain in the ass. It is fun getting under her skin, though. In fact it's so fun, I might actually enjoy it as much as I enjoy being on the ice.

Or maybe that's the booze talking.

My phone slips out of my hand and my eyes slowly close. The second my phone dings, they shoot back open. I reach down, slapping my hand around beside the couch until I find it.

> Legs: I'm not sure how you got my number, but lose it please.

Man, she's harsh, but I have no intention of losing her number. I've never let a girl linger on my mind as long as she has. I can't quite put my finger on what it is about her, but I chalk it up to her being different from all the other girls I've slept with. I told her to go, and she went.

The thing that gets me is, she actually stayed away when all of a sudden I just want her to be close. For some reason, her attitude only intrigues me further. And the fire that burns in her eyes every time she looks at me feels like a challenge.

I always did love a challenge because winning is how I make my magic. And I want to win Brogan.

I close my eyes, thinking about the first night I met her and how good it felt to bury my cock inside her sweet pussy.

Now all I can think about is how I want to do it again. Damn, that girl turns me on. So much so, I'm hard as fuck just thinking about her. Which is saying something with how drunk I am. I shouldn't even be able to get it up, but nope, I'm hard as nails.

Kicking off my pants and boxers, I get a firm grip on my cock. My thumb skims over my piercing, the barbell rolling with each stroke feeling better than sin.

My hand glides up and down my erection while I pull the image of her standing naked in my room from memory.

Only this time, she's wearing my game jersey. I let the mental picture linger for a minute, because fuck, she's hot.

I'd slowly peel my jersey over her head, exposing her milky, smooth skin. My eyes roam her body, landing on her chest. I'd give my left nut to suck on one of her perky tits right now. I'd drag my teeth across her budded nipple until she screams in agony-filled pleasure and begs me to do it again.

I envision the curvature of her hips that run down to her widespread thighs. If she were here, I'd bring both of her knees to her shoulders and bury my face in her dripping center.

Pumping myself faster, I see her again, standing in the dimly lit parking lot after my game. I remember the way she smiled and how something shifted inside me. I'm not sure what it was, but I wouldn't be opposed to feeling it again.

More so, I'd love to feel her tight lips wrapped around my cock.

Her slim fingers would wrap around my length, her other hand gripping my balls as she massages them. I can already feel her long nails pressing into them as I bring my newest fantasy to life.

I grip myself tighter, moving quicker, as I imagine it's her mouth sucking me off. Her mouth would be so warm and inviting. Those fiery eyes staring up at me with want in them.

I'd let her get her fill before tossing her on my bed and sliding into her. I'd fuck her like she was mine. *All mine.*

Heat shoots through my core and every muscle in my body tightens as I release, shooting cum into my hand. Using my shirt, I wipe it off and toss it to the corner as my reality begins to set back in.

It feels a little like that night. But this time, I wouldn't let her leave. I wouldn't run from that look she gave me because now I know that Brogan is a girl worth fighting for.

Now, I'm not sure how I'll ever settle for not having her in my bed again.

CHAPTER 8

BROGAN

MY ALARM BUZZES and it feels like I've barely slept. Between my late-night text conversation with Kamden, to my middle-of-the-night message from Hayes, I'm surprised I even woke up to my alarm.

After a long, drawn-out yawn, I open my eyes and snatch my phone off my nightstand, pulling it from the charging cord. I quickly swipe away my notifications so I can torture myself by rereading my conversation with Kamden last night.

> Kamden: You're unbelievable, Brogan. The fact that you're the one pissed right now is beyond me.

> Me: Quit playing innocent. All I did was lose a stupid bet and go to a hockey game. You invited your ex to your dorm.

> Kamden: I didn't invite her. She showed up. What part of that don't you understand?

> Me: I don't believe anything you say anymore.

> Kamden: You know what? Fuck this. There are a thousand girls in this school who would love to be in your position.

> Me: Oh, you mean in the position of their boyfriend running around with his ex. Sure. I'm sure a thousand girls would love that.

> Kamden: I'm not your boyfriend. Not anymore.

> Me: You haven't been my boyfriend for the past week. The minute you decided to ignore me instead of facing your problems like an adult you stopped being mine because you were too busy thinking about yourself. Have a nice life, Kamden.

I stop reading there because it only gets more painful after that. Although I said I was done with him when Avery and I left the arena last night, our relationship still felt unfinished.

Our conversation last night sealed the deal, though.

My dorm door comes flying open and Avery bursts inside like she's running from an axe murderer. "B," she cries. "Oh my God. Are you okay?"

I glance around the room, wondering if said axe murderer made his way in here without me seeing. "I'm…fine," I tell her warily.

"You poor thing. You haven't seen it, have you?" Her ass lands on the corner of my bed and she holds her phone in the air.

My eyes lock to the screen, and a shiver runs down my spine. My hands tremble, but I somehow manage to snatch the phone from her grasp to get a closer look.

"Where did you get this?" I gasp, barely able to catch my breath as the video of me pleasuring myself plays on repeat. I shake the phone in my hand, swallowing down the huge lump forming in my throat. "Why would Kamden do this to me?" I shout.

Avery's face contorts as she looks at the video. "That's Kamden?"

"Of course it's Kamden," I growl. "Who else would it be?"

She leans her head slightly to the right, observing the footage. "It's so hard to tell because it doesn't show his face."

"Who all has seen it?" I ask in a panic.

"Brogan," she gulps. "It was shared on Rosewood U's Flash-Chat page. It's since gone viral! It's everywhere."

My entire body breaks out in chills. *This can't be happening.* This can't seriously be happening right now. I cup my face in my hands, struggling to find enough oxygen to calm my racing heart. My eyes close, only to open immediately. I'm trapped in my own nightmare.

"Babe, you don't look so good," I barely hear Avery say. Her words sound so far away even as she's sitting right beside.

"I feel dizzy," I tell Avery. "I think I'm gonna pass out."

Avery lowers me down until I'm lying on my back, staring blankly at the ceiling.

Minutes pass. I'm not sure how many but enough for me to realize this is really happening.

"I'm transferring," I mutter into the pillow I've pulled over my head.

Avery grabs it and tosses it on the floor, so I cover my face with my hands. Then the bitch takes my arms and pins them to the sides of my body. "You are not transferring. With some time, this will blow over."

My face scrunches. "How much time do you think?"

"Eh..." She lifts a shoulder. "A couple weeks. Months at worst."

"Months?" I whimper. "Jesus Christ, Ave, how did this happen?"

Then it hits me.

My body shoots upright and all the blood rushes to my head. "I can't believe he did this."

"The guy's got balls, I'll give him that."

"No kidding. He's a heartless asshole."

"No." Her eyebrows hit her forehead as she looks back at her phone. "The guy has some big-ass balls. Hairy too. He should give those a trim. Gross."

"Oh my God, Avery," I hiss as I slap the phone out of her hand. "Stop watching that."

I fling myself back onto the mattress, burying my face in my hands again. "This is a fucking nightmare," I scream.

Digging my fingertips into my eyeballs, I make an attempt to pull myself together so I can find a way to save my reputation. But first, I need to know what I'm dealing with. I sit back up and hold out my hand. "Show me the whole thing."

"Maybe we should give it a little—"

"Show me!" I snap, curling my fingers. "I need to know, Ave. And once I do, I'm killing him."

"Now calm down, Brogan." Her voice softens. "You're not killing Kamden…because I'm doing it for you. I already have plans for him. There's duct tape and a shovel in my trunk. I bet the hockey team would help us bury him too."

If anyone can make me laugh at a time like this, it's Avery. I should probably keep a close eye on her, though, she's been waiting for this moment for a long time. She might actually kill him.

After tapping onto her phone, she hands it to me and humiliation takes hold as I watch myself on the screen. This video alone has twenty-three thousand views and has been shared over two hundred times. Of those two hundred shares, I can't even begin to imagine how many other views and shares there are. The math is making my head hurt.

As I'm watching, my head tilts slightly to the left, a smile tugging at my lips. "I actually look pretty fucking hot," I confess. "If this were anyone else, I'd say *get yours, girl.*"

"Right?" Avery blurts out. "I was thinking the same thing. I mean, I didn't watch the whole video because that's just weird, but, babe, you look hot as fuck. I'm surprised guys aren't banging down our door right now."

Avery was right, though. Kamden is shown in the bottom

corner of the video, but you can't even tell it's him because all it shows is his stomach. *Ope. There's a penis.*

The worst part is, this doesn't even make him look bad. If anyone figures out that it's him, he will be held to a high honor while I'll be ridiculed and shamed. Kamden has a smoking hot body and the girls are going to flock right to it. The guys will offer up high fives and might even crown him for his big cock. I don't even want to think about what the female population at Rosewood U will say about me.

A knock at the door has me stuffing Avery's phone underneath my ass, as if I'm hiding something that nobody has seen.

Avery jumps up and heads to the door, but I stop her. "I can't face anyone right now."

She moves closer and presses her eye to the peephole before shooting me a glance. "It's Lucia and Jared."

I sigh. "All right. Let 'em in."

Avery opens the door, waves them inside, then pokes her head out, looking up and down the hall. "The paparazzi haven't arrived yet," she teases before closing the door. "But rest assured we will beat their asses if they do."

It's great that she's making jokes, but at some point, I will have to leave this room and it won't be funny anymore.

"Girl," Lucia says with her arms spread wide. She's coming at me like my grandma just passed away. "How are you, hon?"

I let her hug me and give her a couple pats on the back. "I think my mind is in a state of shock right now. But what can I do, ya know?"

"I'll tell you what you can do," Jared begins. "You're gonna pull yourself together and walk out of this room with your head held high. If the world sees that this video has knocked you down, they'll keep you down. But if you show them you're unfazed, they'll get bored with it."

"Good point," Avery tells him as she sits down at her vanity. "Just get up and get ready and go to class like nothing happened."

My eyes widen and my heart races. "I can't go to class. It's too soon. The video is still getting shared. What if someone in one of my classes sees it for the first time *during* class. No." I shake my head. "I'm not leaving this room today. Maybe not even tomorrow."

"What about cheer?" Lucia asks.

"I'll text Coach Wendy and tell her I'm sick. Unless she's seen it, too. Oh my God!" I cry as I fall back onto the mattress. "Why is this happening to me?"

"Kamden Donnelly," Avery grits out. "That's why."

My eyebrows pinch together tightly and I grind my teeth so hard I'm certain I just chipped a molar. "Kamden Donnelly is going to rue the day he double crossed me."

My face twists with frustration as I grab my phone to find that I have even more notifications. I never even checked the ones that came overnight. Tears well in the corners of my eyes because I know what's behind the dozens of texts and voicemails.

By now, my parents have probably heard. My sisters, my brothers. This is worse than a nightmare. This is a living hell. I can't read them right now. But what I can do is give Kamden a piece of my mind.

Opening our text log, I practically pound out a message to him…

> Me: I should report you for harassment and slander after this shit you pulled. I knew you could be an asshole, but I had no idea you were so coldhearted. How could you do this to me?

Then I block his number because I know he'll deny any wrongdoing. I don't even care to hear his pathetic lies. I just want him to know that I know it was him.

The damage is done. Now I have to clean up the mess.

CHAPTER 9

HAYES

I'm RELUCTANTLY POURING myself a cup of coffee and I don't even drink the shit. Something needs to kick this killer hangover in the ass because I already missed my first class of the day and I can't afford to miss any more. Coach is already on my ass about my grades and if they slip any further, I'm fucked.

The house is blissfully quiet, thank the Greek gods, because so much of a mouse crawling across the floor might make my head explode.

With my cup of coffee in hand, I go into the living room and sit back down on the couch where I slept last night. If my pounding head wasn't proof enough that I was off my ass wasted, the lapse of memory is. I don't even remember leaving the bar. I don't even know how the hell I got back to the house.

As I bring the mug to my mouth, the scent wafts up my nose and my stomach curls. "Screw this nasty shit," I mutter as I set it down on the end table beside me.

I lean back, paralyzing myself to the couch as I try to recall the events of last night. I remember talking to Brogan after the game. Then Kamden showed up and we brawled in the parking lot.

My finger skates across my bottom lip and I notice the slight bump. Wonder how Kamden's looking this morning. I'm pretty sure I jacked up his nose.

After that, the guys and I went to Legends and it's all a blur from that point on.

I pat my body down in search of my phone, but it's not on me. *Shit. Did I lose it last night?*

I spring to my feet and stand up, immediately regretting that decision because the pounding in my head intensifies.

I scan the living room, searching for my phone. My eyes dart from the couch to the coffee table and then to each recliner. When I don't see it, I drop to my hands and knees, scouring every inch of the carpet.

Relief floods through me when I see the end of it poking out from underneath a cushion. I pull it out and drop my ass to the floor, leaning my back against the couch.

No missed calls or messages is a good thing after a night of heavy drinking. But when I see that a text exchange was created with Brogan, I blow out a pent-up breath of air and slump further into the floor.

Bracing myself for whatever I may have said to her, I open the chat log.

> Me: Your boyfriend is an asshole.

Okay. Not bad. And truthful, I might add.

> Legs: I'm not sure how you got my number, but lose it please.

That's it. I'm actually surprised as hell I left it at that. I would have expected my drunk ass to at least respond because I've been told I become extremely defensive when I'm drinking.

It seems Brogan is the only person I texted last night and I'm grateful as hell for that. The combination of deep regret and being hungover is literally the worst. It's the main reason why I usually don't drink more than a beer or two. Especially during peak season for hockey. I don't like who I become, or the choices I make.

After lying on the floor for a few minutes, my headache subsides enough for me to pull myself up and get in the shower so I can make it to at least two of my three classes today.

"He's alive," Lenny bellows as I walk into my clinical psych class. I hesitantly pull out a chair beside him because I know he's gonna give me shit.

As suspected, he claps a hand on my back with a thud and lets out his booming laugh that echoes loud enough in the room to grab everyone's attention. "My man, you were a mess last night. There is drunk—then there is *Hayes Madden drunk*."

I sink into my chair and let my head fall back with a smile. "Good times, huh?"

Evan—one of the Kappa Rho frat members, a housemate of mine, and teammate—sits down in the empty seat beside me. We bump knuckles and he asks, "What's up, brother?"

"Just another day," I tell him before returning my attention to Lenny.

"We sure as hell had a good time," Lenny says. "I don't know about you, though. All you kept talking about is some chick named Brogan and that fucker Kamden Donnelly."

Fuck. Was I seriously talking about her?

Lenny continues, "You must have it bad because I've never heard you talk about a girl like that. Or any girl, for that matter."

That's it. No more alcohol for a very long time.

"It's probably best if we just pretend last night never happened." I wave a hand, trying to dismiss the whole thing, but Lenny knows me too well.

"Nah, man," he roars. "I need to know more about this girl."

"Did you say Brogan?" Evan asks, grabbing my attention. "As in Brogan Astor?"

I tip my chin. "I don't know her last name, but I imagine there aren't many Brogans on campus. What about her?"

He holds his phone out, showing me a video of some chick rubbing her clit. Then the girl's face appears. I snare the phone from his hand aggressively, giving the video a double take to make sure my eyes aren't deceiving me. "Holy fuck. Where'd you get this?"

Lenny grabs Evan's phone from me and his eyes widen, a smile creeping on his lips, and I immediately snatch it back from him and swipe the screen to shut it off.

"What the fuck? Lemme watch," Lenny grumbles.

I hold up Evan's phone, my hands trembling. "How *the fuck* did you get this video?"

"The university FlashChat page," he responds, and the casualty in his tone unnerves me. "My feed is full of it. Different clips and memes have been shared all morning. Rumor has it, Kamden Donnelly shared it."

That son of a bitch.

Evan reaches for his phone, but I hold it back. "Report this shit. Every time either one of you sees this video, report it. And if I see anyone..." I raise my voice so the whole class hears me. "And I mean anyone, watching this video, I'll smash your fucking phones with my bare hands."

"Watch your language, Madden," Professor Clements calls out.

I'm hit with a sudden urgency to go talk to Brogan. It seems we might actually agree on something for a change—Kamden Donnelly is a fucking prick who deserves to suffer. Who better to make that happen than his disgruntled ex.

Slamming Evan's phone to the table, I push my chair back and get up. "Report it!" I grind out before gathering up my shit.

Our professor stares at me so I level him with a glare. "Unless you're encouraging people to share unsolicited videos of women without their consent."

He swallows thickly, eyes darting across the room. "No, Madden, I would not encourage that."

Giving him a nod, I turn to the door. "You've all been warned."

Lenny's jaw drops and Evan frantically begins typing on his phone, no doubt spreading the message that this shit won't stand while also reporting the video.

Walking steadfastly out of the room, I go out the main doors and head to the concrete staircase where students often gather. There is a couple dozen out here, casually hanging out, reading, and playing on their phones.

I walk behind each one of them, curious if they're watching her.

My heart hammers against my rib cage when I step behind three guys who are crowded around a phone the middle one is holding. "What the fuck!" I growl as I reach between them and grab the phone right out of the douchebag's hands.

"Hey!" One of them lets out a high-pitched squeak. He's pretty scrawny and looks like he should be in middle school, not college. He holds out his hand, face flushed with anger. "Give me my phone back."

The other two hang back and keep their mouths shut because they know what's good for them.

I grip the phone tightly in my hand. "You're lucky I don't shatter this thing right now. Mark my words, if I ever see you nitwits watching that video again, not only will I destroy your phones, I'll break your goddamn teeth."

Scrawny Boy shakes his head. "Fine. We won't watch it. But do you plan on threatening the entire university? Because we're not the only ones."

I shove the phone into his chest and he catches it before it falls. "If that's what it comes to. Don't fuck with me."

Jogging down the steps, I pull out my phone and text Avery. Brogan told me to lose her number last night, so I doubt she'd respond to me now. Her best friend will, though.

Me: Hey, it's Hayes. I'm not sure if you're aware of what's going on but there is a very graphic video of your girl surfing around campus.

As I wait for a response, I head to the student center to get some food. I'm fucking famished and I can't deal with this shit day and a hangover without food.

CHAPTER 10

BROGAN

"Go away!" I holler as the knocks on the door continue. This is the fourth time today and I still don't even know who was out there. It could have been someone from the squad. Could have been one of my coaches. Or it could have been a guy thinking I'm easy and down to fuck.

I pull the pillow back over my head, drowning out the rhythmic pounding, but the thuds grow relentless and urgent.

It's only been half a day and it already feels suffocating in here, as if the walls are slowly closing in around me.

Knock. Knock. Knock. "Open the door, Legs."

Springing up, the pillow falls beside me. *Did I hear what I think I heard?*

"Who's there?" I call out, eagerly waiting for a response.

It comes immediately. "It's Hayes. I've got something for you."

I wouldn't be surprised if he's referring to his nine-inch pierced cock. He probably saw the video and thinks I'm just gonna fall back on the bed and spread my legs for him...*again*.

My shoulders slump and I roll my eyes. "Whatever it is, I don't want it."

"Even if it's a chocolate croissant and an oat milk mocha latte?"

How the hell does he know I love chocolate croissants and the way I drink my coffee?

My brow furrows and I tilt my head to the side. "Who have you been talking to?"

I slowly peel the blanket off me and stand up, moving at a snail pace as I creep toward the door.

"Talked to Avery and she told me you weren't feeling well. I thought maybe I'd stop by and cheer you up."

"You're the least cheerful person I know, Hayes. What are you up to?" I'm at the door now and I could open it if I really wanted to. But I don't. That latte and croissant sure sound tempting, though. I can almost smell the sweet goodness.

"Just trying to help out a friend."

"We're not friends." I bend down and look in Avery's vanity mirror, running my fingers under my eyes to erase the smears of mascara.

"Just open the damn door. Your coffee is getting cold and I know how much you hate that."

For the first time all day, my lips twitch with a smile. "For being a complete stranger, you sure do know a lot about me. Should I be concerned?"

"Probably," he deadpans.

I click the lock and drag the chain then wrap my fingers around the door handle. Drawing in a deep breath, I pull the door open and come face to face with Hayes, who isn't looking so hot. His eyes are bloodshot and glossed over and his lips are redder than usual. He's dressed down in a pair of gray joggers and a black Devils hoodie.

I press my hand on my hip and narrow my eyes. "Didn't I tell you last night to leave me alone?"

Clutching a brown paper bag from Clara's Cafe under his arm and holding a hot latte in his hand, Hayes leans into the doorframe. "I think your exact words were, *lose my number, please.*" The corner of his mouth tugs up in a grin. "I will say, I did appreciate your manners in that text."

"In that case, can you *please* go?"

His eyebrows pinch together as he straightens his back. "Why are you so mean to me, Legs?"

I tap my chin. "Oh, let me count the reasons. How about if we start with the fact that you call me Legs."

"What's wrong with Legs? It's not insulting." His eyes drag down my body and I feel the heat of his stare between my thighs. "If anything, it's a compliment."

"Okay then. I'll let that one slide for now. Let's go back to the first night we met. It all started when you stole a cup from me…"

"Ahh…" He holds up a finger. "Now, if I remember right, you were gawking at me for, like, ten minutes with your hand on the stack of cups. Can you blame me for getting impatient? I needed a beer to deal with all the drama in that room and you were in my way."

The sound of voices hits my ears and I poke my head out in the hall to see a group of girls walking in our direction. One of them has her phone in her hand and she lifts her eyes to mine.

"That's the girl in the video," I hear her say. "I told you her room was down here." Laughter echoes down the hall and in a swift motion, I lunge forward and grab Hayes by the pocket of his hoodie and jerk him into my room. The door slams shut behind us and as we stumble, hot coffee splatters onto my shirt.

I hold my arms out as the liquid seeps through the fabric and hits my stomach. "Now look what you've done."

"Accountability isn't your strong suit." With his hand held out to keep the coffee from dripping down his arm, Hayes scoffs. "What the hell was that all about anyways?"

"Those girls, umm, we don't get along." It's a lie. I don't even know who those girls are, but it seems my dorm room has become a museum for video sluts and everyone wants to see the main piece.

Hayes bites the corner of his bottom lip. "Hmm. Okay."

My defenses kick into high gear. "You think I'm lying?"

Best-case scenario, Hayes hasn't seen the video and never will. Worst-case scenario, he's here out of pity because he *has* seen it.

"Considering I heard one of them say, 'that's the girl in the video' and another say, 'I told you her room was down here.' Yeah. I think you're lying."

Defeat hits me all at once. My shoulders drop and I sink my ass into my mattress. "You heard that?"

"Yeah." He nods. "I heard that."

"I assume that means you know? About the video, I mean?" My face heats, my ears getting hot as the tears I thought were gone fight to come back. I won't cry in front of him, though. I won't.

His face scrunches as he says, "It's sort of why I'm here. How are you holding up?"

I scoff. "As if you care."

"I'm here, aren't I?" The way he says the words, as if he is disarming himself and actually trying, it makes my shoulders slump a little. If Hayes Madden feels sorry for me then this really is bad.

My cheeks feel flushed, followed by a sharp jab to my chest. I look down, unable to make eye contact as I ask the burning question, "Did you watch it?"

His silence has my eyes shooting up. "Hayes! Tell me you didn't watch it!"

He brings his hands to his chest, bag and coffee still gripped. "I'm a man, Legs. A man with the curiosity of a cat. But in my defense, it was only a peek. In fact, I even stopped a few other guys from watching it."

Hands folded in my lap, I lift a brow. "Oh yeah? What'd you do?"

"Beat the fuck out of 'em with a hockey stick then shoved a puck in their mouths."

Always a comedian.

I blow out a heavy breath of air before falling onto my back. "Honestly, I'm not even mad that you saw it," I tell him truthfully. "I wish nobody had watched it, but there is only one person to be mad at in this whole situation."

Hayes comes closer and I lift my head to meet his gaze. "Kamden?"

"Yup."

Cautiously, he takes a step forward, though he looks at me like I might bite his head off for it. Now, I'm considering it. But he brought treats and if I kill him now, he could drop them and that would be a waste. "I take it that was him in the video?"

"Well, yeah," I say with a bite of sarcasm. "He *is* my boyfriend." Blinking back tears, I try to keep my composure. "At least he was."

"Hey," Hayes says softly as he comes closer. He sets the bag and cup down on my nightstand and runs his hand over the spilled coffee on his sleeve. "It's his loss. The guy's a prick."

My throat tightens and I struggle to swallow around the lump that feels like it's the size of my fist. "I just wish I would have realized it before I let him in."

"Before you let him in your..." He looks down between my legs and I pin him with an intense scowl. "Sorry. The mind of a man."

"No, not *that*." I grimace. "Before I let him in my heart. I guess that's what I get for wearing it on my sleeve."

I don't even know why I'm saying all of this to Hayes. I don't even know why he's standing in my room right now. I don't even like him.

He falls silent, clearly not comfortable talking about emotions, or any serious matters. I sort of pegged him that way. Every word that falls from his lips is either laced with dark humor or coated with teasing insults.

I feel that, though. Talking about feelings isn't really my thing either. It's just that right now I'm feeling so much and if I don't get some of it out, I might literally go crazy. These four walls have been staring at me all day as I try to wrap my head around everything that's going on. It's tumultuous enough to make anyone spill their guts to the first person that walks through the door.

"Anyways," I say as I sit up and crack a smile to lighten the mood. "Thanks for the croissant and the coffee. It's like you read my mind or something."

"No worries." He slices his hand through the air. "Though, your friend warned me you wouldn't drink it if it was cold, so it's probably no good now."

I reach for the cup and when I grab it, I notice it's still fairly warm. Giving it a soft blow through the lid, I take a sip and while it is cold, I say, "It's perfect."

Wait. Am I being nice to Hayes? By golly, I think I am.

Hayes looks around the room rabidly. "Who is this show for?" He quirks a brow with a glint of a smile on his lips. "Is Brogan Astor actually being nice?"

Dammit. I knew I should have just spit the coffee out and told him it was gross.

"Hey now, I happen to be a very nice person."

He gives me this squinted look that happens to make him appear even more devilishly handsome, even in his state. It's not fair. "I'm almost positive you were in the middle of listing all the reasons you're mean to me, when you abruptly pulled me into your room like you were ready to ravish me."

I nearly choke on my cold coffee as I spit, "Ravish you?"

"You were pretty aggressive."

"I was desperate."

"Rigggght," he drawls. "Desperate to hide from those girls you don't get along with."

"Something like that." My tone shifts to a more serious note. "I'm mortified, Hayes. Things have been rocky with me and Kamden, but I had no idea he'd stoop so low. My reputation is completely destroyed."

"Ever heard the saying, bite the bug that bit you?"

"Yes." I laugh. "But doesn't that pertain to a hangover?"

"It does and I've got a killer one right now. But I think that saying can take on another meaning. Kamden bit you." He shrugs. "So bite him back."

"Oh, I'm gonna bite him. I'm gonna bite him so hard my teeth marks will become a permanent tattoo on his skin."

He smiles, but it's not one full of his normal sarcasm. This one looks like he is actually concerned for me. "That works too, but hear me out. What better way to get back at your ex who wronged you than by *getting with...*" He air quotes. "...his biggest enemy?"

Now I'm really laughing. Full-blown hysterics. "You've officially lost your mind." The serious look on his face is a little unnerving. "Wait. You're joking, right?"

"Do I look like I'm joking?"

He doesn't and that's a little scary. I need to end this conversation before I'm sucked into another one of Hayes's horrible ideas. The last time he had a spontaneous suggestion, I ended up naked in his bed.

"Okay, Mr. Comedian." I drop my feet on the floor and stand up. "You probably have classes to get to, yes?"

He shrugs, lying on my bed as if he owns it. "Skipped 'em all today."

"To come here to bring me coffee and to offer yourself up for revenge against my ex? I think you wasted your time."

"I think you speak too fast. Think about it, Legs. This could be good for both of us. We both want Kamden to suffer and he will if you just say yes."

I laugh, though there is no humor in the sound. "Say yes to what, exactly? Sleeping with you?" God, just saying it makes my skin crawl. It's not that I find Hayes hideous—the exact opposite, actually. Part of me is a little afraid that if I did sleep with him again, I could potentially fall for him, and that's the most honest I've been with myself throughout this entire situation.

I can't fall for Hayes. Not only is he a player, but he's... Hayes. He's annoying and cocky. He is oddly charming, though, even if his charm is followed up with a sexual innuendo or an arrogant remark.

"Not exactly," Hayes continues. "I mean, I'm down to fuck if you are, but that's not what I was implying."

"Who just casually asks someone if they're down to fuck?" I shake my head at his forwardness. Doesn't he ever get embarrassed by the shit he says? And why am I suddenly embarrassed? I'm not the one who said it, but I definitely feel heat rise in my cheeks.

"I mean, isn't it better to ask than assume? I prefer to have a conversation about it first to make sure both players are on the same team."

I clutch my heart, sitting back on the bed. "Such a romantic."

"You want romance?" he asks, and I immediately shake my head no. "Oh, I can romance you, Legs." He sits up, leaning in like he's gonna kiss me and I back away so fast I bump my head on the headboard.

"Don't ever do that again," I growl, though I can't help but smile. He's so…weird. But right now, I sort of like his quirkiness. For a sliver of a moment I actually forgot all about the video and how my life is in shambles.

Hayes laughs. "Chill out, Legs. I'm not really gonna kiss you."

I'm not sure why there's a pang of disappointment in my chest. I don't want him to kiss me. Hell no. So why am I looking at his mouth right now? His lips curve upward and my eyes shoot up to his to find him staring back at me. Fuck. He noticed. And knowing him, he'll call me out for it.

"Unless you want me to," he continues.

"Easy pass," I quip as I grab my coffee and take a sip. I need something to do with my hands—and my eyes. I can't look at him right now.

"Lemme know if you change your mind."

He just never stops. I smile behind the lid of my cup but don't say anything.

"Anyways, as I was saying. You wanna do this? Stick it to Kam where it hurts?"

He called him Kam. Only people who are close to him call

him that. Most everyone calls him Kamden. I'm probably just overthinking it, but it's a little strange.

"Tell me this plan you concocted again." I know I'm going to regret even asking, but I might as well hear him out. He did come all this way with food and coffee.

"Let's make a video." His hands fly in the air before smacking down on his thighs. All the while, my jaw is sitting in my lap.

"A video?" I pick up my jaw before I burst out laughing. "Yep. You've lost your mind."

"Do you have any idea how much that would piss Kamden off? Not only would he be angry, and a little hurt, but he'd also be embarrassed as hell that his own video was followed by something so much sexier. You can't deny we've got chemistry in bed. He'll wanna crawl in a hole when he sees how hot we are together." Is it bad that equal parts of me want to give in to this idea, but also want to slap him across the face for it.

"It's really sad that I can't even tell if you're joking or if you're serious. But I hope like hell this is a joke."

His shoulders lift and the expression on his face isn't one of humor. "It's a solid plan."

"Let me get this straight." I set my coffee down and stand up to pace in front of him. "You want me and you to make a sex video and share it with the entire school?"

"Or we just send it to Kamden and see where it goes from there."

I freeze, turning to him like a fucking robot because my body just went that stiff. "You really are serious right now?"

He holds out his hands as if he is the picture of innocence while we talk about making a sex video and sharing it publicly. "Hey, I'm just trying to help."

"Noooo," I drag out the word. "You're trying to send Kamden into a fit of rage. Do you want him to kill you or something? Because he probably would if we did…that. Which we're *not*."

Hayes drags his fingers through his hair, silently staring at his feet. "You're right." He lifts his head. "It was a stupid idea. I'm hungover as fuck. Maybe even still a little drunk."

"It was a stupid idea," I tell him, but to save his dignity a little, I add, "don't worry, Hayes. Karma is a bitch and Kamden will get his."

He nods as he takes steps toward the door.

This sudden shift in his demeanor is a little unsettling. There's some real animosity between him and Kamden and I think it goes deeper than I could ever imagine.

"Hey, Hayes," I say, stopping him in his tracks. "What happened with you two anyways?"

I doubt he'll tell me, but it's worth a shot.

"That's a story for another time. You gonna be all right?"

"Oh yeah." I smile. "Don't worry about me. I'm like a rubber ball. I always bounce back."

"I believe that." He shoots two fingers in the air before pulling the door open. "Later, Legs."

The door closes behind him, and I whisper, "Later, Hayes."

I'm not sure who that decent human being with terrible ideas was, but it sure as hell wasn't the Hayes Madden I've grown to love to hate.

CHAPTER 11

HAYES

I'M STEPPING off the bus and into the cold drizzle of rain coming down when my phone chimes with a text. I reach into my pocket and pull it out.

Legs: Can you come back over? I need to talk to you.

Without a second thought, I type out a response.

Me: On my way.

Just as the bus doors begin to close, I jump back on and take the ten-minute ride back to Hallstrom Hall. By the time I get there, the sun has set. I have no idea why she would want to talk to me, but maybe I gave her a bit of a reprieve from all her feelings earlier.

Moving as fast as I can, I head down the hall to Brogan's room. As if she was watching from her window, her door comes open and she pokes her head out.

"Everything okay?" I ask as I walk steadfastly toward her.

She nods. "I changed my mind. I think we should do it."

Excitement swirls in my stomach. I quirk a brow, curious if we're on the same page. "Changed your mind about what?"

She looks both ways down the hall for added measure before saying, "Not out here." Then she disappears back into her room.

My chest tightens with a mix of confusion and excitement as I walk back into her dorm room. I push open the cracked door and see her sitting on the edge of her bed, legs crossed. Her messy hair falls in waves around her face and even with the coffee stain on the front of her oversized t-shirt, she looks gorgeous.

Wondrous eyes sparkle as she looks at me. "I wanna do it."

I close the door, making sure it latches before taking slow and deliberate steps toward her. "I'm gonna need you to be more specific here, Legs."

Brogan leans back slightly on the bed, pressing her palms to the mattress. "I wanna make the video."

I gulp, biting anxiously on the corner of my bottom lip as my gaze trails down her body to the hem of her shirt. The fabric falls just below her hips and when she uncrosses her legs, pressing the tips of her toes firmly against the floor, I see the outline of her pussy. She curls her hips inward, trying to conceal herself, but it's clear she's not wearing any panties. The realization makes my pulse quicken. "I umm…maybe we should talk about this first."

"What's there to talk about? It was your idea." She looks almost embarrassed and that's the last thing I want her to experience after the day she's had.

"You're right. It was." I scratch underneath my chin, fighting the urge not to stare at what she's failing to hide under there. The thing is, I didn't really think through what I was saying in here earlier. The words sort of just came running out of my mouth like an uncontrollable case of diarrhea. I wasn't even surprised when she shot down the idea. But now, I'm fucking speechless that she's agreeing to it.

"So what's the big deal? It's not like we haven't had sex before. We'll just be recording it this time." Her eyes bore into mine, but her words are what strike a chord with me. This is a big deal. It's a huge deal, in fact. The girl I can't get off my mind, who swears she hates me, just offered to have sex with me to make someone jealous.

"Like, right now?" I stammer, prolonging this for reasons I can't even comprehend. I guess I'm still processing what's going on. I'm not even sure why I'm still standing here. I should have her on her back with my cock inside her this very second. Yet, something is holding me back.

She lifts her shoulders lazily. "Sure, why not?"

My eyes shift to her nightstand and I see a half-empty bottle of potent vodka. It's all starting to make sense. This girl must really be hurting right now. I was gone fifteen minutes, tops, and she's already drunk.

I move in front of her and take a few steps until I'm standing between her legs while my dick twitches. Reaching down, I tip her chin up with two fingers. "How much have you had to drink?"

Her soft blue eyes look up at me, appearing lost and sad. "Does it matter?"

"I think it does. Why don't you eat your croissant and sleep this off then we'll talk tomorrow when you're thinking more clearly?"

Her arms reach out, wrapping around my lower waist, and a subtle growl climbs up my throat. She tugs me closer, but I put up resistance, even though it's tempting as fuck to fall into her.

"Why are you being like this?" she asks. "Is it because I'm damaged goods now?"

"God no," I spit out as I run my fingers through her tangled hair. "Trust me, Legs. You are tempting as fuck. I just don't want you to have regrets tomorrow."

"I'm not drunk, if that's what you think. I just took a couple shots so I could be more relaxed when we…ya know."

My head falls back and I take a deep breath. *She's fucking killing me right now.*

"If you can't say it, we can't do it," I tease in an attempt to lighten the mood and settle down my dancing cock.

Her doe eyes peer up at me. "Always giving me a hard time."

"Someone has to." I grin. "Seriously, though…" I comb my fingers through her hair again, already regretting what I say next. "Sleep on it and I'll stop by tomorrow and we can talk again."

She gnaws on the inside of her cheek, looking at me unsurely. "You're not really as cruel as you want people to think you are, are you, Hayes Madden?"

There's a pang in my chest I wasn't expecting. *If she only knew.* "Depends on who you ask."

"If someone asked me, I know exactly what I'd tell them."

Narrowing my eyes, I assess her. "Do I dare ask?"

She smiles. "I'd tell them not to judge you so quickly. Then again, that could just be the alcohol talking."

Lifting my finger in the air, I point it at her jokingly. "Ahh. So you are drunk."

She pinches her fingers together and squints. "Little bit."

"All right, Legs." I swiftly grab her by the waist and lift her to the head of her bed before pulling the blanket up. "It's been an eventful day for you. Get some sleep and I'll check in tomorrow."

I go to turn around, but I'm stopped when Brogan says, "Hayes."

I raise my brows. "Yeah?"

She sighs, her eyes already heavy, which makes me feel good about this choice. If I'm having sex with Brogan, I want her sober. I want her to look into my eyes the same way she did that first time and even though it terrifies me, I want her to make me feel what I felt in that moment again.

"Thanks for not judging me when I judged you so harshly."

I walk up to the side of her bed, brushing some of her hair back before my finger strokes her chin. She leans into my touch in a way I'm not used to. Brogan isn't a puck bunny just trying to get with a hockey player—she isn't just *some* girl. "You had every right to judge me, Legs. I'm the first to admit I have asshole tendencies."

She chuckles, before looking up at me. "Don't we all?"

I grin, and though I have no idea why, I lean down and plant a kiss on the top of her head. It's something I've never done before, but something in my gut tells me she needs this. She needs to know that not every guy out there is like Kamden. And though I'm no hero, I know for a fact that I would treat Brogan better than Kamden ever did. "Yeah. I guess we do. G'night, Legs."

Turning around, I open her door and step out into the hall. Before I close it, I can hear her sleepy voice mutter. "Night, Hayes."

I should get a fucking award right now because I am hard as fucking nails and just turned down sex with my dream girl, for what? To be a good guy? Shit, what is this woman doing to me?

CHAPTER 12

HAYES

I T 'S BEEN four hours and I've reported over a hundred videos of Brogan on FlashChat. I've even exchanged a few unkind words with some of the people who have reposted it. I'm supposed to be meeting some guy named Dirk in front of the library in twenty minutes so he can "kick my ass before he pounds his cock into Brogan's wet pussy." His words, not mine.

If it weren't for the downpour outside and my level of exhaustion, I'd actually show up. Doubt he will, though.

It's all good. I just photoshopped a picture he shared of him eating an ice cream cone to him eating a dick instead. For extra credit, I added the wording, "I like big dicks and I cannot lie."

Immature? *Maybe*. Funny as fuck? *Hell yes*.

Oddly enough, it's the first thing I've ever shared on my account that isn't hockey related. Once I'm confident I've made a dent in the videos, I search up Brogan's page. I find it almost instantly and click to view her profile.

It's obvious she hasn't been on here recently because it's flooded with pics of her and Kamden. *Wait a damn minute.* Legs never told me she cheers for the Devils' football team. I shouldn't be surprised after witnessing her love for the sport, but I sort of am. It's hard to imagine her being peppy and faking smiles.

After giving her a follow, I scroll through more of her pictures, noticing how happy she looks while wondering if it's all for show. From what I can tell, she's got a couple sisters and some brothers. Seemingly normal home life. Then again, we only share what we want people to see.

I stop on each photo of her and Kamden, torturing myself. The more I look at him beside her—touching her, kissing her, hugging her—the angrier I become. How does a guy like that get a girl like her? She's far too good for him and his holier-than-thou attitude.

A notification pops up telling me Brogan is live. *Shit, girl. What are you up to now? You're supposed to be sleeping off the booze.*

Without hesitation, I click to view her live footage while my heart pounds in my chest in anticipation of what I'm about to watch.

She appears on the screen and a smile instantaneously lifts my cheeks. Her damp hair is framing her face, leaving me to assume she just got out of the shower. She's not wearing any makeup and looks more beautiful than ever.

"Some of you might be surprised to see me on here considering what's been circulating. If you don't know what I'm talking about, then consider yourself lucky. You see, my ex-boyfriend decided he would exact revenge on me for reasons I don't understand, by sharing a very graphic video. It's hard to tell when you watch it, but that tiny little thing in the corner belongs to Kamden Donnelly."

"Atta girl," I bellow as I laugh my ass off.

Brogan narrows her eyes at the camera as if she's speaking directly to one person in particular. "Kamden, I just wanna say thank you."

What? Why the hell is she thanking him?

"Thank you for giving me the opportunity to speak out against all the people who have slut-shamed women, or told them that sex before marriage is a sinful act and you'll be condemned to hell. If you're one of those people, I feel sorry for you. I just skimmed through dozens of messages from horrible judgmental people telling me how I should off myself because I'm a waste of skin. Or how ashamed I should be. And do you know what I have to say in response? Shame. On. You."

Damn. She's getting deep and I fucking love it. I shift on my bed until I'm sitting with my back to the headboard and concentrate on her beautiful face. That fire in her eyes is back, and I have a feeling that this time it's there to stay.

"We need to end the stigma that sex is something to be embarrassed about. Sex is a natural and healthy part of life and I will not be a pariah because I choose to engage in it. My body is my body. And your body belongs to you. Do what you want with it. Cherish it, touch it, love it. That's *your* right."

This girl is cool as fuck. I'm so damn proud to know her. She could hide away and wait for this whole thing to blow over, but instead, she stood up for what she believes in and probably helped a lot of people in the process. I've never met anyone quite like her.

"With that said, I also believe we're all entitled to a certain level of privacy. If someone decides to share videos or images of their body, then I support that. In fact, I fucking love it. However, sharing such recordings without consent is not only wrong, it's harmful. As much as our sexual health matters, our mental health matters too. All of this to say, don't be an ass—don't be a Kamden Donnelly." She kisses two fingers and holds them up. "I won't hide. So, I'll be seeing you."

The video ends and I actually miss her already. I don't know what Brogan is doing to me, but I've never felt anything like this before and it's scaring the shit out of me.

I'm stuck in a trance when my phone chimes in my hand. I snap back to reality and see that it's a text from Brogan.

> Legs: How bad did I suck?

I smile as I type back a response.

Me: You were awesome!

And I mean it too. It's not often I give compliments, but she deserves one tonight. Brogan is fierce. Kamden messed with the wrong girl.

Legs: Thanks for tuning in ;)

Is she flirting with me right now? She can't still be drunk, right?

Me: Glad I got on when I did. Would have been bummed if I missed it. Brogan Astor calling out half the school and shaming them better than my mother ever could.

It takes a second for the next text to come in, and I find myself waiting with bated breath. This is only the second time that Brogan has initiated a conversation with me and I want it to last. It's weird because I'm not normally into getting to know people.

Part of that might come from me not wanting to share anything about my life outside of this university, which makes it hard to connect. How can you expect someone to open up to you if you're a closed book?

But I find myself wanting to know more about this girl, and even scarier, I want her to get to know me in return.

Legs: I'm sober by the way.

I laugh.

Me: I'm proud of you.

Her reply comes quick this time.

Legs: I'm sober and I still want to do it.

I sit up straight, rereading the message over and over. There is no way she actually wants this. I was semi-joking when I threw the idea out there, even though I played it off like I was dead serious. I wasn't even fazed when she shot it down, but now, I'm surprised as hell that she's all but begging to do it.

Legs: Are you there?

Fuck. Is she messing with me right now? I don't even know how to respond.

Me: I'm here.

Legs: So when is this happening?

Me: You're serious?

Legs: Dead.

Leaning back, I groan, my cock already at full attention just with her texting me. I don't even have to see her face or hear her words. *Nope.* Apparently all it takes to do me in is a fucking text. *I'm so screwed.*

Me: Sleep on it. Let's talk tomorrow.

Legs: You said that yesterday. It's one in the morning. It is tomorrow.

This has to be her anger and hurt talking. Besides, this isn't really how I want this to go down with her. I don't want to be just some revenge plot.

Me: Sleep on it.

Legs: Are you scared, Hayes Madden?

Me: You do scare me a little bit.

Legs: I do? How so?

Me: You're the only girl in the world to ever put me in my place. Now I'm stuck here and I'm not sure what move to make next.

Legs: Make the video with me. Let's stick it to Kamden. Do you know that asshole actually had the audacity to come onto my live and say it wasn't him who shared the video? Everyone will believe him. He's Kamden Donnelly.

Kamden. Right. This is all about sticking it to Kamden. This isn't about us. I mean, why would it be? Brogan and I don't even like each other. Our disagreements sure don't feel like they're fueled by hatred, though. In fact, I'm positive there is nothing this girl could do to make me hate her at all.

Me: Tomorrow.

That's all I've got. My thoughts are running rampant right now and the growing bulge between my legs isn't helping.

Legs: Meet me at Clara's Cafe at nine and we can nail down the details.

Me: Details?

Legs: For the video. Don't you dare back out on me now, Hayes. This was your idea and while I may have laughed about it at first, the more I thought about it, the more I realized we should do this. It's just sex. Don't worry, it doesn't have to be anything more than that.

Me: What if it already is...

My finger hovers over the send button for a second before I backspace and retype:

Me: See you at nine.

CHAPTER 13

HAYES

THE SCENT of bacon wafts through the kitchen as I enter, making my stomach growl. My eyes immediately pin to a blonde chick standing in front of the stove in nothing but what appears to be a bikini thong and a black-and-white checkered apron.

God damn. I drag the pad of my thumb across my bottom lip, cleaning up any drool that might have slid out. It's when I glance at her legs that this weird feeling crosses my mind. They aren't the legs I have been fantasizing about being wrapped around me while I fucked the girl they belonged to.

"Good morning." She eyes me up and down. I've never seen this one before. It's nothing new to find random girls in the house, and I'm actually surprised she's the only one I've come across this morning. "Hungry?" she asks with a glimmer of hope in her eyes.

"Nah. I'm good." There's no time to eat. It's already five after nine and I can already picture Brogan in a booth tapping her foot on the floor as she checks the time on her phone.

I need to fucking go, but I can't find my damn keys. It would take me at least fifteen minutes on the bus and she'll probably jet before then.

My gaze roams the area around the blonde chick. "Have you

seen a set of keys connected to a key chain with a hockey stick on it?"

She sets the spatula down on the countertop then reaches for a kitchen towel that's been hanging off the handle of the oven for at least a couple of weeks. "I haven't. But let me help you."

"Don't sweat it," I tell her as I crouch down, looking around on the floor, but she scours the room anyway.

Another girl walks in wearing just a sports bra and a pair of gray sweatpants that hang off her hips. This one I have seen before. I can't quite put my finger on her name, though. Stella? *No.* Sara? *No.* I'm pretty sure it started with an S.

"Well, well, well," she sings. "If it isn't Hayes Madden."

"Good to see you again…" I click my tongue on the roof of my mouth.

"Sierra."

I snap my fingers. "Sierra. That's right."

"It's been a while," she says as she walks in circles around me. "In fact, didn't I leave a pair of red panties in your room last time I saw you?" There isn't a glimmer of shame in her expression. The opposite, actually. She appears pleased with herself as she flashes the blonde chick a snarky look. I could be wrong, but I get the feeling these two are not friends.

"Ugh. Maybe." My eyes roll with a huff of frustration. I don't have time to deal with horny puck bunnies right now. "Go look for yourself."

I move to the living room and dig my hand into the crevices of the couch cushions. Where the hell are they? My mind races in a panic as I try to remember where I put them last. The last time I rode my bike was Sunday. That was four days ago. I try to take the bus whenever I can because it saves on gas but if I'm running late, it's nice to have a quick ride.

Dammit. All I can remember about Sunday night is almost running over Brogan. I think I came home and the guys had a shitload of people here and I went straight to my room.

Suddenly, a pair of arms wrap around me from behind and a warm whisper hits my ears. "Come look with me."

Son of a bitch.

Temptation has been strong as hell lately and I truly deserve some sort of recognition for the level of willpower I've got. A week ago I would have already had this girl bent over my bed. Now, I'm sweating balls trying to find my keys to go to a coffee shop to discuss a sexual transaction. What has my life become?

I straighten my back and stand up, hoping her arms will fall from around me, but she only pulls me closer. "Can't."

"Can't? Or won't?"

I draw in a deep breath before saying, "Both. I've got a class to get to. If you're really that desperate, go crawl into bed with Finch."

The front door comes open and I expect it to be one of my housemates, but instead, I look over to see Brogan standing in the doorway. Baffled eyes dart from Sierra to me. "Sorry. It was open and…"

"It's fine. Come in." I sidestep around the couch and out from Sierra's hold.

"Actually, I'm gonna go." She shoots a thumb over her shoulder. "You were late and I just figured I'd come to you instead."

"I thought you said you had to get to class," Sierra says with her hand pressed to her hip.

I shake my head, annoyed as hell with this girl. I wanna scream at her to shut the fuck up, but I don't because it's my own fault. I've developed a reputation with a lot of the girls on campus. I talk a sweet game, get them into my bed, then pretend they don't exist. Problem is, the majority of them always come back for more. That might be my hockey player ego talking, but it's my reality.

"Hey!" Sierra barks. "Aren't you the girl in that video with Kamden Donnelly? I can't believe you actually let him record you doing that."

I turn a scowl toward Sierra, finally saying the words. "Would you shut the fuck up!"

She practically jumps back a step, stunned by my outburst. "Excuse me!"

"Yeah, I'm gonna go," Brogan says again. She backsteps out the door, pulling it toward her, but I quickly eat the space between us and pull it back open.

"Don't go."

Her eyebrows dip low. "You're obviously busy and I have things to do."

Running my forearm across my forehead, I swipe away the beads of sweat forming. Why do I feel like a child who was just caught doing something he shouldn't be doing? "I'm sorry I was running late. I lost my keys, and…"

"Breakfast is ready." The sweet and sultry voice comes from behind me and I follow Brogan's gaze to see the blonde chick in an apron coming toward me with a plate of food. "Now I know you said you weren't hungry, but breakfast is the most important meal of the day." She comes to my side and reaches out to squeeze my bicep. "Especially for strong and sexy athletes like you."

Brogan rolls her eyes. "Goodbye, Hayes."

CHAPTER 14

HAYES

"Wait a damn minute." I walk out of Blondie's hold on me and head for the door. The second my feet hit the top step, I slam the door closed behind me and shout with my hands in the air, "I thought you wanted to talk?"

"Not anymore," she grumbles as she begins down the sidewalk.

Not wearing any shoes, I jog after her, feeling the cold dampness seep through my thin socks. "Legs, would you stop walking for a damn minute?"

She finally stops with her back toward me.

"What?" she huffs.

I catch up to her and grab her arm to spin her around to face me. "Why are you so pissed?"

"Do you remember the first night I met you when you got pissed because I was wasting your time?" She crosses her arms. "Well, now you've wasted mine."

"Come on now," I chuckle airily. "I'm fifteen minutes late. No reason to get mad."

I give her a quizzical look, wondering how heated she'd get if I called her out for what I think is actually going on right now.

She crosses her arms over her chest and grimaces. "My time is precious."

"Is that what this is really about? Your *time*?"

"Of course it is. When you tell someone you'll be somewhere, showing up isn't optional. A person's word means everything. What more would it be?"

I suck my bottom lip between my teeth, lift my wet foot and look at it for a second, then finally say, "I think you're jealous."

"Jealous of those girls?" Her cheeks flame before a dry laugh climbs up her throat. "Not a chance."

"You sure about that?"

With a heavy huff she spins on her heel and continues walking away from me as light rain begins to come down. Unfortunately for her, I'm not letting her get away that easily.

Back at her side, I throw an arm around her shoulders, knowing it's going to piss her off, but not giving a damn. "Just admit it. You're jealous."

She tosses my arm off of her like it's a dirty rag. "Hey, if you wanna sleep with all the puck bunnies that show up on your doorstep, have at it. Just don't expect me to be one of them."

This attitude she's giving me is a big change from the way she was talking last night. Part of me knew she wouldn't follow through with it. I think the other part of me was scared she actually might and I'd have to decide between listening to my dick or my brain. Maybe this needed to happen. Maybe Brogan needed to get a glimpse into the life I live to realize she doesn't want any part of it.

"I assume this means you don't want to make the video now?"

"Oh, no, Hayes," she scoffs. "We're making that damn video." She takes a few steps forward, leaving my mind spinning. Suddenly, she stops and shoots me a glare. "Are you coming or what?"

I look down and point at my feet. "I don't have fucking shoes on and it's raining now."

"Jesus, Hayes. Why didn't you put them on before you walked out of the house?"

"I didn't have time," I shout. "I had to chase after your stubborn ass."

"Well, what are you waiting for? Go get them!"

"I will when I'm goddamn ready! For Christ's sake, woman. Give me a break."

"Woman?" she growls.

I grip the sides of my head. "You're so damn infuriating."

"And you're…" She growls as she searches for the word.

"I'm what?" I curl my fingers, snarling as I howl into the rain. "Let me have it, Brogan."

She looks at me with disgust in her eyes as she shakes her head. "You're such an ass."

"I'm an ass?" I gasp. "Aside from the first night we met, I've treated you with nothing but respect and kindness while you've insulted me and judged me. But *I'm* the ass." I can't help but laugh about it because it's actually fucking hilarious.

She steps into me, her baby blues peering up. "Yeah. You are." Her voice is soft, tranquil almost.

I blow out a heavy breath, tossing my hands in the air. "You're impossible, Legs."

"That's better," she whispers.

I quirk a brow. "What's better?"

"You called me Brogan. You *never* call me Brogan."

"I thought you hated it when I call you Legs." I can't keep up with this girl. She talks in fucking circles and her moods swing like fucking Tarzan.

"I do." She pauses for a beat. "But I hate it more when you don't."

As if she suddenly noticed the rain falling, she looks up at the sky and out of nowhere, she's bursts out laughing. "Oh my God, we're insane."

"Yeah. You are." I reach for her hand, biting back a smile. "Now get your insane ass inside before you're drenched."

She puts up some resistance as I attempt to pull her back to the house. "I don't wanna go back in there."

"Why? Because of those girls."

"You saw the way they looked at me. All judgy and shit."

"Hey." I tip her chin up. "What happened to the badass who went live last night and said she wasn't hiding?"

"It's easy to pretend when you're behind a screen."

"Nah…" I shake my head. "I saw the look in your eyes and heard every word you said. You weren't pretending. You're a hell of a lot stronger than you think, Legs. Now put on your big girl panties and come back inside with me. If I go in there alone, those chicks might tie me up and never let me leave."

"You and that ego of yours." She cracks a smile but finally walks with me, even if her fingers aren't wrapped around mine. "Don't act like you wouldn't love every second of it, though."

We walk up the stairs, but I stop before opening the door. "Not anymore."

"What's that supposed to mean?"

My shoulders rise and fall and I cock my head to the side as I try to make sense of it myself. Lately, the desire to have a new girl in bed every other night has faded. Ever since Brogan came back into my life, she's all I think about and I'm not sure what to make of it. Sometimes I don't know if it's because I enjoy getting under her skin, or if it's because I find more enjoyment in her getting under mine.

"I don't know yet," I finally say. "But I'll let you know when I figure it out."

Her nose scrunches and she looks at me with those same eyes she did the night we slept together. As if she's reading my innermost thoughts, or at least trying to. It's equal parts terrifying and mesmerizing.

Appearing lost in my gaze, she finally says, "You're such a puzzle, Hayes Madden."

I chuckle as I push the door open. "Tell me about it. If you find any missing pieces lying around campus, let me know. I need 'em back."

Once we're inside and out of the rain, I immediately peel my soaked socks off and toss them beside the door. "Make yourself comfortable. I'll grab a couple towels."

Reluctantly, Brogan sticks close to the door. "I can't stay, Hayes. I've got a class at noon and I should probably go home and change first."

I look at her skeptically. "It takes you two hours to change?"

"Amongst other things." Her fingers run through her wet hair as she pushes stray strands off her forehead.

She feels uncomfortable here, as she should. This house is no place for a girl like her. You can almost smell the testosterone and I know every guy who lives here would try to get in her pants.

I cross the room toward her and as I approach, I can see the lines of worry etched in her face. "Don't worry about those girls, or any other girls that might be here. I'm sure they're all otherwise occupied at the moment."

"It's not about them." Her arms hug around her middle, and I get the feeling that this is about more than the puck bunnies.

"Then what's the big deal? I thought you wanted to talk about the video."

She looks away from me, out the window. "And I thought you didn't wanna do it."

As I step forward, she steps backward until her back hits the door. I notice the rapid flutter of her heart through the fabric of her sweatshirt.

Something shifts inside me and as I'm watching her, witnessing her defensiveness front and center, all I want to do is make that video. Not because I want to send it to Kamden, but because of the way she's standing there with droplets of water running down her face, looking sexy as fuck.

A familiar heat shoots through me as my cock throbs against the tight fabric of my boxers. I never thought I'd be turned on by someone who is such a pain in the ass, then she came along.

"Since when do you care what I want?"

"I don't." She scoffs, putting on a tough girl facade, but I see right through it. In fact, it's now become my life mission to peel back her layers of vulnerability, since she's somehow begun breaking down the walls I've built around myself. Walls I swore I'd never let anyone so much as touch.

Chest to chest, I put one hand on the door, then cage her in like a timid mouse with the other. I watch her throat as she gulps, lustful eyes staring into mine.

This is so unlike her. Brogan is always so sure of herself and isn't easily intimidated. What Kamden did to her left more scars than I think even she realizes. "What is it then?" I rasp, peering down at her. "What's wrong?"

"Nothing." She blows out a laugh. "Why are you acting so strange?"

In an instant, she ducks down and escapes the cage I've put her in. My head drops to the door momentarily, then after a strong exhale, I push myself off it and spin around.

If I don't agree to making this soon, she might be the one to change her mind. It could very well be my only way of ever having her again, and just the thought of that is agonizing.

It hits me—like a puck out of nowhere. *I'm falling for Legs.*

Holy shit. I've got it bad. I haven't had feelings for a girl since I was seventeen years old. Maci fucking Grey. Man, that girl was a bitch.

She broke my heart in ways I didn't know a heart could break. That is until three days later when it literally shattered to pieces because I lost Mom.

I roll my shoulders and work out the ache in my chest.

Taking a deep breath, I spit out, "New deal." Before Brogan has a chance to intervene or ask questions, I continue, "You're mine for forty-eight hours. Hang out with me when I want, and do what I want, and when the two days are over, if you still wanna make the video, we'll do it."

Her features twist, displaying her disgust. "Are you serious? You want me to be your sex slave for two days?"

I shrug. "Sex wasn't on the table, but I'm game if you are—"

She holds up a hand, cutting me off. "You do realize I've

gotten twenty-three messages just this morning from ready and willing men who would make this video with me at the drop of a hat?"

My fists clench at my sides just thinking about her asking anyone to take my place. "The fuck they will."

She smirks. "Now who's jealous?"

She's right, I am jealous. This video was my idea in the first place. Like hell will some random punk put his dick in her.

I won't tell her that, though. She'll get defensive and claim she can do whatever she wants because it's her body. She isn't wrong; I just won't stand for it. Brogan is mine. She just doesn't know it yet.

I could easily, and honestly, throw the same logic at her. There are just as many girls out there who would sell their souls to the devil for a night with me. Yet, I only want one and she could have me for free.

I won't tell her that either.

Instead, I move toward her again. "Look, Legs." I begin reciting some of my smooth words from the first night we met. "Let's just call it like it is. You're hot. I'm hot. There's obviously still some sexual tension burning between us, so don't even consider asking some stranger to fuck you just to piss off your ex when I'm ready and willing."

She sputters a laugh. "You need to stop right now before you embarrass yourself further."

"Ahh. You remember?"

"How can I ever forget? I think I blushed *for* you that night."

I smooth my hands down my damp shirt in a slick manner. "Hey, it worked." Shifting to a more serious note, I say, "Is this really that important to you?"

"No," she quips. "It's really not. But following up on my video last night, I may not be as badass as I came off. I meant what I said, though. I'm not ashamed of my sex life, or the fact that I can pleasure myself better than any man ever could. I guess I just want Kamden to see that he didn't hurt me. Even if maybe he did, just a little."

I open my mouth to speak, but she shuts me up before I can get a word out. "Don't," she stammers. "Don't try and convince me that your nine-inch pierced cock—"

"It's actually nine and one quarter inches," I say amply as I roll my hand in the air. "Continue."

She shakes her head and tsks. "As I was saying. Even though my body count is on one hand, I'd advocate for women with numerous partners any day. Sex feels good. Humans *want* to feel good and if they say they don't, they're lying. As for me and you, we already did it. You're my number four and you'll always be my number four."

"Hmm." I nod. "I think I just got a new lucky number."

"I don't want a random stranger, Hayes. And I wouldn't really consider offering myself up to one. I'd only do this with you."

It's a little fucked up that she made me feel special just now. She does put up a very good argument. I just can't shake this feeling in my gut that this will backfire on her.

"No one else sees this," I tell her. "You send it to Kamden and Kamden only. I think we both know his ego will be too bruised to show anyone else."

She smirks. "Especially once he sees all nine and *one quarter* inches."

"Can't argue with that."

"Okay." She claps her hands together, holding them in place. "I really do have to go. Do we have a deal? For real this time?"

"You tell me. Are you mine for the next couple days?"

She pauses, thinking for a minute. "Absolutely no sleepovers. And you can't interfere with my classes."

I quirk a brow. "Or cheerleading?"

It's still so hard to believe she's a cheerleader. I'm making it a point to go to the football team's next home game just so I can see it for myself.

Brogan tsks. "Someone's been doing their research."

"You're an open book on FlashChat. Literally, *I have seen it all.*" My eyes drag down her body, a smirk playing on my lips.

"You're a dick." Her fist flies at my shoulder, landing with a soft blow that I laugh off. "Just answer the question. Do we have a deal?"

Against my better judgment, I reach my hand out to her. "We have a deal."

She lays her open palm in mine and I look her dead in the eye, grinning from ear to ear.

We're gonna make that video, Legs, but I'll bet on Finch's life, we'll be the only ones to ever see it. After a couple days with me, you'll be saying, Kamden who?

As soon as she leaves, I continue the search for my keys. Not only is my bike key on the ring, but so is my house key.

When I walk in the kitchen, I'm surprised to find them sitting on the counter. Next to them is a note that reads:

> **Hayes,**
> **Found these under the couch. You can thank me by**
> **buying me a drink Friday night after the game.**
> **Xoxo,**
> **Sierra**

I crumple the paper up and toss it in the trash bin, not giving it a second thought.

CHAPTER 15

BROGAN

SOMEHOW I SURVIVED my classes today. Even with the whispers and stares, I kept my chin up and showed everyone I was unfazed. At least on the outside.

On the inside, I was a fucking mess. However, something I didn't expect happened that made it all a little more bearable. There were some girls who waved and said hello that I've never seen before, which led me to think my words made a positive impact on a few. But honestly, if I could help change one girl's opinion about herself and her sexuality then this shitshow is worth it.

Well, I felt that way until I got to cheer. Practice was brutal today. Coach Wendy really stuck the fork in us with this halftime routine. We're not even close to perfecting it, and she expects us to perform it at Saturday's home game.

An abrupt thud on my door has me jumping off my bed.

"Coming," I holler. I set my brush down on Avery's vanity and approach the door, no longer afraid of who might be on the other side.

The day the video surfaced, I was terrified every time someone knocked on this door. Now, I'm ready to face the world with my head held high. There's peace in empowerment, and I'm feeling it now more than ever.

Stealing a peek out the peephole, my peace is quickly replaced with a sudden urge to wage war.

I rip the door open and come face to face with the last person I want to see. "What the hell do you want?" I spit at Kamden, who looks as if he's ready to battle it out as much as I am.

The heavy bags under his eyes tell me he hasn't had much sleep. Good. I hope he's getting the same horrid messages I was getting before I went live and took a stance.

His jaw clenches. "Take down the fucking video, Brogan."

I assume he's referring to the recording of my live stream the other night—I reposted it, three times. Now I might post it three more. Or one for every meme I see of my naked body. I haven't quite decided.

"Screw you!" I go to slam the door shut in his face, but he wedges his foot in the way.

With his palm pressed firmly to the door, he pushes and sends it flying wide open as he grits out, "Take down the video and tell everyone you made a mistake."

With my arms tightly folded across my chest, my jaw tightens. "And why the hell would I do that?"

"Because it's a lie!" he shouts. "I didn't share that fucking video of us. I don't know who the hell did, but it sure as hell wasn't me."

I roll my eyes, standing tall. How dumb does he think I am? "You seriously think I'm buying that bullshit? No one had that video but me and you. I also never consented to you recording us. Seems like I was right not to trust you."

"Oh, grow up. It was hot and you know it."

I might agree that it was hot, but I'm also a firm believer that consent matters and he never even asked, not even when I pointed it out.

"I don't believe you," I say, ignoring his statement because even if it's true, it doesn't give him the right to share it.

"Someone must have gotten access to your phone because it

sure as shit wasn't me, Brogan. I might be an ass sometimes but not even I would stoop that low."

"Or maybe someone had access to your phone," I snap. "You know what, forget I said that because I know it was you, Kamden."

"And why the hell would I share a video of myself jerking off? Think about it." His face is red, his hair sticking up like he's been pulling at it. *Good.* Maybe if people gave him shit about what he did to me then he'll understand how I feel.

"I have thought about it," I bite back, "and all I can come up with is, you hate me more than you love your dignity."

"First of all, I didn't hate you until that video surfaced. For all we both know, your new fuck toy shared it. You have been hanging out with him a lot."

My teeth grind and I narrow my eyes. "Hayes would *never.*"

I'm not really into defending Hayes, but why would he share that video just to show up right after and offer to help me? Some could say a mastermind would think that way, but this is Hayes. He can hardly remember to show up on time, much less launch an elaborate scheme.

"Right. Because you know him *so* well. Well, I've got news for you, Brogan. I know him better and he wouldn't even hesitate if he knew it would drive a wedge between us."

"Well, I've got news for *you*, Kamden," I mock him. "Hayes didn't have to drive a wedge between us. You did that yourself."

He shakes his head, refusing to take responsibility for anything that he did, only solidifying my hatred toward him. He is nothing to me anymore.

Kamden shakes his head. "Don't count him out so quickly. It was either him or you. Maybe one of your many nights of drinking went too far and you did it to get a little attention from the guys on campus."

"How dare you!" Without thinking, my hand connects with his face in a loud smack. I take a step back, feeling the sting radiate through my palm while I grit my teeth. This is the third time now Kamden has made me out to be a slut, and it fucking stops here.

Cupping his cheek, he glowers. "You're fucking crazy. I think that psychopath Hayes is rubbing off on you since you two are spending so much time together."

I jab a stern finger in the air, pointed at the door as my voice rises, "Get out!"

When he just stands there, a sly grin on his face, I shove my hands to his chest and push him to the door. "If you ever come back here again, I'll get a restraining order against you!"

As soon as he's out the door, I go to slam it closed, but he stops it, once again. "You do realize who my father is, right? Take down the video of you slandering my name, or you'll face expulsion and a lawsuit."

I shove my whole body into the door, finally latching it before dragging the chain lock across it.

Tears of anger immediately spring from my eyes as I slide down the door and sit in front of it.

Maybe it was wrong of me to call Kamden out like that on FlashChat. Even after what he did, I had the opportunity to be the bigger person and I chose to retaliate publicly. It's possible he didn't share the one of us, but he's still the reason it exists in the first place.

He can come for me and bring Daddy along for the ride, but I won't fight lying down.

As for my message promoting sexual positivity and advocating for women who have been shamed for enjoying something so natural, I have no regrets. And I'm sure as hell not going to delete it because Kamden told me to.

Suddenly, the handle shakes violently and the door rattles in its frame. I sit up, wiping my face with shaking hands. With a creak, the door opens slightly, stopped by the chain lock. Avery's voice hits my ears. "B, Let me in."

I push myself off the floor and swipe away the tears under my eyes. As I go to close the door, it nudges back open. "You have to shut it, Ave."

The sound of her giggle has me smiling. "My bad."

We've done this a hundred times, but her impatient ass always expects me to unlink the chain with the door cracked open.

She pulls it shut and I drag the chain across before the door comes flying open. I'm met with wide eyes and hands that grip my shoulders. "What the hell was Kamden doing here?" Before I can even answer, she tilts her head to the side and says, "Why are you crying, babe?"

I draw in a bumpy breath and sniffle. "He demanded I take down the live recording I shared and then threatened me with a lawsuit and expulsion."

"That son of a bitch," she grits out before spinning around and taking a step out the door.

I grab her by the hood of her sweatshirt and jerk her back into the room. "Oh no you don't."

"Let me have him, B. Let me fucking have him."

I laugh through the heartache in my chest. "He's long gone by now."

Her shoulders slump in defeat. "Just say the word and I'll barebow him with an arrow straight to the chest."

"That extracurricular archery course is going straight to your head." I can't help but chuckle, which is why I love Avery so damn much. Even when I just got threatened and slut-shamed by my ex, she still finds a way to make the tears stop.

"Seriously, though, B. Don't take down the video. Do you have any idea how many girls came up to me today and asked me to thank you for what you said?"

"Really?" My voice squeaks, a smile playing on my lips. "How many?"

"One," she quips, and my expression drops a little. "But that's more than none."

"Yes, Avery. One is more than none." I laugh. "I'm not taking down the video, though. I thought about it, and in the end, I decided to take my chances."

Avery walks over to the bed and drops her bag on top of it.

"Kamden is such an ass. He has some nerve coming to our room and threatening you. Do you think he'd actually try and get you expelled?"

I shrug. "Maybe. He is sort of a jerk like that. And he definitely has the means. I don't know much about his dad, and I've never met him, but I know he has money and power, and with his countless donations to Rosewood U, there's not a doubt in my mind the school would act in his favor."

"Let's not forget, B. You have connections, too. Your stepdad is the mayor of your hometown and your mom is a district attorney." She sits down on her bed, kicking off her shoes and crossing her legs. "You could win, and even file a counterclaim and sue him for what he did."

I shrug, sitting next to her. "That's the thing. Kamden is claiming he isn't the one who shared the video of us."

"Oh for fuck's sake," she grumbles. "Please don't tell me you actually believe him."

I think about it for a second because when he came in here, the last thing I wanted to do was believe a word he said. I still don't. But part of me feels like he was telling the truth, and even if I want to take that part and tell it to fuck off, Kamden looked truly bothered. "Yes and no."

Her eyes roll to mine. "Brogan Ann Astor."

"That's not my middle name." I laugh.

"Oh. Well, what is it?"

"Alexis."

"That's pretty." Her tone shifts abruptly to a more serious note. "Brogan Alexis Astor, please don't buy into Kamden's bullshit. The next thing you know, you'll be the one apologizing to him then you'll be back in his bed the next day."

"No." I shake my head. "Not anymore. I've forgiven Kamden for standing me up, being an ass, and even lying to me, but he went too far this time. Even if he isn't the one who shared the video—"

"But he is," she cuts in.

"*Even* if he isn't the one who shared the video, he said some unforgivable things to me and made me feel like the biggest slut in the world. I would never take him back. Besides, I've—"

"Fallen for Hayes Madden," she cuts in again.

I exhale heavily. "No. I have not fallen for Hayes Madden."

At least, I don't think I have. Though I can't deny that yesterday I felt things I didn't think he could make me feel. I'll never admit it to Hayes, but I actually was jealous of those girls at his house. It literally felt like one of them reached their nails into my chest, clawed out my heart, and slapped it on my sleeve for him to steal. And he almost did when we were standing at the top of the steps in front of his door in the rain. The way he looked at me…no guy has ever looked at me like that before.

I can't go there right now. If I do, it will throw our whole plan offtrack and I'm sticking to it. Now more than ever, I want Kamden to feel pain.

"Don't worry," I say to her. "I'll never take Kamden back. Let's just leave it at that."

Her lips press together tightly as they draw up in a crescent-moon smile. "You're better off, B."

"I know I am." I get up and decide that comfy clothes are the answer to my problems right now.

It doesn't make it hurt any less, though. It's not even my relationship that's doing me in right now, it's the way it all fell apart.

Rummaging through the middle drawer of my dresser, I pull out a pair of boxer shorts and a Willow Creek High t-shirt. After tossing them into my mint green bathroom tote, I grab my shower caddy from one of the built-in shelves on my desk.

"I need to shower and go to bed so I can sleep off this day."

"Have you eaten?" Avery asks with the concern of a mother in her tone.

Dragging my feet, I head to the door. "Just a croissant for breakfast."

"Go shower and I'll get us some food. I've got an idea that will make you forget all about Kamden Donnelly for the night." Her brows do a little dance and I'm afraid to even ask.

"Be nice," I warn, pointing a finger at her. "I know how crazy your ideas can get."

Avery's lips curl up into a mischievous grin, revealing the prominent dimples on her cheeks.

I can't resist shaking my head as I leave the room, trying not to smile at her antics.

Our senior year of high school, during spring break, Avery had the grand idea to take a road trip to Vegas because she swore on everything that we could gamble there at the age of eighteen. She was wrong. But it just so happened that the first place we went wasn't checking IDs and instead relied on signs, which neither of us paid any attention to. When Avery actually won three thousand dollars, the cashier was ready to pay her out and that's when she was asked for identification.

We were told we had to leave and Avery had to forfeit her winnings. Avery, being the loudmouth she is, argued with the cashier and they threatened to call the police and press charges, which would have landed both of us in jail for the night. After a lot of convincing, I got her to leave and we were walked out by security.

We laugh about it now, but I sure as hell wasn't laughing that night.

I walk down the hallway to the shared bathrooms, relieved to hear that none of the showers are in use. I don't mind sharing a bathroom with everyone on our floor—growing up with siblings prepared me for it. However, I do prefer having the space to myself when I use it. Even when I do have privacy in the bathroom, I still try to hurry.

There's always at least one or two people that come in to use the toilets and nothing grosses me out more than cleaning my body while the scent of shit wafts through the steamy air.

My stomach curls just thinking about it.

Coming to college has been a real wake-up call. As much as I thought I was ready for the real world, I'm finding there's still a lot to navigate. I couldn't wait to get out of my parents' house so I didn't have to live by their rules anymore, but I'm finding that making up my own rules is more difficult than following theirs.

Before college, I never would have let a guy record me naked, but I decided to let it slide. Now look at where it landed me.

So many people my age think they are ready for the big world, but to me it feels a little too big. There is comfort in someone else making your own meals, having your own room, and your own shower, even if you have to share it with your stepbrothers. There is stability—balance.

That's something I realize I'm craving as I step out of the shower and start packing up my stuff to go back to my room. I just want some balance. I want the thoughts to feel less chaotic and I want the world to stop spinning quite so fast.

It's sort of crazy that I feel most balanced here when I'm with Hayes. Even when I was pissed at him for being late the other morning, I knew exactly what I wanted. He makes me think one step ahead all the time. Even though he still surprises me here and there, it doesn't feel like an earthquake trying to knock me down. Things between us just flow. One sarcastic response to the next.

As I walk out of the bathroom and down the hall to my room, the smell of pizza floods my senses and my stomach growls. I open the door, ready to run and kiss Avery for ordering it, but I come face to face with Hayes fucking Madden who is sitting on my bed wearing a big-ass cheeky grin.

"What's up, Legs?"

My lips press into a thin line as I drop my bag on the floor. "Just the thing to cheer me up, huh?" I sneer at Avery as I shoot my thumb toward Hayes. "He's supposed to do that?"

"He brought us pizza." She beams as she digs her teeth into a large slice. "Oh," she continues as she chews. "And look what's on."

I follow her gaze to the television that's mounted in the corner of our room and see *Hocus Pocus* playing.

With everything going on, I completely forgot Halloween is coming up. This is my favorite month of the year and I haven't even decorated or made any plans. I guess watching my favorite Halloween movie can set the mood for that, but watching a movie with Hayes feels so...awkward. Are we at that level of friendship yet? Are we even friends at all?

I step farther into the room, closing the door behind me. "Why are you really here, Hayes?"

He stands for a second, grabs a slice of pizza from the box sitting on Avery's desk, then sits back down on *my* bed. "Avery texted me and said she needed my help cheering you up. You were right." He shoots a look at Avery. "She does seem sort of down."

"I'm fine," I stammer. "I can't believe you invited him here. Let me guess, you told him about Kamden coming here, too?"

Hayes jumps to his feet mid-chew. "Why the hell did Kamden come here?"

"Guess you got your answer." Avery snickers. *God help me, I might actually smack her this time.*

"Did he seriously come here?" Hayes asks adamantly. "Is he the reason you look like you want to punch a wall? What the fuck did he say to you?"

What I want to know is why he cares so much.

"Yes, he came here," I tell him. "But it's not a big deal. And I am *not* about to punch a wall, that's a pussy move."

I steal a look at Hayes who is holding a piece of pizza in one hand and trying to conceal something on my bed with the other.

"What are you doing?" I cross the room toward him and pull away the corner of my blanket he so carefully folded up. "You dropped pizza on my bed and now you're trying to hide it?"

A growl climbs up my throat as I grab a couple napkins next to the pizza box and scrub vigorously at the sauce stain.

"You really need to lighten up, Legs."

I scoff as I direct his attention to the red stain on my baby pink comforter. "You dropped pizza on my bed."

"So what?" he huffs. "It's just pizza. You need to chill out and have some fun once in a while. Why's everything so serious with you?"

"She gets like that," Avery whispers, but I hear her loud and clear.

I shoot her a glare before dragging my eyes back to Hayes. "I'm not always serious and I happen to have a lot of fun. It's just been a rough couple days."

Part of me feels like I should apologize, but my damn pride is getting in the way. I flip the corner of my comforter back up, hiding the stain before plastering a big-ass smile on my face. "See."

"Oh yeah," he drawls teasingly. "Hide that stain, baby. We're partying hard now."

I can't help laughing. Hayes does a good job of cheering me up. I'll give him that.

"Well, you two," Avery begins as she slips her foot into a knee-high boot. "This has been fun, but—"

"No you don't!" I point my pizza at her as I swallow down a bite. "You don't get to leave. Uh-uh. You can't invite someone into our room then bail."

"After what's been going on, I just didn't want to leave you alone. The thing is, I've sort of got plans tonight."

She could have reached out to any number of our friends, yet she called Hayes. And while I don't exactly despise him anymore, I still don't want to lie in my room and watch a movie with him…alone. He makes me nervous. Which is crazy because guys don't usually have that effect on me.

Planting my hand on my hip, I give Avery a death glare. "Plans with whom?"

"A guy…" She pauses for a beat. "…named Evan. Remember the night after the hockey game when Hayes said his friend was checking me out. Well, he called the other day and now we're going out for dinner."

"I hate you," I grit at her.

"Hey," Hayes sings. "I thought you only said that to me. Welcome to the club, Avery." He holds up his hand and she smacks him a high five.

My face feels hot. Hell, my entire body feels hot. I can't

believe she's actually leaving us alone together in this dimly lit room with pizza and a movie playing. She thinks she's *so* sneaky, but I know exactly what she's up to.

I could easily rest on the certainty that Avery likes Hayes and she doesn't like many guys when it pertains to me. Her opinion means the world to me and she's almost always spot-on—hence what happened with Kamden.

I look at Hayes briefly, admiring the way he carries himself. He's so confident and sure about everything he does and says. It doesn't hurt that he's breathtakingly gorgeous.

No. I can't think like that. We're about to have sex and record a revenge video. I'm not falling for Hayes. I can't be. *Can I?*

CHAPTER 16

HAYES

Why is she looking at me like that?

I raise an eyebrow, turning my head slightly as I try to get a read on her expression.

"You two have fun," Avery says as she backs out the door and pulls it closed.

Brogan's gaze snaps to the door before coming back to me. "Looks like it's just the two of us."

She seems uneasy. As if this situation is uncomfortable for her. But that's just too damn bad. We had a deal, and if I know her like I think I do, she'll stand by her word.

"Looks like it," I tell her, watching with skepticism as she drops the crust of her pizza in a trash bin beside a desk. "You just wasted a perfectly good crust."

"Oh, I don't eat the crust." She speaks casually as she walks around her bed and sits down on the side opposite of where I am. "It's gross."

Baffled, I turn my body just enough to see her. "What do you mean it's gross? You eat the rest of the pizza, right? You do realize it's made from the same ingredients?"

Getting comfortable, she tugs the comforter until it's nestled around her lower half. She pats one side, tucking it under her body, before tucking in the other side.

"I know that. But the crust doesn't have any toppings. It's not the same."

I'm half tempted to reach into that trash bin, pull out her crust, and eat it just to prove a point, but I won't go to those extremes. I'm beginning to realize no one can change Brogan's mind about anything once it's made up. And even if she were wrong in a situation, I'd probably still let her be right. Not without giving her a little shit first, of course.

Scooting up the bed, I sit beside her with my back against the headboard. With my ankles crossed and my hands folded in my lap, I watch as she squints at the TV, glancing over at me out of the corner of her eye. I don't even ask her if it's okay to sit here beside her because being the stubborn girl she is, she'd probably use the opportunity to tell me to move, in which case we'd start a full-on argument.

Because of my schedule, I don't watch much TV, aside from bits and pieces of live sports. Now that I'm sitting here watching a movie, I'm certain I wouldn't want to watch it with anyone else right now. My only wish is that I was on the other side of her so I could see her while I'm pretending to watch the movie.

Brogan's voice slices through the silence, amidst the movie playing. "Have you ever watched *Hocus Pocus*?"

"Ugh, yeah," I tell her, eyes on the screen. "My mom loved this movie. It's a shame she'll never get a chance to watch the second one." I look at her, noticing her pinched expression. I save her the discomfort of having to ask and say, "she passed away when I was seventeen."

"I'm sorry to hear that. I can't imagine how hard it is to lose a parent at such a young age."

I nod. "It's not easy. That's for sure." I shift the subject off of me and onto her. "Are your parents still together?"

"Nope." She moves her body up until she's sitting flush beside mine. "My mom remarried two years ago to a really good man and I gained four stepbrothers."

Those must have been the guys I saw in the pics. I had a feeling they were family.

She continues, "My dad is dating a model in her early twenties whom I've met twice. So that's fun."

I snort a laugh. "Wow. Is your dad Richard Gere, by chance?"

"No," she chuckles, "but he is a good-looking man with money."

Lifting a finger, I say, "Ahh. That explains it. And how is he as a father?"

"You sure are asking a lot of personal questions."

"You don't have to answer," I tell her.

After thinking for a minute, she says, "He used to be a good dad. Or at least, that's how I remember him. When he and my mom got divorced, it sort of felt like he divorced us too. We still talk. And don't get me wrong, I love my dad very much. We're just not as close as I think we could be. What about you? Are you close with your dad?"

"I don't really know him," I tell her truthfully.

"I'm sorry to hear that." There's pity in her voice and I don't like that. The last thing I want from anyone is pity.

"Don't be sorry. I'm not. I know who he is. I know where he lives. But I really don't care to know *him*."

She nods, not taking any offense to my annoyed tone. "I get that. Not everyone who comes into our lives is meant to stay and we don't have to feel bad about that."

"He never even came into my life until the year my mom passed away. Up until then, I didn't know or care if he was dead or alive. Then one day, he just appeared and decided to try and be a hero." Shaking my head, I ball my hands into fists, trying not to let the memory of that moment overwhelm me. "I put that asshole in his place real fast."

Brogan sits up, turning toward me. "And you haven't seen him since?"

"Oh, I see him. He likes to show up whenever it's convenient for him just so he can make himself look good to his wife. We don't talk at all, but I know he's there."

Brogan puts her hand on my arm, her fingers gently grazing my skin. I look down, and she pulls away, but the warmth of her touch lingers.

"So," she says sharply, cutting through the tension. "Did you live on your own after your mom passed away?"

Shaking off the feeling of her touch, I clear my throat. "I lived with my aunt. Well, technically, my mom and I both did. I didn't have much of anything growing up. My mom couldn't hold a job long enough to make a deposit on a rental, so we stayed with her sister for, like…three years. When she passed away, I continued to stay there until I graduated high school and moved here."

Brogan crosses her legs, fully abandoning the movie in favor of giving me all her attention. I find I like it more than I expected to. "I'm glad you had your aunt to get you through all that."

"She didn't get me through anything. I got myself through it. My aunt was always part of the problem, so don't give her too much credit."

I squirm a bit. I don't even know why I'm opening up to her like this. I thought I'd be okay with it, but this is the stuff that feels raw, scary even.

She looks over at me, studying my expression. Sometimes I swear she can read my mind with how perceptive she is.

I need to change the subject fast. "How many sisters do you have?" I ask her. "I was stalking your FlashChat page and noticed some family pics."

"Two sisters." She smiles and her eyes light up. "Elodie and Lake. Elodie is in college and Lake is a senior in high school."

"I gotta say…" I chuckle. "You and your sisters have some unusual names."

She laughs along with me. "Yeah, my mom wasn't very kind to us in that regard. Lake is actually short for Lakin and Elodie is my mom's middle name."

"And Brogan?"

"Brogan is my mom's maiden name."

"Hmm." I nod. "That's actually kinda cool."

"It is. I sort of like having a name no one else has. Less confusion." She swats me playfully. "And you're one to talk. Hayes isn't exactly on the top ten list of popular boys' names."

"I can't even argue that one. I have no idea where my mom got my name." I scratch the back of my head, smiling. "It was probably some old-school tobacco or liquor brand."

"Well, I like it." Her smile makes something in me warm, like I'm finally earning that magic my mom talked about. "I think it suits you."

I lift my chin, biting the corner of my lip. "I think that's the nicest thing you've ever said to me, Legs."

Her face drops and she swallows thickly. "I must be pretty damn cruel if that's the nicest thing I've said to you."

"You do like to give me a hard time." I nudge her, trying to lighten the mood again.

Her neck cranes back. "I do? Yeah, you're right. I do. I guess it's the middle child in me."

"Being an only child, I don't have that problem. Instead, I have the attitude of the oldest, middle, and youngest."

"Ahhh. That explains a lot." She starts to laugh and I find that it might be my new favorite sound. "Well, at least you have the brothers of your fraternity."

"Fraternity?" I spit out, confused. "I'm not in a fraternity."

Her body shoots forward and she turns to face me, legs crossed. "Yes, you are."

"No," I deadpan. "I'm definitely not. I live in the house, but I'm not part of the brotherhood."

Confusion cripples her features. "Why do you live there then? Why aren't you in the dorms?"

I shrug, no shame in my voice as I say, "I got kicked out of the dorms. I'm surprised your buddy Jared didn't tell you."

"No. He didn't tell me anything, except to stay away from you." She taps the tips of her fingers together devilishly. "I bet it's good, though. So what is it, what did you do to piss Jared off?"

"To put it simply, I fucked his ex-girlfriend in our dorm and she may have been high as a kite at the time, but I had no idea she had drugs on her when it happened. I was tested multiple times because of hockey and it all came up clean, but it all kinda went downhill from there."

Her mouth drops open. "Wait a damn minute. Jared's gay. He's been seeing a guy named Luca for the last couple weeks now."

"He's bi. He and his ex actually dated for a year before *he* dumped her."

"That's horrible, Hayes!" She glowers at me with judgment in her eyes. "Why would you do that to him?"

"In my defense, I didn't know who the fuck it was. It was dark as hell and this chick climbed in my bed, rubbed up on my dick, and I was at her mercy after that. Had no idea it was her until Jared came in and flipped on the lights."

Her face scrunches. "Is that really grounds for getting kicked out of the dorms?"

"No, but because she had drugs on her at the time and she was in my bed, I was guilty by association and I didn't have money or influence to help me out."

She curls her nose. "But why Kappa Rho? Why not just find an apartment and get a roommate?"

"Can't afford it," I say mildly. "I don't have the luxuries a lot of students have. I'm not here on a scholarship. The dad I told you about, he's paying my tuition. I didn't wanna accept the favor, but I had no choice if I wanted a future in hockey. So I took the money with the plan to pay him back every single penny if I go pro."

"*When* you go pro," she corrects me. "Speak it into existence. Manifest that shit."

I turn to face her, loving this side of Brogan, the side that wants to put up a fight. "I stand corrected. *When* I go pro, I'm paying him back. Until then, I work part-time during the off-season just to eat and afford the rent I pay for that hole-in-the-wall at Kappa Rho."

She goes quiet for a minute, that look of pity in her eyes again. But it quickly fades and she smiles. "Well, I'm really proud of you. A lot of people would call it quits and drop out, but you do what you have to do to keep going."

"Damn, Legs. I think that's the second nicest thing you've ever said to me"

"See." She grins, pushing me gently with her hand. "I can be nice."

My eyes skate downward, from her eyes to her mouth. The tip of her tongue darts out slightly and she drags it between her lips. *I wanna kiss her so fucking bad.* I wonder how she'd react…

"Wow," she blurts out, snapping me from my thoughts. "The movie is already over and we didn't even watch it."

I glance to my left at the TV. "Oh yeah. So it is. Guess that means we'll have to try again another night."

She nods quickly. "It has to be before Halloween, though. Because once that holiday is over, it's Christmas all the way."

I look at her through squinted eyes. "Don't tell me you're one of those?"

She chuckles. "One of what?"

"A Christmas creep."

Her brow furrows and I want so badly to reach my thumb up and smooth it out. "Now you're just making stuff up."

"No. No. It's a thing. Christmas creeps jump straight from Halloween to Christmas, completely skipping over Thanksgiving."

"Nobody *skips* Thanksgiving," she says with defensiveness in her tone. "It still happens and it's still celebrated. It's just that, Thanksgiving is a day that's celebrated. Christmas is an entire season of joy and laughter. It's filled with lights and love and hot cocoa and all the good things."

I know these Christmas creeps are dead set in their ways, so I put my hands up in surrender. "I won't argue with you, Legs. I'm just gonna let you win."

She smirks. "Now you're catching on."

There's a beat of awkward silence before I cut through it and say, "I guess I should head out so you can get some sleep."

As much as I don't want to leave, we're in a good place, and I should probably quit while I'm ahead. Besides, I've got a full two days with her coming up.

Brogan licks her lips and I find myself watching the action, again. The fire inside me intensifies with each passing second with this girl and if I don't leave now, I might not be able to refrain from kissing her. But it's too soon. She's fresh out of a shitty relationship and her heart is more guarded than ever.

So, instead of making a move, I play it safe and fling my legs over the side of the bed and stand.

Leaning down, I press a chaste kiss to the top of her head and whisper, "see you at my game tomorrow." When I stand, I give her a wink before heading to the door to put my shoes on.

"Your game?"

"Our two days together begin tomorrow." I slide one shoe on, then the other before pulling open the door. "Your seats will be waiting."

CHAPTER 17

BROGAN

THERE HE IS. All geared up and ready to go. I never realized how sexy hockey players are when they're out on the ice. They glide with so much ease and precision, all while maintaining their tough and rebellious personas.

Beside me Avery is hooting and hollering like she's a born and raised hockey buff. Last time we were here, in these exact seats, she had her face in her phone the entire time and couldn't wait for the game to be over. Funny how a date with one of the players has made her the team's biggest fan. It works out well for me, considering I *have* to be here. Though, I really wouldn't want to be anywhere else.

I like watching Hayes play. He's extremely talented and it's obvious he's passionate about the sport. When I came out to watch the scrimmage. Hayes was such an enigma to me. I didn't know anything about him, and what I did know, I judged harshly just because of a single encounter.

Now, I truly want him to succeed in everything he does. He's got fire in his soul and I have no doubt he's going to move mountains one day. Hayes is so much more than the bad boy everyone else sees. I feel pretty special that I get to witness what's behind the armor he wears.

"Stuck-up bitch at two o'clock," Avery mumbles with her hand cupped around her mouth.

I look to my right, expecting to see someone I should know.

"Wait. I think she's at six o'clock," Avery says, "or maybe that's nine." I push my hands to the armrests and stretch myself up, still not seeing anyone. "Jesus, I don't know how to read analog clocks," she gripes. "She's coming toward us."

When I look to the left, which is *not* six o'clock or nine o'clock, I see Gabby maneuvering her way through the seats in our direction.

Bracing myself, I take a deep breath and keep my eyes on the ice.

"Hey, girls," she says with a perky tone. She squats down in front of the empty seat next to me, her wavy blonde hair bouncing around her face. "Enjoying the game?"

I roll my eyes at her, already annoyed with the fake smile plastered on her face. "What do you want, Gabby?"

There's a tense moment of silence, aside from the chants surrounding us, then she finally says, "I owe you an apology, Brogan."

My eyes widen in shock as they connect with hers, my surprise readable. Gabby has never once said anything remotely kind to me, so the fact that there is a potential apology hanging in the air right now is mind-boggling. With a pinched expression, I nod toward the game. "Out with it then. We're sort of in the middle of something."

An exasperated sigh slips through her lips. "I'm sorry for the way things ended between you and Kamden."

She's not apologizing for how cruel she's been to me. I don't think she's really apologizing at all. If anything, she's gloating.

My shoulders draw back and I turn to her with a heavy scowl. "That's your apology?" I laugh dryly. "Duly noted. You can go now."

She shifts on her feet, still crouched beside me. "I truly am, Brogan. I know the pain of losing him. I still feel it in my chest. I just want you to know if you ever need to talk, I'm here for you."

"Girl," Avery howls. "Get the fuck away."

Gabby leans slightly to get a look at Avery. "Excuse me? Do I even know you?"

Avery practically turns her whole body in her seat and pins Gabby with a scathing glare. We have all been at Piggy's at least ten times together. Gabby is just being a petty bitch, as always.

"Hell no, you don't. But I know enough about you to know I don't like you."

My best friend really is the best. However, I can hold my own. "Gabby," I seethe. "Why don't you take your shitty apology and shove it up your ass?" I tap two fingers to her shoulder and give her a gentle push, causing her to fall back slightly.

Her chest rises and falls with effort as she straightens her back. "And to think I came over here with an offer of friendship." She purses her lips. "I'm actually not sorry at all Kamden finally came to his senses. In fact, you should probably know, I spent the night with him last night and our bodies connected on a whole new level."

I burst out in laughter as I clap my hands together. "Wow. Congratulations, Gabby. You win. Now you better hope like hell a video doesn't surface," I air quote, *"of your bodies connecting."*

An insolent smile adorns her face. "Kamden would never do that to me."

"Must not be video-worthy," I cough the words into my hand.

Avery laughs beside me while any glint of humor on Gabby's face fades. Avery puts her hand over her mouth but doesn't speak quietly. "I bet she just lies there and takes it while making stupid noises too high pitched for human ears. I'd put money on Kamden investing in ear plugs."

Gabby's face turns the shade of a tomato as she straightens her preppy pink polo. "I do not," she stammers.

I roll my eyes again before paying attention to the ice as I murmur, "I bet it was just magical for one of you."

"Oh, it was and if anyone should hope it doesn't surface, it should be you because it would put your video to shame."

"Oh, you watched me pleasure myself?" I spit out in sarcasm, not even bothering to look at her because she doesn't deserve it. But when she doesn't walk away, I can't help myself. Crossing my arms, I smirk at her. "I hope you took notes."

Heat rises in her cheeks, turning them a deep shade of crimson. Her eyes narrow and her lips curl in a snarl. "Ya know, your message about empowering women in regard to sex really resonated with me, but now I'm starting to think it was all an act."

"If you felt empowered to come over here and tell me that a man who tried to publicly humiliate me by putting my body on display for others without my permission was good for you in bed then I don't really think you got the message, Gabs." I fake a yawn, eyes back on the game. "Can you go away now?"

With a heavy foot, Gabby stomps back down the aisle, bumping into anyone in her path. I look at Avery and we both just laugh.

Seconds later, Hayes scores and we're both on our feet with our hands in the air.

He skates toward his team's bench, his stick tapping gently against the ice with each glide. As he approaches, he slows down directly in front of me. His eyes meet mine and a mischievous grin spreads across his face.

I smile back at him and he winks, sending my heart into a frenzy of chaotic beats.

"I don't understand why you're fighting this so much," Avery says, and I turn to her with a scorned look.

"Fighting what?"

"You and him." Her voice is soft and sincere. "Hayes likes you a lot, B."

"He does not," I spit out with a laugh. "Hayes and I can't stand each other."

Avery shakes her head, real disappointment in her features. "You can keep telling yourself that, but one morning you're going to wake up and realize he's the one person you don't want to live without."

Dwelling on her words, I turn to the left and look at Hayes laughing with his teammates. His helmet is dangling from his hand, his hair damp and matted against his forehead. Each heavy breath he takes is a testament to the hard work he's putting into the game.

His eye skate to mine and a rush of pulsating heat floods through me.

Hayes has steadily been in my life for almost two weeks now. For a sliver of a second, I try to imagine a lifetime without him, and it's almost crippling.

It's hard to pinpoint what I would miss the most about him. Maybe his sharp wit and sarcastic banter? His dry sense of humor that always somehow makes me laugh? Or maybe his gorgeous physique and captivating eyes? No. I think it would have to be his infectious laughter. No matter what emotional state I'm in, it always seems to make me smile.

I'd miss it all. I'd miss *him*.

I sit back down, feeling the weight of my emotions crash into me. And when the game wraps up, giving the Devils their first true win of the season, I don't even have it in me to jump up and down in excitement with Avery.

My mind is spinning and my heart feels heavy, as if I've already lost Hayes and he's not even mine.

"Come on." Avery beams as she takes my hand and practically drags me to the end of our row.

"Where are we going?" I ask breathlessly when we finally reach an open space.

I spot the team, out of skates, taking pictures in front of a brick wall with a large Devils logo on it.

"Getting pics with our favorite players."

I grumble, forcing resistance between us as I pull back. "I think I'll pass."

"Fine. Stay here." She lets go of me and pushes her way through the crowd to get to Evan.

As I scour the crowded area, my eyes fall on Hayes. He's down on one knee beside a small boy, both of them sporting matching jerseys with Hayes's number, twenty-eight. With a proud smile, Hayes wraps his arm around the boy's shoulder and they smile for a photo. I can't help but grin as I watch them.

The second he stands, his eyes find mine like they're magnetized. His brows lift and the corner of his mouth twitches in a smile.

Holding my gaze, he walks toward me. A few people call out after him, asking for a picture, but their words slip through empty ears as he eats up the space between us.

"Good game tonight," I say with a pressed smile.

"Hey, thanks. Glad you could make it out."

Looking away, I shrug. "As if I had a choice."

"You didn't." His hand wraps around my waist, strong and sure as he pulls me close. "But I'm glad you're here, nonetheless." He cracks a cheesy grin. A cameraman steps in front of us with a large camera set up on a tall tripod. "What d'ya say? Wanna take a picture together?"

"And what makes you think I want a picture with you?" I tease.

"Nothing," he says coyly. "But I want one with you."

He steps up to my side and wraps his hand around my waist fully, sending a tiny spark of electricity through me. I curl into him with my hand resting gently around his torso, posing for the cameraman.

He moves in closer, his breath tickling my ear as he whispers, "Meet me at Legends in thirty minutes." Before I can even respond, his lips brush against my cheek, leaving a tingling sensation on my skin. My heart races and I'm frozen in place as I watch his confident steps carry him back into the crowd of fans.

Avery and I walk through the heavy wooden doors and step into Legends, immediately enveloped in a mix of loud chatter and pulsing music.

The walls are lined with a grid of televisions, each one broadcasting a different sporting event, but there is no sound coming from them, instead the surround speakers are bumping out "Circles" by Post Malone.

A group of rowdy people wearing Devils gear is huddled around a table, shouting and high-fiving to the win tonight, and Avery pulls me in their direction.

My eyes gravitate to Hayes as if they knew exactly where to find him. He's out of uniform, wearing a pair of torn blue jeans and a Devils hockey t-shirt. Looking like sin dipped in chocolate. How did I ever even stand a chance at staying away from him?

Walking toward the group, he balances an overfilled martini glass in his hand and doesn't seem to notice me right away. I'm actually surprised to see the glass in his hands; I took Hayes to be a beer drinker.

As we draw closer, I notice him walk up behind a girl. He leans close as if he's whispering something to her and my stomach twists into knots. The second she turns around, I see her familiar face. She's one of the puck bunnies that was at his house the morning we were supposed to meet at Clara's.

He hands her the drink and she runs her dirty hand down his bare arm. I curl my lip in disgust, though my wrenching gut is no match for the sheer anger I'm feeling right now.

My thoughts drift back to the night we first met and how he so easily dismissed me after we had sex. I was starting to forget that side of him existed, but he just showed me, once again, who he truly is and who he will always be.

I tug on Avery's arm. "I think this was a bad idea," I shout over the noise, holding my stare to Hayes. "Maybe we should just go to Piggy's."

She must not even notice the intense flirtation happening directly in front of us because she keeps on pulling me toward them.

"Try to let loose and have some fun, B. Like old times." Dropping my hand, she gleefully skips her way to Evan.

Old times didn't involve Hayes Madden and letting loose was effortless. Somehow he's turned me into this uptight girl I don't even recognize. I'm constantly on the defensive, and now apparently, I get mad when I see him flirting with other girls.

With Avery already at Evan's side, I use this opportunity to go outside for some fresh air. If I have to, I'll wait out here for her all night. I'm halfway to the door when I'm halted by a hand on my shoulder. "Leaving so soon?"

I spin around and come face to face with Hayes. His head tilts to the side as he reads my expression, loud and fucking clear. "What's wrong, Legs?"

"You think you're *so* smooth, don't you?" My shoulders rise, caging in my neck as rage consumes me. "I'm just some foolish girl you're trying to turn into one of your little puck bunnies, aren't I? Or am I just a revenge tactic against Kamden? Which one is it, Hayes?"

I may have gone too far, but my emotions are speaking for me.

Hayes takes a step back, dropping his hand from my shoulder. "What the hell are you talking about? Did someone say something to you?"

"No!" I stammer. "No one has to say anything to me. What I see with my own eyes is telling enough."

I feel stupid even being upset. What did I seriously think was going to come out of this? Hayes and I aren't together. We will never *be* together. I don't even think we're friends.

"Look…" He holds his hands up in surrender, a scorned look on his face. "I don't know what happened between the arena and here, but I think you're mistaken."

"Just go back to your little puck bunny for the night." I steal a look over his shoulder. "Her drink is almost gone."

He follows my gaze before returning with a smile. "Are you talking about Sierra?" He shoots a thumb in her direction. "I owed her a drink for finding my keys the other day and she wouldn't let up. I went and got it for her so she'd leave me the hell alone." His lips twitch with an egotistical grin. "Are you jealous again, Legs?"

"Of course I'm not jealous!"

Dammit. I should have kept my big mouth shut. I won't deny I feel a sense of relief. But now I have to explain why I reacted like a jealous fool when I don't fully understand it myself.

He pokes a finger into my side, making me squirm. "Come on, Legs. Just admit you're jealous."

"Stop it!" I swat at his hand, biting back a smile. "I'm not jealous. I was angry," I tell him truthfully. "You invited me here and I saw you flirting with her and it pissed me off."

"Baby, that's called jealousy."

He is eating this up right now. I can tell just by the shit-eating grin on his face and the way he's got his shoulders pulled back so confidently. Being vulnerable and putting myself out there is probably my weakest trait.

"Whatever." I crack a smile and grab his hand. I can see it in his eyes he is telling the truth and as Sierra stares daggers at me, Hayes pays her no attention. "Just buy me a drink too and we'll call it even."

He chuckles, pulling me to walk in front of him toward the bar. "I'll get you whatever you want, Legs."

It's said just against my ear and my whole body tingles. Hayes Madden's charm might just be the death of me.

CHAPTER 18

HAYES

"Here's to Hayes sealing our win," Finch bellows with his bottle of beer in the air. "One hell of a hockey player and an even better friend." Everyone clanks their bottles and glasses in the air and I just coyly sip on my bottle of water.

I'm not a fan of attention, unless I'm on the ice, and I certainly don't want any praise unless it's coming from an NHL scout.

Glancing to my left, I look at Brogan who's got her body turned to Avery beside her. Her head leans back as she laughs at something comical.

I wonder if she realizes how beautiful she is. A lot of girls know they're hot and they use their looks to their advantage. Girls like Sierra and Gabby. Brogan is different, though. Her beauty seems almost incidental to who she is.

Suddenly, it hits me. I could be anywhere I want with this girl right now because she's on my watch, and we're sitting in a crowded bar with a bunch of drunk idiots.

Yesterday I was trying to think of the best way to use these next couple days with her, and I came up with some pretty good ideas. One of which, I think she's going to love.

Getting to my feet, I lean down into her space and steal her attention. She peers up at me with wide, curious eyes. "Let's get out of here," I tell her.

While I enjoy coming to Legends after the games, the loud noise and crowds grow tiresome after a while and right now, I want to be anywhere other than here with her.

She sets her empty glass on the table and just when I think she's going to put up a fight, she says, "Okay."

I grab the back of her chair as she tells Avery she's leaving, then I pull it away from the table so she can stand.

Taking her hand in mine, I shoot two fingers in the air at my boys, and before they can ask questions, I lead Brogan out of the bar.

When we step outside, I move my hand to her waist, keeping her body close to mine. Legends is in the heart of the nightlife district, so the sidewalks are always bustling with people.

Brogan shivers in her leggings and Devils sweatshirt and I feel like an ass for not bringing a jacket for her to wear. I pull her closer, tucking her body under my arm to shield her from the cool night air.

"So where are we going?" she asks as we walk against the crowd and away from the string of bars.

"I have a surprise for you," I tell her as I look down at her for her reaction.

She looks up at me, her eyes sparkling. "Have I ever told you I hate surprises?"

"Honestly." I laugh. "I'm not surprised by that in the least. But I think you're gonna like this one."

We approach my bike and she stops walking. "Are we getting on that?"

"Yeah. Why not?"

She gulps. "I've never ridden on a motorcycle before."

"Technically, it's not a motorcycle," I tell her as I open the top box on the back of my bike. I'm happy to see I've got a heavy flannel shirt in there. I take it out and hand it to her, hoping she'll wear it without putting up a fight. I'd hate her to be any colder on the ride. "This old girl is much faster. I'll take it slow for you, though." I wink.

To my surprise, she slides her arms in the sleeves of my flannel and tugs the opening closed. Knowing it'll blow in the wind, I reach out and begin snapping the buttons on it. "If you kill us…" she begins.

"Then you'll kill me. Got it, Legs." I slide my spare bucket helmet over her head and tighten the strap under her chin, pausing to admire her for a second. She looks cute as fuck right now.

"I can't kill you if you're already dead." She adjusts her straps until the helmet is sitting comfortably on her head. "I was going to say something more along the lines of, I'll haunt the Devils' hockey team and make them lose every single game."

"Ohhh," I groan teasingly. "You're pure evil."

I swing my leg over my bike and settle onto the leather seat. "Now climb your sexy ass on and hold on tight." I grab my own helmet off the handle and slide it over my head before slipping on my leather riding gloves.

Brogan takes her sweet time sitting down, but once she's nestled behind me, I reach back and grab her arms, knowing she won't wrap them around me of her own free will. Then I bring the engine to life.

Her hands grip so tightly around my waist I feel her fingertips press through the fabric of my shirt. With her chest flush against my back and her chin touching my shoulder, I hear her voice over the roar of the bike. "You think I have a sexy ass, huh?"

I roar a laugh. "I was waiting for you to mention that."

Twisting the throttle, I speed up, feeling the wind whip past us. Brogan's grip on me tightens as she clings to my body like her life depends on it. "Hayes!" she shouts with laughter. I like having this sort of control over her. Even more so, I love the way she holds on and how she says my name with joy and excitement. Something about it just makes me want to go even faster, to show her what it feels like to fly. But I'm going to be careful with this one.

As we cruise down the roads, my grin stretches from ear to ear. Taking a longer route crossed my mind because I'm not ready for Brogan to let go of me, but I'm a gentleman and don't. I know she's cold, and I'm anxious to see her reaction when she realizes what I have planned.

Pulling into an empty parking space in front of Hallstrom Hall, I kill the engine and help Brogan ease to the ground before flipping my leg over the bike in a smooth move I've practiced way too many times. After taking off my helmet, I unfasten hers and hook them on my bike.

"My dorm, huh?" She smirks. "What exactly are you up to, Hayes Madden?"

"You'll see." I take her hand and lead the way to her room.

CHAPTER 19

HAYES

ONCE WE'RE inside her room, Brogan turns on a lamp beside her bed and I immediately begin searching Avery's half of the room for the backpack I had her put in here earlier today. Avery may be Brogan's best friend, but she and I were in cahoots to ensure that Brogan is happy and it looks like we pulled this off perfectly.

I can feel her eyes following me as I peer under Avery's bed and around the clothes scattered on her floor. "What are you doing?"

Shooting a look over my shoulder, I see her standing with her hands on her hips. "You do realize you're snooping around my room right in front of me?"

"Uh-huh," I mutter as I stand up, still searching.

When I don't find it on Avery's side of the room, I move to Brogan's side, hoping she doesn't shove her foot up my ass while I'm scanning under her bed.

My hand slaps against an open notebook, so I slide it toward me. While it's not what I was looking for, it's caught my eye. On one of the pages are drawings of dresses with intricate designs and cuts. The other page holds sketches of the backside of each article of clothing.

"Hey!" Brogan snaps as she flips the notebook closed. "That's personal! Hayes, why did we leave the bar just to come back to my room so you could search it in front of me? This is weird."

I point to the book that's now in her hand. "Did you draw those?"

"No," she blurts out, pulling the book close to her chest. "I mean, yes. But they're not for you to look at. Or anyone, really."

"I didn't realize you could draw so well."

"I, uh." She swallows thickly, sighing a little. "I always liked fashion design as a kid and once I got my first sketchbook, I wasn't able to stop."

I've told Brogan a little bit about my future goals, but she's never once mentioned hers. Maybe that's because I haven't really asked. "Is that your major then? Fashion design?"

"Actually, no." She glances down at the book before shaking her head. "My major is fashion merchandising."

"Hmm. I don't know what that is but I assume it means you still design clothes, right?" I know nothing about the fashion industry at all. I once tried to watch an episode of *Project Runway* with a girl because no one could find the remote and I was too hungover to care, but after they put something that looked like a whole-ass peacock on a chick's head, I had to turn that shit off, it got too weird.

"It means I will help the people who design the clothes sell the clothes."

My expression twists in confusion, just as my brain does. "But why? Those are amazing, Legs." They're way better than the peacock thing I saw, that's for sure. "You should be the one designing them. Then let someone else sell them for *you*."

She blushes, a subtle smile coming to her face as she opens up the book and flips through a few pages with no peacocks in sight. I step up next to her, looking through the different textures she has blended together and the way some of the fabrics she brought to life cling to her models.

She has everything ranging from what a Victoria's Secret model would wear to what I imagine a mom would wear. She's clearly talented, being able to draw this kind of range, but not only that, I swear I can even feel some of the textures she added in.

"You really think they're good?" Her eyes rise to mine and I am damn near tempted to grab her face and tilt her head to look at the paper just to make sure we are seeing the same thing.

"Hell yes, they're good. It's like some of them have come to life on the page."

Her lips twitch with a smile. "Thanks. I've always loved sketching out different clothing designs. Some are a little off-the-wall, but each one is special to me."

I may be stuck on this peacock thing, but none of her designs are anywhere near that "off-the-wall."

"As they should be. Now tell me this, if you love creating the designs, why the hell are you pursuing a merchandiser degree? Or whatever it's called."

"Honestly…" She shrugs. "I don't really know. I think it just comes down to fear of rejection."

Placing my hands on her shoulders, I make her face me. "Legs, Legs. Legs. Do you think every Division One hockey player gets drafted into the NHL?"

"No," she gasps. "Of course not."

"Do you think *I'm* going to get drafted into the NHL?" I look at her seriously, not asking for a compliment here. I know I play well, but getting drafted isn't just about skill, there is a little luck involved too. I don't want her to tell me what my teammates tell me; I want her to be honest.

She grimaces as she lifts a shoulder. "I don't know, maybe. Maybe not."

Standing tall, I wink at her. "Do you think that's going to stop me from trying?"

She grins up at me, that fire of a challenge in her eyes. "You tell me. Is it?"

"Fuck no," I howl. "Not a chance. I'm giving this shit all I've got and then some. If I don't make it, there's no way in hell it'll be due to a lack of trying. Sure, I've got a backup plan with a sports communication degree, but I hope I never need it."

She lets out a breathy laugh, but then her finger falls to trace over a purple jumpsuit design with a belt looped through the waist.

"I hear you and I know what you're saying, and yes, you're right. You don't know the outcome if you don't try. I get it." She takes a deep breath, still looking down at the notebook. "But isn't it scary working so hard for something that requires a level of talent you're not certain you have?"

Brogan finally lifts her head and I feel like I need to make sure I say the right thing here. Deciding what risks we will take is just part of life, but not taking any risks means we aren't living.

"Isn't it scarier to waste that level of talent and never make it because you never tried?"

She exhales heavily as she closes her notebook and slides it on the nightstand. "It's all just...scary."

"Life is scary." I pull her close to me so we are only a few inches apart. "But that doesn't mean we just stop living because we're afraid."

Grinning, she shakes a finger at me. "You need to stop that."

"Stop what?" I lean down into her space.

"Making me think. It's too late in the day and I'm too tired."

Fuck am I tempted to kiss this girl. How is she everything I didn't realize I needed?

I lift a shoulder. "Just think about it later then. Some things are worth the risk, and in your case, I think the risk is extremely low."

As I'm turning back around, I spot my black backpack sitting beside the door. "There it is," I mutter. *I wonder how many times I walked right past it.*

Snatching it up, I toss it on Brogan's bed. Once I've got it unzipped, I tip it upside down and dump the contents onto her duvet that is somehow no longer stained from the pizza.

"Oh my God, Hayes. What is all this?" She begins rummaging through the various items on her bed.

Her fingers land on a pack of fake spiders with a cotton-spun web before setting it down and picking up something else. There are some orange and black LED lights, some skull and ghost cutouts, and a banner that says "Happy Halloween." Amongst a few other random things I grabbed at the dollar store.

I sit down on her bed, my eyes following her every move as she looks at each item. The way her face lights up with child-like excitement makes me feel like the luckiest man alive for being able to witness it.

"When Avery called last night and asked me to grab a pizza and come over, she mentioned watching a Halloween movie because it's your favorite holiday. It struck me as odd when I arrived and saw absolutely no Halloween decorations in your room."

I didn't think too much about it until we were watching the movie and she had this look in her eye like she wished she could bring it to life.

"I know you've been feeling sort of down lately and I thought maybe we'd decorate and get your mind off things for a little while."

She sets the last item down—a package of yellow caution tape—then turns to me with her hands clasped over her heart. "This is seriously the nicest thing anyone has ever done for me, Hayes."

I shrug it off, not wanting too much credit. "It's no big deal."

Shaking her head, she moves to stand right in front of me. "It is to me."

Our eyes lock and time seems to stand still as the air between us grows heavy. Even while all my friends are out partying and having a good time, there is no place I'd rather be and no one I'd rather be with.

Brogan makes me feel settled, like the racing storm inside my head that I am always trying to push down breaks in her presence.

I wasn't supposed to fall for this girl, but she entered my life and wreaked havoc on my heart, and now, I'm not sure how I can ever let her leave.

By the way her chest is rising and falling rapidly, I'm more certain than ever that she feels it, too.

In an instant, Brogan blinks away and snatches up the fake spiderweb, waving it around with a widespread grin on her face. "Should we get started?"

I smack my hands to my thighs and leap to my feet. "Let's do it."

We start with decorating the door—running caution tape over it and adding a couple of paper skeletons. Then we weave the fake spiderweb in the corner above her bed and stick the little eight-legged plastic spiders all over it.

Just for the hell of it, I stick one in Brogan's hair.

Twenty minutes later, we're sticking paper cutouts on her wall and she still hasn't noticed.

I grab my phone from her bed and snap a pic of her mid-stretch as she tacks a banner on the wall.

Then I duplicate the photo, crop it zoomed in on the spider and send it to her in a text message. Her phone pings from her nightstand and she hurries over to it, leaving the other end of the banner hanging from the wall.

While she's checking her phone, I finish what she started and evenly position the banner over the window. Just as I push the tack in, I'm hit in the backside with a pillow.

"You think you're so funny." She giggles as she tries to get the spider out of her hair.

I crouch down and snatch the pillow up, flinging it back at her. She dodges out of the way, but I'm quick on my feet and already grabbing the other one off her bed. With a swift movement, I raise it above my head and slam it onto her. Still laughing, she tumbles onto her side, shielding her face as I gently pummel her with the pillow.

"I surrender," she squeals.

Just as I toss the pillow down, she grabs it and begins beating my legs with it.

"So much for surrendering." I drop to my knees and snare her wrists in each of my hands, forcing her to drop it. Breathlessly, I stare down at her. "Are you done now?"

Blowing strands of hair away from her mouth, she nods.

"You sure?" I lean in, assessing her crazy eyes to see if she might try another round. I honestly wouldn't mind it.

"I surrender, for real this time." She blows out another breath and I help her out by letting go of one wrist so I can push the hair out of her face.

Her lustful eyes peer up at me as she catches her breath. "Thank you."

"Don't mention it," I tell her as I eye the plastic spider still in her hair. I pluck it out only to set it down on her nose with a mischievous grin.

She wriggles and squirms, causing it to fall on her shoulder. "You're such a dork."

"And you're such an easy target," I tease.

I notice the way her eyes dart to my lips, only to shoot right back up. "You'd be singing a different tune if you didn't have me pinned to the floor."

"Oh yeah?" I jut my chin out in a challenge. "What are you gonna do about it?"

Brogan bites her lip. "Let me up and I'll show you."

"Nah. I sort of like you underneath me on your back." Preferably biting her lip while she screams my name, but beggars can't be choosers.

"Oh my God, Hayes." She giggles and swats me with her free hand.

It's the truth. In fact, I think this is my new favorite way to look at her. Not only is she crazy beautiful with her messy hair scattered around her head, but she truly is at my mercy.

Heat radiates through my body and I can almost taste the desire on her lips. My fingers twitch as the temptation to touch her soft skin gnaws at my insides.

With my free hand, I reach out and stroke the backs of my fingers against her cheek. "Ya know. I could kiss you right now and there isn't a damn thing you could do about it."

She swallows hard, her body tensing underneath me. "Do it and find out."

I was not expecting that response. *Damn.* I think she actually wants me to kiss her. After days of torment, it's finally happening.

Leaning down, I brush my lips against hers, but before I can add pressure, she turns her head to the left.

My head shoots up and disappointment floods through me. "What was that all about?"

When she looks back at me, she's smiling. "I guess you found out."

"Not funny." I go to push myself up, but before I can, she grabs my face and pulls my mouth to hers, taking me by complete surprise.

My body falls into hers, covering her like a warm blanket as the curves of her lips mold perfectly to mine. Every nerve in my body feels like it's been lit on fire. Warmth spreads from our kiss down to my cock and it hardens instantly.

It feels like I've been waiting for this moment for ages, even though it was only recently I even realized I had feelings for Brogan. I knew from the start she was different from any other girl and I can't deny that I've been magnetized to her. Wherever she is, I want to be. If she's not there, I don't want to go. She consumes me—every thought, every dream, every second of every day.

I run my fingers through her hair, getting a gentle but firm grip on the back of her head. Lifting up, I bring her closer and deepen our kiss. Our tongues dance, our lips gliding effortlessly together.

The ache in my groin tells me I need to stop this before it only gets worse. But before I can, the door to the room flies open and Brogan startles out of the kiss before pushing two hands to my chest.

"Ooopsies." I hear Avery's voice from behind me.

My body rises, hovering over Brogan's, and she immediately wriggles her way out from underneath me.

We both stand—Brogan wiping the back of her hand across her mouth, and me scratching my hand wondering why she reacted like we just got caught hiding a body.

"I'm so sorry," Avery says as she walks quickly to her side of the room. She gets on her knees, fishing for something under her bed. "Don't mind me. Just keep doing what you were doing."

Brogan and I share a glance and a grin spreads across both of our faces as we fight not to laugh.

Avery's head pops up and she stands, holding a pair of tennis shoes. "I knew they were under here somewhere."

"Ugh. Whatcha got planned, Ave?" Brogan asks with a raised brow.

"Evan and I are going to a haunted corn maze and I don't want to break an ankle in these shoes." She turns her foot up, showing off her black high heels. "Do you two want to go with us?"

I look at Brogan who is shaking her head. "I've got an early game tomorrow and need some good sleep. Probably shouldn't."

I back her up by saying, "Yeah, and I'm pretty beat after tonight's game."

Avery's gaze shifts back and forth between me and Brogan, a devious smirk spreading across her face. "I think I'm picking up what you're putting down. You two want some time alone."

"No," Brogan sputters a laugh. "Why would Hayes and I want time alone?"

Avery moves hastily across the room. "Oh, I think we both know why." She turns the handle and pulls the door open. "By the way, I like what you two have done with the place." With that, she leaves.

As soon as the door latches, we both burst into laughter. But when the moment passes and the humor has settled, I move to her side as she pretends to organize random items on her dresser. "Does it bother you that Avery walked in on us kissing?"

She doesn't even look at me—just keeps moving stuff around. "Not at all. What makes you think that?"

"Ugh. How about the way you rolled out from under me like you were on fire?"

There's a tense beat of silence and she's still fucking with things on her dresser, so I put my hand on her shoulder and turn her to face me. "What's this all about?"

She averts her gaze, thinking for a minute before saying, "That shouldn't have happened." Her words are like a knife to my chest. "Kamden I just broke up, and you and I…" She waves her hand between us. "…we don't want this. Right?"

I nod, spitting out the first word that comes to mind. "No." I clear my throat. "Hell no. Of course not."

Something in her expression falls, like I just said the wrong thing, and I know in my gut I did. But there is no going back. "I'm glad we both agree. Because I'm actually starting to enjoy your company, and the last thing I want to do is make things messy."

I'm not sure if that was a compliment or an insult. It could go either way. I enjoy her company, too, but I don't tell her that. Instead, I step away from her, trying to wrap my head around what's happening.

There's no fucking way she didn't feel what I felt when we kissed. She can't deny the sexual tension between us or the way our eyes connect and it's like we're reading each other's souls. Yet, she is denying it. She's saying it never should have happened. But why are her eyes telling me a different story?

She's not ready. There hasn't been enough time. I just hope forty-eight hours is long enough to change her mind.

That kiss needs to stew a little bit on her mind. I want her to think about it—dream about it. Then wake up and wish for it to happen again.

"I'm gonna get going." I walk over to my shoes and begin sliding them on with the laces still tied.

"You're not mad, are you?"

My eyes snap to hers and I immediately notice the sadness behind them. "Hell no." I force a smile as I go back to her bed and grab my backpack. "Not even a little bit. Just beat after the game and I could really use a long shower." I fling my bag over my shoulder and cross the room, stopping where she's at in the middle.

Cupping her cheeks in my hands, I press my lips to her forehead, holding them there for a second before I take a step back. "Get some rest and I'll see you tomorrow."

She walks me to the door and pulls it open. "Thanks for tonight. It was probably one of the best nights I've had since coming to Rosewood U."

"Me, too, Legs." *Me fucking too.* I walk out the door and take a few steps down the hall before she stops me.

"Hayes?"

I look back at her, hoping like hell she's had a change of heart and she wants me to come back.

With half her body in the hall, she leans into the doorframe. "Our deal still stands, right? You said you'll see me tomorrow, so I assume that means we're still making the video?"

An ache ripples through my chest as my heart drops into my stomach.

"Sure," I tell her. "Our deal still stands."

She quirks a brow. "I was thinking maybe next Thursday after the Kappa Rho Halloween party?"

"Next Thursday it is."

CHAPTER 20

BROGAN

MUSIC ROARS through the speakers and my squad and I jump into formation. Adrenaline surges through me as the crowd cheers us on.

Twisting to the left, I kick my leg in the air and throw my hands to the sky, waving my pom-poms, all with a big grin on my face.

Even as we're down 21–10 in the last minutes of the second quarter, my smile never falters.

The stadium falls dead silent as the other team's quarterback scrambles and completes a pass for ten-yards on the fourth down.

"Go, Legs!" I hear the distant voice call out from somewhere in the stands.

My cheeks heat up and I feel every pair of my squad's eyes on me. I look out in the stands, searching frantically for Hayes— because I *know* it was Hayes.

A second later, I find him decked out in Devils colors with his fist pumping in the air, eyes locked on mine. I shake my head at him, suppressing the ridiculous smile that threatens to break free. All the while he has no shame as his grin stretches from ear to ear.

I can't believe he's even here. I've never seen Hayes at one of our games and he's never given any inclination that he cared to watch one. Then again, he isn't really watching the game. It appears he's just watching me.

"Girl, what was that all about?" Lucia sings as she steps up to my side, shaking her pom-poms as we keep our eyes trained on the field. "Is there something going on with you and Hayes?"

"No. Not really. We're just friends." It's weird using that word in reference to Hayes. But, yeah. I think we are friends. Though, our kiss last night sure as hell felt like more. As I lay there on my back with his body hovering over me, it felt like time was standing still.

I waited with bated breath, hoping he'd kiss me, then he did. Of course, I had to fuck with him a little bit. I think my move only intensified the moment, though. It was a perfect kiss. Almost too perfect because it scared the shit out of me.

I don't know why I told him it shouldn't have happened. I guess my reaction was rooted in fear that he didn't feel the same way. But now, as I glance at him in the stands—watching me with deep intensity—I don't think he's too far behind my fall.

Feeling like I'm under Hayes's scrutiny, I do my best to remain focused on our cheers. When halftime rolls around, we slay our performance on the field. So much so that Coach Wendy tells us we get the day off tomorrow from practice.

In the end, we lost the game 21–18. It sucks, but I'm not sad over it. I actually enjoy seeing the look of defeat on Kamden's face as he walks off the field.

Knowing Hayes is here somewhere, I try to get through our post-game festivities quickly in hopes of catching him before he leaves. On our way to the locker room, we all make plans to go to Piggy's after the game, but I'm not so sure I'll be able to since I'm under Hayes's orders for the rest of the day.

It's probably for the best. I'm not so sure I want to be part of that scene right now. Even though my viral video seems to have died down, Gabby seems to be doing everything in her power to keep it alive. Even now as she's gossiping with her clique a few lockers down from mine about how I wouldn't dare show my face at Piggy's.

"Ignore her," Lucia says as she hangs her uniform in her locker. "Make an appearance with me and Jared and make that bitch eat her words."

I close my locker door and fling my backpack over my shoulder. "I don't know if I have the patience for her childish behavior right now." I shrug. "We'll see."

I head out the doors and immediately see Hayes sitting alone on the bottom bleacher in the gymnasium. The second he notices me, he stands up.

"Well…" I do a little jump kick. "How'd I do?"

He laughs. "You killed it, Legs. Just like I knew you would. Ya know, I had a hard time imagining you as a cheerleader, but now that I've seen it with my own eyes, I don't think I can picture you *not* being a cheerleader."

I stand proudly at that. "I'll take that as a compliment."

He ruffles my hair playfully. "Just don't let it get to your head."

"Duly noted. The same way you don't let it get to your head that I think you're somewhat decent at hockey."

He laughs while reaching over to grab my bag with one hand and slinging it over his shoulder as we exit the gymnasium. "Exactly."

I can't help but smile at the small gesture. It's actually pretty sweet.

Not wasting any time, I ask the million-dollar question. "So, what's on the agenda today?"

"You tell me."

"I don't understand. I thought it was your decision." I lead him to a side door so that we can get past most of the people in the atrium without as much of a rush.

"It is. But you've gotten a taste of my life and post-game activities, now I wanna get a taste of yours."

I look up at him as we make our way to the atrium. "Are you sure about that?" I ask, voice low.

"Hell yeah. Your crew gathers at Piggy's, right? Want to go back to the place I saved your life."

Rolling my eyes I have to try not to smack him. "You mean outside where you shoved me violently into the building?"

"We can reenact the night. See if there's anything I'd do differently." He eyes me the same way he did when I was beneath him on the floor and heat pools in my core.

I laugh. "Sounds like you've thought about it. Is there something you would have done differently?"

Hayes pushes open the door to the parking lot, holding it open for me. "Honestly, nothing," he quips. "I think things are working out just the way they should."

I look up at him and smile. "I think so, too."

As I step out of the rideshare car, my eyes immediately land on the neon sign above Piggy's. It's still too early in the day for it to glow, so it just sits there dark and unlit.

Hayes comes to my side and takes my hand, calming my nerves slightly. I've never brought an outsider to Piggy's. Let alone a hockey player. It's always been me and Kamden.

"Ready?" he asks.

Mentally preparing myself for the inevitable gossip and stares coming my way, I suck in a breath, filling my lungs. "Let's do this."

Even at three o'clock in the afternoon, the bar is jumping. The majority of people are cheerleaders, football players, and assistant coaches, but there's a few random customers sitting at the bar.

I search haphazardly for Lucia and Jared in hope that they're at a table we can steal a seat at. The last thing I want to do is stand around and become the center of attention.

A sigh of relief escapes me when I spot them in a booth at the back of the bar. "This way," I tell Hayes as I take his hand to pull him in their direction.

We're walking at a leisurely pace when Kamden steps in front of me. His eyes pin to Hayes. "You've got some nerve coming on *my* turf, Madden."

"Fuck off," Hayes grumbles as he gives Kamden a light shove.

Kamden slaps Hayes's hand and seethes. "Don't fucking touch me."

I step in front of Hayes as a barrier between the two of them. "Stop it, you guys, please." I speak softly in hopes of de-escalating the situation. "Can we just coexist for one night?"

Looking at Kamden now, it's like a veil has been lifted. Every inch of his gorgeous physique makes my skin crawl. His eyes no longer hold me captive, and I see the despicable person he is behind his charming facade.

"Screw that." Kamden jabs a finger in the air. "I'll never coexist with that fucking bum."

"You're fucking dead." Hayes lunges toward him, but I shift my body just in time, keeping him behind me. He stops right where our bodies meet, and I feel a little bit powerful knowing that I can hold back this strong man. I've seen him take down guys five times my size with ease, but he is gentle with me and doesn't push.

"Stop it!" I raise my voice.

Kamden pins me with a scathing glare. "You've only got yourself to blame here. All you had to do was keep your legs and your mouth closed. But you spread them far and wide for this dipshit. Then you went public and spread bullshit lies about me."

"You better watch your fucking mouth when you talk to her." Hayes gets antsy behind me, shifting from one foot to the other. His body tenses as he tries to get past me, but he's mindful of my presence and holds himself back.

It sort of pisses me off that not one person has come to help keep these two apart. Then again, they're all Team Kamden. If he and Hayes throw down, I've got no doubt the entire football team will jump in to defend him.

As for Lucia and Jared, they're off in la-la land right now and none the wiser to what's going on.

Kamden clenches his fist, though he's looking me dead in the eye. But Hayes puts his hand on my waist from behind me and pulls me closer to him, offering me a sense of security.

"You've got until tomorrow afternoon to take that fucking video down," Kamden seethes. "Do I have to remind you who my fucking father is?"

Hayes's hot breath hits the back of my neck as he grits out, "Do I have to remind you who *my* fucking father is?"

"Oh, I know who he is." Kamden smirks deviously. "Unfortunately for you, he's forgotten who *you* are."

The next thing I know, Hayes breaks free from behind me and lunges at Kamden. With a fierce grunt, he grabs Kamden by the waist and slams him into a table. Plates of food and filled drinks crash to the floor, shattering glass and splattering liquid all over.

Rolling onto the floor, they continue to wrestle, but Hayes has the upper hand being on top. I watch as his arm cocks back and his fist flies forward, connecting with Kamden's cheek.

I shriek, slapping a hand over my mouth while people finally step in and attempt to break the two of them apart.

After a very long minute, they're separated, and Hayes is pulled to his feet unscathed while Kamden is sporting a swollen cheek.

"Keep hiding behind your girl, asshole." Kamden gnashes as a couple of his teammates hold him back. "She can't protect you forever. In fact, you might not wanna turn around with this one. She's quite the backstabber."

Hayes seizes my hand and pulls me through the gathered crowd and to the door. "Fuck him and this place."

We don't stop moving as our feet lead us quickly down the sidewalk. Hayes's heavy breaths flare his nostrils. Finally, I pull back on his hand, stopping him. "Can we just stop walking a minute, please?"

He looks past me, almost as if he's too ashamed to look me in the eye. Dragging his thumb across his lip, he wipes up a smear of blood—just like last time these two went at it. "That fucker always goes for the lip."

I brush off some crumbs on his shirt, looking him over to make sure the glass didn't cut him. "Other than your lip, are you okay?"

"I'm fine," he deadpans. His chest rises and falls at rapid speed and I can see that his adrenaline is still pumping.

We're silent for a minute, collecting our thoughts before I ask the question weighing heavy on my mind. "How long has this feud between you and Kamden been going on?"

He stares blankly behind me, shaking his head. "I honestly can't even remember when it started." His eyes skate to mine and he grabs my hand, stroking my palm with the pad of his thumb. "He's already ruined enough of our night. I don't wanna talk about him anymore."

I nod. "Okay. So let's do something. Something fun to get our minds off...*that*."

The corner of his lip curves upward. "I think I know exactly how to do that. I just need to make a call first."

CHAPTER 21

HAYES

Walking into Delta Ice Arena, I'm flooded with all the memories I've made in this place. But I have a feeling that tonight, I might make my favorite one of all.

"Now will you tell me what we're doing?" Brogan asks anxiously at my side.

I laugh. "You seriously haven't figured it out yet? What could we possibly do at an ice rink?"

Her eyes widen. "*Noooo!* Are we ice skating?"

"Damn straight we are." I pull her hand, leading the way to the locker room where all my gear is stored. "I've gotta make a quick stop to grab my skates, then we'll go get you sized up."

Her brows rise. "Is the skate rental even open?"

"A buddy of mine works security here and he owes me a favor for going to his son's school last year to talk about ice hockey."

Brogan sits on a bench outside the locker room while I grab my skates, a sweatshirt for her, and my practice jersey just for added effect.

When I walk out, I motion for her to stand and I pull the sweatshirt over her, then top it off with my jersey. I take a step back and look at her and it's like my fantasy has come to life. She looks sexy as fuck.

"So tell me, Hayes. How many other girls have worn your jersey?"

We round the corner and I see Johnny standing beside the counter holding a ring full of keys. "You're the first, and likely the last. I'm not very good at sharing."

My response makes her smile.

"What's up, Johnny." I stretch my hand out to him and he returns it with a shake.

"I could get in some deep shit over this, Madden." He narrows his eyes. "You've got one hour."

Johnny turns the key in the door to unlock it, then gestures for us to go inside. I wish I had a pair of skates that aren't worn and smelly to offer Brogan. Unfortunately, she'll have to wear a pair of shitty rentals.

I help her get the correct size then we head out to the rink to get them on.

"I think you should know something," she begins as I lace her up. "I'm a terrible ice skater and it's in your best interest to just let me hold the wall."

"Hell no." I chuckle. "The only thing you'll be holding out there is my hand." I look up and flash her a smile. "By the time we're done, you'll be skating better than the team's ice girls."

She looks legitimately terrified. "Don't hold your breath on that."

I reach for her hands and pull her to her feet. "You'll be fine. I've got you."

Balancing carefully on the toe of the blades, she stretches her left arm out to brace herself if she falls. Not that I'd ever let that happen.

"You're just full of surprises, Hayes Madden."

"Is it safe to assume you've been enjoying our forty-eight hours together?"

A smile spreads across her face when she looks at me. "I

really have." Her voice is soft and sincere, her eyes glistening with excitement.

I step onto the ice first, then take both her hands and guide her out. "Well, it ain't over yet, baby."

She squeals as her blades glide a few inches and her legs slowly drift apart.

I glide backward, leaving delicate lines on the ice. Her legs tremble as I lead her farther and farther away from the edge until we're in the center of the rink.

"Hayes," she bellows as her feet begin to move in opposite directions.

"Bring them legs together, Legs. You can do this."

With a swift jerk, I pull her body to mine. Our chests collide and I wrap my arms around her waist.

The lights dim and I look across the rink and see Johnny near the light panel, his thumbs in the air. I didn't ask him to do that, but I'm not angry he did.

Brogan cranes her neck, looking at me. "Are you trying to romance me, Hayes Madden?"

I don't know what it is about the way she says my full name, but I fucking love the way it rolls off her tongue.

"Maybe I am. After all, we have a pretty big date coming up."

"Ahh," she chortles. "The video? I was starting to think maybe you forgot."

"How can I? You mention it every time we're together." I try not to say this with the same amount of distaste I have at the idea of being her puppet and nothing more. But maybe that is what I did to her when we first met, so it's only fair.

She shrugs. "A deal is a deal."

"Right." I nod as I pull her to the end of the rink.

Part of me wonders if she'd even be here with me right now if it weren't for our deal. I can't complain—I asked for this. In fact, this entire thing was my idea. The video, forty-eight hours together. I guess I just didn't think she'd actually go along with it. But here we are. Me, falling hard. And her, holding on for the ride thinking it's all some game.

Putting pressure against my hands, she tries to move faster so I keep up with her pace. "Look at you being a little dare devil," I tease.

"I think I'm starting to get the hang of it," she says confidently.

She tries to move even faster, but I slow her down just a tad. "Easy, Legs."

Just as I do, her legs drift apart again and the next thing I know, she's falling to the side. I reach out and grab her by the waist, lifting her up until her back is straight.

Her body falls into mine and she holds on like her life depends on it. Wide eyes stare back at me and just when I think she's going to panic, she bursts out in laughter. "I'm terrible at this."

"Nah. You're doing great. You haven't hit the ice yet, so count that as a win." It takes everything in me not to press a soft kiss to her hair right now with her so close. I don't even know why I want to, but I do.

She peers up at me with adoration as I hold on to her. "How's your lip?" Her hand comes between us and she gently runs her finger over the cut.

I gulp, wanting to tell her that her lips are the Band-Aid it needs. Instead, I just say, "Better now."

We do a few more laps and before I know it, the lights return to full brightness. I find Johnny again and he nods, signaling us to get the hell out of here before he loses his job.

With gentle ease, I help her off the ice, and she sits down on the closest chair, nearly breathless. Most people don't realize how much of a workout a few laps can be, especially when you're new to skating. "I can't believe we just did that."

I crouch down in front of her and unlace her skates. "What do you think...you ready to try out for the ice girls' cheer team?"

"Not a chance." She laughs. "But I did have fun."

I smile. "Me, too."

Our ride is waiting for us outside the main doors of the arena; only this time, I'm not getting in with her. I've realized something about Brogan that I'm not even sure she knows about herself. She likes to have people around and I don't think she would ever tell me to leave. I think if I want to make this real for her, I need her to want to ask me to stay. Not just that, but I want it to be a conscious choice, not just one of convenience.

Once she's seated in the back, I lean into the doorframe. "Night, Legs."

"Wait. You're not coming?" Shocked eyes look back at me.

I shake my head. "Think I'm gonna quit while I'm ahead tonight."

"Ahh." She quirks a brow even as something sad crosses her features. "An underachiever?"

"Something like that." I wink before closing the door and tapping the roof to signal the driver he can leave.

I could have dragged the night out and spent the rest of it with her—God knows I wanted to. But after the way she reacted to our kiss last night, I think she needs to miss me a little bit. I gave her a memorable two nights. Now I just need to hope it was enough.

CHAPTER 22

HAYES

WITH CLASSES and a full training schedule for us both, Brogan and I haven't seen each other most of the week. But I think my plan is working in my favor because she's texted me first on multiple occasions this week.

We have joked around and even called on the phone while walking between classes a few times. I never really wanted a girlfriend before, but I think I'm finally getting the appeal. She makes my life exciting with her constant sass, but she's also someone I can open up to about things like my grades stressing me out.

She is so much more than I gave her credit for that first night, and I'm starting to find I really like all the sides of Brogan Astor. Which is why I cannot wait to see her tonight for the Halloween party. No matter how many times I asked, she refused to tell me what she's going to be dressed as, but she promised it was something special just for me.

Speaking of my little spitfire.

"Hayes," I hear her holler over the crowd of people. When I turn, my heart literally skips a beat.

Goddamn. I bite my fist, watching as she crosses the room in her sexy costume.

Is she wearing a bathing suit? It looks like a baby pink one-piece suit that does a terrible job of holding her tits. They're one jump kick away from popping out. I need to get a look at her backside because there is no way those black fishnet stockings are covering her ass cheeks the way stockings should. I dig the pink bunny ears and a black bowtie around her neck, though. And don't get me started on those black heels. I'm not opposed to her wearing those and using my hands tonight.

Fuck. How the hell am I supposed to have a good time while every man in this house ogles her?

Part of me wants to go downstairs and grab a jacket from my room, so I can wrap it around her. The other part of me just wants to take her away from the party altogether.

I've missed her like crazy and based on the excitement in her eyes as she approaches, I'm confident she missed me, too.

"Damn," I drawl, stroking my chin as my eyes drink her up. "That costume should be illegal."

"I'm glad you like it. Any idea what I am?"

"Ugh," I side-eye her. "A sexy bunny, obviously."

She shakes her head, a grin on her lips. "I'm a puck bunny. *Your* puck bunny."

Jesus. If she wasn't already appealing enough, she just got a hell of a lot sexier.

Her hands immediately land on each of my arms, her eyes roaming up and down my body. "Your costume is the one that should be illegal." She nibbles delightfully on her bottom lip. "I think a priest may be my newest fantasy."

"Well," I lean close and whisper in her ear, "what do you say we make that fantasy a reality? Tonight's the night, Legs."

That's right. Tonight is the night she either walks out of my life for good with the revenge she so desperately craves. Or, the tides turn in my favor and she'll finally realize she wants to be with me instead.

"That it is," she says enthusiastically. "How are you feeling about it?"

I shrug, looking past her. *Like any guy would feel when he knows he's about to fuck the girl of his dreams for the first time since realizing she's the girl of his dreams.*

"Just ready to get this over with," I tell her.

"Wow, Hayes." She smacks my arm playfully. "You sure do know how to turn a girl on."

"Oh, you're gonna be turned on all right." I wink at her and pull her a little closer. I'm not ready to get the sex over with; I'm ready for our deal to end, so I can see if this is real or not.

This girl has no idea what's in store for her.

I might not have a history of good relationships, but ask any girl I've ever fucked and they'll openly admit it was the best sex they've ever had. I bet Brogan would even agree. Tonight will be no different; however, I plan on taking my sweet-ass time as I savor every second with her.

"Be right back," she says, "I need a drink."

As she goes to walk past me, I throw my arm out, catching her around the waist. "Oh no you don't." I spin around and turn her with me.

She growls in response. "I can't get a drink?"

"Not alone, you're not. This place is crawling with horny men who wouldn't hesitate to smooth-talk a girl like you into their bed."

She plants a hand on her hip, taking a stance. "Men like you?"

"Exactly." I hook an arm around her neck and curl her body into mine and walk with her to the kitchen.

"You do realize I'd have to be willing in order for them to get me in their bed unless they drug me or something?"

"And that level of trust in mankind is why I'm not letting you out of my sight tonight. Understood?"

"Yes, Daddy," she murmurs.

I bite my fist again and growl. "I'm gonna need you to repeat that later tonight." Adjusting my pants, I attempt to conceal the erection she just gave me.

We walk into the kitchen and it looks like half the party is in here. A group has gathered on the back deck, surrounding the kegs of beer. On the counter, there are endless bottles of liquor and a line of people waiting to get to them.

"Liquor or beer?" I ask Brogan as I lead her to the front of the line.

She picks up a bottle, and after examining it, she sets it back down and picks up another.

"This." She passes me a pint of cheap white rum. I hold it up, reading the alcohol content, and when she's not looking, I pour a half shot worth into a plastic cup. I want us both to be fully present tonight, which is exactly why I'm only drinking water. I fill the rest of the cup with room temperature Coke, leaving enough room for a couple ice cubes, then once it's mixed, I hand it over to her.

With her drink in hand, Brogan wanders aimlessly, chatting with random people as she sips her drink.

Sticking to her side, I watch her like a hawk. I've never felt the need to protect someone to the extent I do with Brogan. Just the thought of lecherous eyes watching her—or worse, some touching her—gets me heated.

As the night rolls on, all I can think about is how badly I want to get the hell out of here and take her back to her dorm.

Avery's already made plans to stay here with Evan, so we'll have the room all to ourselves.

"What's up, Madden?" my boy Lenny says as he walks toward me. "I heard Coach gave you hell again this morning. Something about a fight at Piggy's Saturday night."

"Eh…" I drag my hand through the air. "It was nothing. Just a little bar brawl."

"Tell me it wasn't Kamden Donnelly." Lenny makes a fist and slams it into his palm, repeating himself. "Tell me it wasn't him, Madden."

"In the flesh." I try to wave it off, but Lenny takes Kamden seriously. As he should because he is a thorn in my side.

"Goddamn," he growls. "I think it's time we put that kid in his place. He's been causing too many problems. And to report you to Coach when the season is in full swing. That's some bullshit."

"As I've said before, he'll get what's coming to him." I untwist the cap of my water bottle and take a long swig.

"What's coming to him is an uppercut straight to the jaw." Lenny bends at the waist, balls his fist, and fakes an uppercut. "That boy needs to quit trying to break our best center."

I laugh at him, rolling my eyes. "Nothing that fucker does can break me so don't go getting your ass in trouble trying to stop him."

Finch joins in and the three of us are standing around bull-shitting when I realize I've lost Brogan.

"Fuck," I grumble. "Have you seen Brogan?" I ask the guys as I scour the room.

"She was just here a second ago," Lenny says.

"Haven't seen her all night," Finch adds. "What's up with you two anyways? You got a thing for this girl, or what?"

Without responding, I walk away, but I hear Lenny say, "I'd say he's got it bad. I've never seen our boy so uptight over a girl."

He's not lying—I do have it bad. Which is exactly why I'm franti-cally searching the crowded room for her. It's only been ten minutes, tops. She couldn't have gone far. So why the fuck can't I find her?

I live in this house with thirty-two guys, and I barely know half of them. The ones I have met are notorious for their woman-izing ways. And that's just the people who live here. This place is swimming with creeps.

I need to get out of my own head. She's probably just chat-ting in a corner with Avery somewhere, talking about me and how charming and sexy I am.

Loud hoots and whistles flow from the kitchen and some-thing in my gut tells me I need to get in there. The music is nearly deafening, so much so that it's hard to tell if my heart is thudding or if it's the bass vibrating in my chest.

My eyes quickly scan the kitchen and I catch sight of

Brogan's friend Lucia dancing in the center of a group of guys. As I'm making my way over to her, I spot a pair of pointed pink bunny ears near the door to the deck.

Cupping my hands around my mouth, I holler, "Brogan!"

My words are lost in the noise, so I eat up the space between us, dodging bodies and spilt drinks. "Brogan!" I try again to no avail.

When she turns to the side, I'm certain it's her, but as my eyes drag down her body, they land on a pair of fingers clutching her wrist.

Anger boils inside me, my vision tunneling as I push my way through the swarm of drunk idiots.

As I draw near them, my mind goes blank and all I see is red. With my adrenaline soaring, I curl my hand into a tight ball and connect it with the back of the guy's head. The impact reverberates through my body and my knuckles sting from the force of the blow. It's not until the douchebag stumbles to the right and I get a look at his face that I realize it's Kamden's roommate, Jeremiah.

His jaw tics with intent and he steels his shoulders and barrels toward me. I see him coming, though, and just as he's about to throw his body into mine, I jump to the left and dodge him. He goes crashing into a group of girls and lands on the floor with a thud. Their drinks go flying and each of them keeps him down by kicking him and screaming at him.

Knowing he's taken care of and won't jump me from behind, I turn back to Brogan…who is fucking gone again. *What the hell!*

I'm back to searching for her again when someone grabs my hand. My eyes shoot to the left and I sigh in relief when I see her. "Jesus, Legs. Where the hell have you been?"

She raises my bloodied right hand and presses a kitchen towel to it. "Are you okay?" she asks with worry in her expression.

"I am now. I've been looking everywhere for you. He didn't hurt you, did he?"

"Who? Jeremiah?" She shakes her head and laughs. "No, he

didn't hurt me. But I'm sure he's in some pain after getting slapped across the face by me, then punched in the back of the head by you."

"You slapped him?" A proud smile spreads across my face.

"Damn straight I did. He was trying to get under my skin by telling me Gabby stayed with Kamden the last two nights. As if I give a shit. Then he proceeded to call me a whore, a bitch, oh… and a clout chaser. So I slapped him. Then he grabbed hold of me and started spewing threats. That's when you stopped him."

Heat rushes to my face again and I clench my sore fingers, groaning through the pain. "He's lucky I don't break his fucking face right now."

I look back at where he was lying and see him sitting with his back against the wall, holding an ice pack to his head. It's not often I sucker punch a guy; in fact, I frown upon it normally. But things have changed since Brogan came into my life, and if you touch her without her consent, it's a surefire way to get an injury from a D1 hockey player.

Brogan tucks the corner of the towel around my hand so it stays in place. "Forget about him. Much like Kamden, he's not worth it."

I shake the towel off my hand and let it fall to the floor. "Let's get the hell outta here." With my hand on Brogan's waist, I lead her out of the kitchen. But not before driving the toe of my shined-up black shoe right between Jeremiah's legs. He grabs his crotch and moans in agony before falling onto his side. "I dare you to speak to her like that again, let alone put your hands on her. Fuck around and find out. Your boy sure did."

CHAPTER 23

HAYES

"Are you sure you're up for this?" Brogan asks as she examines my bandaged hand.

"Hell yes," I spit out, without giving it a second thought. Then it crosses my mind that maybe she's not up for it. She's had an eventful night too. "You haven't changed your mind, have you?

She shakes her head. "Nope. Now more than ever, I want to do this."

I'm still not sure why this is so important to her. The only thing I can come up with when I overthink it is that she needs this for closure. The final fuck-you to Kamden.

Gently setting my hand into my lap, she says, "I think it'll be fine for tonight. I'll unwrap it and clean it again tomorrow."

The first thing Brogan did when we got back to her room was pull out a first aid kit from underneath her bed. After gently cleaning my cuts with antiseptic, she wrapped them carefully.

It's honestly not that bad, but I'm letting her do her thing. I sort of enjoy her taking care of me.

I wiggle my fingers, making sure I can still use them with the six inches of gauze she wrapped around my knuckles. I'm exaggerating a little, but not much.

"I'm fine," I finally say as I stand up from her bed and reach for her hands. She gives them to me and I pull her to her feet.

My heart races with a mix of anticipation and nervousness, which is odd for me. I've never been nervous to sleep with a girl. I think that's part of what makes this one so special—she makes me feel things I've never felt before.

I don't even ask her how she wants to do this, or speak about it at all for that matter, I just go for it. Leaning in, I feel the warmth of her breath against my lips. As they touch, a flame is lit inside me and we are in sync in seconds. Her head angles slightly to the right while I tilt mine to the left. Our tongues meet halfway, moving together in a slow and passionate rhythm.

She tastes like molasses and sugarcane—sweet and inviting.

Tracing the thin strap of the bathing suit she's wearing, I slowly drag it down until it rests on her bicep. My lips follow the path of my fingers, leaving trails of kisses down her chin, then her collarbone, finally settling on her chest. I cup her firm breast in my hand, grazing my thumb over her hard nipple.

Then, I move to the other side, dropping the strap and kissing my way downward.

A soft hum parts her lips and I kiss them again.

"Hayes," she mutters into my mouth, and I groan. My senses are overwhelmed by her nails digging into my shoulders. "The video, Hayes."

Her words hit my ears like a drum. *Of course. The video.* It's the whole reason we're doing this in the first place. At least, it's her reasoning.

Brogan takes a step back, her breasts exposed as she leaves me standing here hard as a rock so she can set her phone up on a tripod. Once it's positioned on her dresser, she hits record.

At this point, I've gone soft and my mind is flooded with all the reasons why we shouldn't do this. Reasons why I never really want Kamden to see this.

Bouncing back over to me, she puts her hands back on my shoulders. "Okay." She smiles. "Where were we?"

One look at her tits and my dick gains a pulse again,

springing to life, reminding me if I don't take advantage of this opportunity, I'm a damn fool. It's not just about sleeping with her; it's about making up for how much I royally fucked up the after part last time. And okay, maybe a little bit about giving her the best sex she has ever had so she never wants to leave.

In my mind I imagined taking this nice and slow, while memorizing every inch of her body. Now, I have the urge to possess her and punish her for making me feel so conflicted.

"I think we were right here," I whisper before pressing my mouth to hers and running my hands over her curves. The intoxicating scent of lavender and vanilla wafts around me. I draw in a deep breath, inhaling her.

Gripping the top of her suit, I pull it down farther until it's nestled around her waist. Inching back, I peer down to steal a look at her perfect form.

Her hands travel down my body, unbuttoning my shirt one by one. She looks up at me, her eyes burning with desire.

Sliding my shirt down my arms, she pushes until it falls to the floor. Her hands press to my chest and she drags her fingers down, trailing them over the ridges of my abs. "Have I ever told you how sexy you are, Hayes?"

I'm not sure if the heat of the moment has her being so open, but I'll take it. "I don't think you have."

She smiles at me, running her fingers over her lips as she drinks me in. "Well, you are."

In an instant, she pushes her bathing suit all the way down then she steps out of it. I groan as I watch her intently, my dick a fucking boulder right now.

Gripping the hem of her fishnet stockings, she gives her hips a shake. Keeping her eyes deadlocked on mine, she sits down on the edge of her bed and slides out one leg at a time until she's completely naked.

There's not a doubt in mind she's the sexiest girl I've ever laid eyes on. Each curve, crevice, and blemish molds her to perfection. And her damn legs are some of the hottest I have ever seen in my life.

She stands up, closing the space between us. I run my hands down the smooth skin of her sides before cupping her firm ass and giving it a squeeze.

Nuzzling her face into my neck, she sucks and kisses, moving downward until she's kneeling in front of me.

I suck in a heady breath, watching as she unzips my pants and tugs them to my knees, along with my boxers. My cock springs free, nearly slapping her in the nose. "See what you do to me, Legs."

My hand reaches for her head, my fingers stroking through her hair as she stares at my cock.

She hums. "Is that for me?"

Goodman, I love this seductive side of her.

"All for you, baby." My voice is raspy and thick. It's taking everything in me not to grab her by the hips and bend her over this bed right now. Instead, I let her lead the way because she's doing a fan-fucking-tastic job.

With a tremble in her hand, she wraps her fingers around my girth, sliding them up and down in a slow motion. I thrust into her hold, seeking the pressure I so desperately crave.

"Wrap your lips around me, baby." I encourage her head forward. "See how good it tastes."

Darting her tongue out, she drags it gently around the curved barbell of my reverse Prince Albert piercing. I can tell by the way she's focusing on it, she fucking loves it. I bet she's dripping wet just thinking about how good it'll feel inside her.

Her mouth forms an O and she sucks in the shallow end. It's all I can do to stay standing upright as I watch her take me so well. When she drags her tongue under my sensitive shaft, a shiver runs through me.

"That's it, baby. You're doing so good."

Resting my hand on the back of her head, I encourage her to keep going, feeding her inch by inch until I feel the back of her throat. Stroking the base of my cock, she sucks on the first six inches, bobbing her head up and down.

Licking my lips, I have to focus on not blowing it right here because this girl has become my obsession and the way she sucks cock just made her the center of my damn universe.

I watch her every move, and when her eyes dart to mine, I think I actually grow another inch for her.

Her pace quickens and she strokes me faster, taking me so deep, I feel her gag around me. "Easy, Legs. It's a lot to handle."

I'm about two seconds from blowing, and that's just not happening. So, I gently pull her off, already missing the way her mouth feels. I need this to last, though, and if she keeps that up, I'm done.

"Your mouth is perfection, baby. But I want more."

Quizzical eyes stare up at me and I reach down for her hands, pulling her to her feet before walking her to the bed.

"Lie down for me, Legs."

Biting her bottom lip, she bats her lashes and does as she's told. Lying back, she props herself up on her arms.

Standing in front of her, my hand glides down her side and goosebumps erupt on her flesh. Tracing a path between her thighs, I gently part them. She watches me with rapt attention and for a moment, this doesn't feel like a game, it feels like two souls colliding.

My fingers brush over her perfect pussy, feeling the dampness of her impending arousal.

"Touch me, Hayes." Her voice is a soft mutter. She widens her legs and arches her back, desperate for more. My eyes stay glued to her entrance as I slowly slide two fingers into her dripping center, watching as they stretch her tight pussy.

"How's that feel?"

Her response is a subtle moan and I want more. I push deeper, feeling the tips of my fingers press against her back wall. She moans again, but it's not enough. Curling the tips, I add pressure against her G-spot and rub back and forth.

"Oh God," she cries out, giving me the reaction I was waiting for.

"Now I'm a god, baby?" My free hand reaches up to pluck at one of her nipples.

"Yes," she breathes. I never expected that answer from her, but the way she is soaking my hand, I would say that this night is off to a great start with the "make sure you're the best she ever has" mission.

The pad of my thumb presses against her clit, rubbing in vigorous circles. I watch as a shiver runs through her, and she lifts her hips off the bed. Her head falls back into the pillows and she moves with me, riding every stroke of my fingers as if I were her favorite toy.

When I feel a flood of her release, my eyes move back to her swollen cunt. So inviting and so delectable. I lean down and drag my tongue between her slick folds. She tastes like candy, which makes her my sweet Halloween treat tonight.

I have thought about the flavor of her since that very first night. I'm not always one to go down on a girl, but something about the challenge in her eyes made me need to prove myself to her. Now, I'm going to do it again, and this time, I'm going to keep her after.

"Hayes," she moans as her hands spread far and wide on either side of her. Gripping the sheets, the fabric crinkles between her fingers.

Digging deeper inside her, I pulsate the tips of my fingers against the spot that drives her wild while I suck her sensitive clit between my teeth, warranting a symphony of cries.

Her walls envelop my fingers and her thighs cage in my head as her body convulses with her orgasm. My cock is on fire right now, desperate to sink into her sopping cunt.

Once she settles slightly, I pull my fingers out, grab her by the hips, and roll her onto her stomach. I'm careful with my injured hand, but she is so small, it's easy to maneuver her into the perfect position. Giving myself a couple pumps with my cum-soaked hand, I slide the tip of my head into her drenched entrance.

"You ready for me, baby?"

She reaches above her head, grabbing onto the sheets as she

lowers her face onto the mattress. "I've been ready all night. Fuck me, Hayes. Show me what I've been missing."

Oh my God, she is going to be the death of me.

With a firm hold on her hips, I push in another inch, then another. A breathy groan rumbles out of her and I stop my movements until her ass rolls back, telling me she wants more. So I give her what she wants—inch by inch, until I'm fully seated inside her.

My hips thrust in a slow, rhythmic motion as I loosen her up enough to feel pleasure over pain. Having a huge cock is both a blessing and a curse. I got the piercing to give added pleasure for me when I need to take things slow. It moves every time their walls so much as think about contracting, and it feels like a caress deep inside me.

But I've heard for women it can feel like a guy has another inch or so on him that hits all the right spots, which is clearly what Brogan is feeling now. And the fact that I'm inside her without a barrier is on another level.

On our way over here I told her that if we did this, I wanted to go all in and see my cum dripping out of her in the end. She bit her lip and agreed, clearly turned on by the idea.

Bridging her back, she eventually gets into it and begins rolling her hips, twerking against my groin. If her movements against me weren't proof enough, the sounds of pleasure spilling from her lips solidifies that she loves my cock.

"You like that, baby?" I rasp as I drive myself in and out of her.

"Yes," she cries out.

Stretching my arm out, I tangle my fingers in her hair and tug back slightly. "What's that?"

"Yes," she whimpers again.

I fuck her harder and faster. "I want you to repeat what you did earlier tonight at the party. Now, let's try this again. Do you like that, *Legs*?"

"Yes, Daddy," she sings as she orgasms for the second time tonight. It's enough to send me over the edge. Every muscle in my body clenches, electricity jolting through my core as I release inside her.

My movements slow to a steady pulse as my cock twitches, giving her every last drop I have to offer. If she'd let me, I'd stay buried deep all damn night.

With one final thrust, I pull out slowly, watching our combined releases try to make a mess of her bed. But I don't let that happen. Instead, I catch it and push it back inside her with two fingers, making her gasp.

When I'm done, Brogan collapses onto her stomach, her breaths labored. Before I clean up, I lie down next to her, not willing to fuck up this time by forcing her away, or walking away myself.

I'm on my side when she turns to face me and I see that same look in her eyes that I saw after our first time together. It's like she's reaching for the real and raw parts of me I don't let anyone see. But this time, I want to show them to her.

Scooping her head in my hand, I push myself onto my elbow and raise her face to me. My lips hover over hers for a moment as I breathe in her shaky exhale. With my eyes wide open, I stare into hers, letting her read me and make of this what she will. Then, I kiss her softly. Our lips connecting as a new wave of emotions ripples through me, ones I hope she feels in the pit of her stomach the same way I do.

I pull back slightly, ready to break the moment so I can help her clean up, but she sits up farther and grabs my face in her hands, only to kiss me harder.

Time stands still for us. She gives in to me wholly, the same way I give in to her. When our lips part, I gaze into her eyes, feeling dizzy—like someone just fed me a love potion because my heart is hammering and I'm about two seconds from saying those three little words.

"That was amazing," she says breathlessly.

I drag my thumb across her wet lip and give her one last peck. "You were fucking incredible, Legs."

I don't want to move. I just want to sit here and stare at her for an eternity. I'm afraid once I walk out those doors, she may never look at me like this again.

"What now?" she asks as her fingers stroke the stubble on my cheek. I've never wanted much affection from girls—never liked it. With her, I find myself craving more.

"Now, we get you cleaned up. Get into some comfy clothes, and I kiss you good night."

I watch her throat as she swallows hard. "But...what if I don't want you to go?"

Taken by complete surprise, my eyes widen. "You want me to stay?"

"Maybe for just a little while." She shrugs. "We could watch *Hocus Pocus* again."

"We sort of have to," I tell her. "Because after tonight, Halloween is over and come tomorrow we'll be watching Christmas movies." I groan at the thought of skipping over Thanksgiving, but also love the idea of watching all of the Santa Claus movies with my person this year.

She laughs. "I like the way you think."

Once I'm dressed, I tell her to stay put while I go down the hall to the bathroom to get a warm wet washcloth. When I return, I have her lie down and I run the washcloth over her sticky thighs.

"When did you become such a Prince Charming, Hayes Madden?" I look up to find her peering at me with adoration in her gaze.

"I'm no Prince Charming, Legs. More of Romeo, if you ask me."

"I think I prefer Romeo anyways."

I finish cleaning her up and toss the damp washcloth in a dirty clothes basket in the corner of her room. Brogan puts on a pair of panties and a large white t-shirt while I get the movie going for us.

This time, I lie on the left side, so I can see her while we watch the TV. With my arm around her, she turns on her side, pressing her back against my chest. I hold her tightly, stealing glances at her face every couple minutes. And by the twentieth minute, she's out cold.

I'd love more than anything to stay here with her, but I don't want to rush things. In order for this to work, we need to go slow. She's fresh out of a toxic relationship and I don't want her to think I'm being pushy. Tonight, I'll take this win, and tomorrow, I'll work for more.

As I'm getting my shoes on, I hear a few gruntled sounds and when I look in Brogan's direction, I see her sitting up on the bed. "Where are you going? The movie is still on."

Walking back over to her, I lean down and press a kiss to the top of her head. "You're tired, Legs. Get some sleep and we'll talk tomorrow."

As if she has an epiphany, she suddenly springs from the bed and hurries to the other side of the room. "Fuck. I forgot about the video." She flips on the light and goes to where her phone is set up.

My chin drops to my chest and I shake my head. Of course that's what's on her mind. *The fucking video.* Just when I thought we were moving forward, she goes two steps back.

"I'm definitely going to have to edit it before we send it to Kamden," she says as she tries to get it off the tripod.

"Yeah. Whatever," I scoff. "I think I'm gonna take off. Let me know how the video turned out."

She's too distracted by the video to even hear me, so without another word, I slip out the door.

CHAPTER 24

BROGAN

I'VE REWATCHED the end of the recording three times already, and each time I feel something new.

The first half was hands down the sexiest thing I've ever watched and I've decided if Hayes and I fail at hockey and fashion design, we might have a future in the porn industry. We were *that* hot.

Then there was the very end. Too hung up on my act of revenge, I didn't notice Hayes's expression at the time. When I watch the video back, I see pain at the first mention of the video. I may be reading into this all wrong, but I don't think Hayes wants this shared. And now, after sitting on it for a few hours, I don't think I want to either. What we have is too special to share with anyone else, especially Kamden.

Last night was everything I ever wanted, and exactly what wasn't supposed to happen. Being with Hayes was phenomenal, to say the least. I can't even form a coherent thought of how amazing it truly was. I've never connected with someone like that before, and I don't just mean sexually.

This flawed guy wasn't supposed to turn out so perfect. Yet somewhere behind his rebel persona, I've found the man I always dreamed I'd find. Now I don't know what I'm supposed to do with all these feelings.

"So what now?" Avery asks from where she's lying beside me on my bed. For a moment, I forgot she was even here, and that I just spilled my guts to her. The good, the bad, and the ugly.

I stare blankly at the cracked paint on the ceiling, feeling fulfilled, but hollow. Is it even possible for those contradicting feelings to coexist?

"I can't do it," I spit out with force. A heavy weight lifts from my shoulders and I spring up, letting my blanket fall into my lap. "I can't do it," I repeat, my voice shaking. "I hope Hayes understands, but we can't send that video to Kamden. Fuck revenge, and fuck Kamden Donnelly. He's the past, and Hayes is my future."

Avery sets a calming hand on my back. "Looks like you've made your decision."

I turn to look at her, the smile on her face mirroring mine. I've always known she was Team Hayes. Somehow between the crazy meetups, the two of them formed a friendship that I sort of love.

"I don't know how I didn't see it sooner." I look at her with a pinched expression. "This was never about Kamden. It was always about Hayes. Subconsciously, I think I knew I had to hold on to him however I could and this was the only way I knew how."

"Or your subconscious just wanted to fuck him again." She raises her shoulders nonchalantly.

Clutching my hands over my chest, I fall onto my back in a hazy daze. "Oh, Avery. You have no idea how amazing he was. It felt like my body was singing his praises. I've never in my life experienced an orgasm like that."

My phone buzzes from my nightstand and Avery reaches over to grab it. She looks at the screen before shooting me a skeptical look. "No caller ID."

"Hmm." I sit up and take the phone from her, opting to answer it just in case it's a call from back home. "Hello."

"Don't hang up," are the first words Kamden says. "Please, just hear me out."

Sighing heavily, I turn my frustrated eyes to Avery. "What do you want, Kamden?"

"Oh, hell no," Avery gripes as she leans close to me so she can hear what he's saying.

"I need to talk to you. It's important."

My eyes roll. "Well, I haven't hung up yet, so let's hear it."

"In person. There's something you need to see. Can you meet me at Clara's in a half hour?"

Avery shakes her head and mouths the word "no."

"Let me guess, a summons to appear in court because you're suing me for slander?"

"No," he huffs. "I was never going to do that to you. I was just pissed."

"You were pissed?" I gnash. "How do you think I felt after you shared that video of us?"

"Damn it, Brogan." A bang sounds in the background like he just hit something. "I didn't share the video, but I know who did, and I can prove it."

There's a beat of silence as I look at Avery who I'm hoping gives me a hint at what I should do. She shrugs, not helping at all.

"So will you meet me?" he asks, tone low. "All I'm asking for is ten minutes then you never have to talk to me again, if that's what you decide."

"Ten minutes," I tell him. "And this better not be some sick joke." On that note, I end the call.

Avery gives me a pressed smile and another pat on the back. "Looks like you're going?"

I swing my legs over the bed and stand up. "Looks like I am."

By the time I get to Clara's, Kamden is already there. He's seated at a small round table outside, wearing a black down jacket and a pair of blue jeans. As soon as he spots me, a grin spreads across his face. Springing to his feet, he pulls out a chair for me. "Thanks for coming on such short notice"

I give him a sideways glance as I sit down, wearing my skepticism on my face. "It sounded important. What's up with you?"

He seems eager to get off whatever is on his chest, so he excitedly dives right in. "Remember how you blamed me for posting that video and called me out publicly?" I cross my arms over my chest because that isn't a moment in my life I'm ever going to forget.

My scowl deepens. "Of course I remember, Kamden."

"Well…" He folds his hands together on top of the table. "You need to take it down now more than ever."

"Unbelievable." I purse my lips as I slide my chair back, the legs scraping abrasively against the concrete patio. "I don't have time for this."

Panicked eyes meet mine, but he keeps his hands to himself, which is more than I can say for his friend last night. "You need to take it down because it's not true. I have proof." He mentioned that, but I halfway believed it was a ploy to get me here.

"Well, let's see it then," I say skeptically, still not certain he's telling the truth.

Kamden picks his phone up from the table and hands it to me. "Hit play."

It's a video that looks like it was taken in his and Jeremiah's dorm room. Reluctantly, I play it.

"So you're saying it wasn't Kamden, and you know that how?"

That's Jeremiah's voice.

"I already told you, Jer. It was me." *And that's Gabby laughing. She sounds drunk.* "We were trying to watch a movie and that psycho bitch Brogan kept texting him. I was so pissed that he was letting her take away from our time together. So when he fell asleep, I went through his messages to see what was so important. That's when I found and posted the video."

I slide the phone back to Kamden, not needing to hear or see anything more. I should be elated that it wasn't Kamden. I should be livid at Gabby. But truthfully, I'm not either of those things. And it comes down to the point of me not caring anymore. I don't care what Kamden did or didn't do. As for Gabby, she's the one who is a psycho bitch and eventually everyone around her will figure that out for themselves. I'm over it all. *Him. This. Us.*

Kamden picks up his phone and sticks it back in the pocket of his jacket. "I think that means you owe me an apology."

I reach into my pocket, scoffing as I pull out my middle finger and stick it right in front of his face. "Just because you didn't share it, doesn't mean you weren't part of it, Kamden. I already knew Gabby was a bitch who had it out for me. You said some pretty vile things to me and while yes, I am sorry I publicly outed you for something you didn't do, I'm not sorry for everything that happened after. If anyone should be apologizing, it's you."

His nice guy persona fades in a snap. "Take down the fucking video, Brogan. I'm not going to tell you again."

"I'll edit your name out of the video, but that's all you're getting from me. For all I know, you forced Gabby and Jeremiah to create that garbage, but guess what, I don't even care. One of you assholes shared it, and no matter who it was, you'll all still be assholes."

With my chair still back enough to give me space, I turn away. "I think we're done here."

As I move to leave, I crash right into another body. When I look up, I see that it's Hayes and he is fuming. His hand goes around my waist and he pulls me close to his side.

"What the fuck is this?" he sneers at Kamden.

Kamden's eyes travel to Hayes's tight fists. "Watch yourself, Madden. The last thing you need is another scolding from your coach."

Hayes jabs his finger in the air, jaw ticking as he grits out, "That was a dick move, tattling on me like a fucking pussy."

Kamden stands and I instinctively slide closer to Hayes.

"That's what you get for being a little bitch. Thank your lucky stars I didn't report you to someone higher up."

Hayes turns his attention to me, looking me up and down for any sign of injury. "Are you okay? He didn't hurt you, did he?"

Kamden scoffs as if that's the silliest thing anyone could venture to guess after being alone with him. "No, I didn't fucking hurt her. We just had a little chat."

Hayes tucks me back behind him when he sees I'm not injured, then turns to Kamden. "Did you call her here thinking she'd give you another chance?"

"Fuck off, Madden. If I wanted her, I could have her. I think I proved that the night we met when she left your room and ran into *my* arms."

What the hell did he just say? "I didn't run into your arms." I step out to glare at him. "You rammed into me, nearly knocking me down in the hall. But how did you know I had just left Hayes's room?" I look between the two of them as this horrible feeling starts to build inside me. "Were you watching me?"

He goes quiet, but his silence is telling, which only infuriates me further. "Oh my God," I spit. "You knew Hayes and I slept together that night, didn't you? You acted like you had no idea then you got pissed at me when I told you. But you knew the entire time?"

My mind is spinning while I piece all of this together. Then it hits me. "You didn't accidentally bump into me in the hall when I left his room. You pursued me just because you thought it might piss Hayes off, didn't you?"

His hands go up and there isn't a glint of remorse on his face. "It worked. At least for a while it did."

I was just a game to Kamden. This whole time I was just a pawn and I had no idea.

"You son of a bitch." Hayes lunges toward Kamden, but I

grab him by the hood of his sweatshirt and pull him back. He lets me, but I can practically feel the heat coming off of him.

Kamden curls his lip in a devious smirk. "I guess if I'm a son of a bitch, that makes you one, too."

Hayes takes a step closer, taunting Kamden, and I already know someone is going to get hit today. "Not if I wasn't raised by one, you piece of shit."

I look back and forth between the two of them as they spew venom at each other, trying to comprehend what all these jabs mean.

"That was your choice, not his." Kamden points a finger at Hayes, jabbing him in the chest.

"Ohhh," Hayes growls, pushing him back. "He had a fucking choice. That bastard chose to stay away."

Okay. Now this really doesn't make any sense to me. "What are you talking about, Hayes?"

Kamden snickers as Hayes takes a step closer to me, regret in his eyes. "I take it you haven't told her?"

"Don't," Hayes stammers as he shoots me a quick glance, trying to communicate with his eyes. But that's the thing about us, we only know how to communicate with backhanded comments.

"What?" Kamden says as he walks closer to us. "Are you too ashamed to tell your new girlfriend I'm your brother?"

"Wait, what?" I gasp, unsure if I heard him correctly. "Did you just say *brother*?"

"That's right." Kamden smirks. "Turns out, fucking whores runs in the family."

The next thing I know, Hayes's fist is flying through the air, and before I can do anything about it, it connects with Kamden's face and a crunch rings out around us.

I'm not even mad that I couldn't stop the hit. If Hayes didn't do it, I may have done it myself.

"What the fuck?" Kamden howls as he cups his bloody face in his hands. "I think you just broke my fucking nose!"

"Now who's being a little bitch?" I recant the words Kamden

said to Hayes only minutes ago. "Aren't you tired of your face looking like you had a bad meeting with a wall? You provoke Hayes so much, I'd think you like looking all black and blue."

Kamden scurries away to lick his wounds after murmuring something about reporting Hayes, and I turn to Hayes. My heart hurts when I see his injured hand wounded further. But that doesn't touch the pain I'm feeling after what I just heard.

"So that's it." I raise my shoulders. "I guess I was just a game, after all. I'm not sure who won, though. I guess you'll have to ask your *brother*."

I don't stay to watch his face or see any of the satisfaction he might have gained from this because I think it would actually break me. I was just a pawn in their scheme against each other.

With that, I leave in a hurry, unsure where to go from here.

CHAPTER 25

HAYES

"Fuck!" I slam my gloved fist into the wall. In a fury of anger and hurt, I spin around and swipe my hand out, knocking my backpack off the bench. I pull my gloves off and slam them to the floor.

"Easy, man," Finch says. "We don't need any broken bones right before the game."

"Why the hell did he come here?" I roar. "Why the hell does he *always* fucking come here?"

Finch jumps up, already on defense for me. "Who? Kamden? I'll beat his fucking ass right now."

With my hands pressed to the wall, I turn a look at him and crack a smile. Finch is the last person in the world who would ever initiate a fight. Not only is he a string bean, he's got the empathy of an elephant—and a heart the size of one, too.

"My dad," I spit out, immediately wondering why I even called him that. He's not a dad to me. He never even gave me the opportunity to give him that title.

"Holy shit. He's here?" His eyes widen and look around as if he is going to find him standing in the locker room with us.

I blow out a heavy breath and push myself off the wall.

"Yeah, he's here. He comes to every fucking game then leaves without saying a word to me."

"Maybe he's just proud of his son and wants to watch him play." Finch shrugs, as if it could be that simple.

I shake my head. "The man hasn't shown up to anything my entire life. Then all of a sudden I have an opportunity to do something big and he just appears. It doesn't make any sense."

Finch walks over to me, his brows pinching. "Have you thought about just asking him?"

"Oh yeah." My tone is laced with sarcasm. "Hey, old man. I haven't seen you since I bashed your and your son's heads together at my mom's funeral, but I was wondering if you could tell me why you come to all my games."

"Oh fuck," Finch slaps a hand to his mouth, sputtering a laugh. "You did that?"

"I did. Then, Kamden called the cops on me and I was taken out of the church in cuffs while they got cared for by the medics. Apparently our *dad* decided not to press charges, so I was let go almost immediately. I haven't talked to the old man since then."

"Damn, Hayes. I had no idea." I never talk about any of this stuff, but ever since Brogan walked away from me like I broke her heart, I can't seem to stop feeling these…*feelings*. It's awful. I was already on a hairpin but now it's like every little thing sets me off and all I want is her by my side to make things feel less volatile.

"No one did. Doesn't matter, though. Nothing I did, or didn't do, could bring her back, or change how everything went down."

Fuck. I don't even know why I'm opening up like this. I guess Brogan really has changed me.

"Have you ever thought about just talking to him?" Finch says hesitantly. "I mean, it could be good for you to tell him how you feel. You don't have to do it looking for a response. Just get this off your chest, man."

"I don't know." I shrug lazily before raising my voice to a

more buoyant note. "What I do know is we need to get out there and win this fucking game."

"Hell to the yeah," Finch roars as he pats his hand on my shoulder and leads me back to the ice.

The first period rolled through without fail. We fucking dominated the ice. After snagging a saucer pass from Finch, I glided past our opponents' defenseman and scored the first goal of the night.

I've had a few hiccups because my mind was elsewhere and my hand still hurts like a bitch. All I can fucking think about is how badly I miss Brogan. It's been over a week since we've talked and she won't answer any of my calls. I doubt she made it out tonight, but I imagined she was here and I played hard just for her.

As we headed into the second period, we were leading the Norsemen 2–1. It wasn't until the third period that we got a little too cocky and they tied the game, but my winning goal at the end sealed our success.

They played hard, but we played harder and we claimed victory, once again.

Walking out of the locker room with my backpack flung over my shoulder, I lift my eyes to find Christian Donnelly, aka my dad, gaping at the glass case of trophies the Devils won over the years. He's wearing a black business suit and shiny black shoes that probably cost more than my bike.

Letting my backpack slide off my shoulder, it falls to my feet. I leave it there as I walk toward the old man with heavy steps. "Take note of the national championship trophy from last year, I won that one for the team. How many of those has Kamden won?" I rub it in just a little, hoping regret stews inside him.

He spins around and we come face to face for the first time in four years. He's grayer than the last time I saw him. And when he smiles, the deep creases in the corners of his eyes show his age.

"Hayes," he beams. I hate the way he says my name, as if he has the right to use it. My mom gave me this name. The woman whose addiction he enabled. The addiction he can no longer feed, because she's dead.

"That was a great game tonight, son."

"Don't call me that," I grit out. "I'm not your son."

His expression drops and he tilts his head slightly. "Look, Hayes," he begins, and I'm tempted to rip his fucking tongue out if he says my name one more time. "I know our relationship has been rocky—"

I hold a hand up. "Stop right there. We don't have a relationship. Never have, and never will. In case you've forgotten, you ran out on us, forgoing that opportunity."

"I'd love more than anything to change that, if it's not too late. There is just so much you don't understand, Hayes." He looks at me with pity and it only makes my anger with him triple.

"God damn, stop saying my name!" I raise my voice as people come and go around us, but I don't give a damn. "Stop fucking talking!"

He falls silent, appearing stunned by my outburst. I take a second to calm myself down. With a low but stern voice, I say, "I spent my childhood unsure if my dad was dead or not. I hoped and prayed he was alive and that one day he'd show up and save my mom from the life of addiction—saving me in the process. Then, I saw you one day. You were giving my mom a handful of cash, and without a word to me, you left."

I try not to think about the pain it caused when I found out who he was and how little I meant to him at that moment.

"A few minutes later, she ran out to do some errands and when she returned, she was high as a fucking kite. The next month, the same thing. Over and fucking over until I finally asked her who you were and she told me the truth. That you were my dad. But you didn't come to rescue us…"

His brows are pinched, his head tilted to the side like he's confused. "But I did, Hayes."

"Shut the fuck up," I shout. "You didn't come to rescue us.

You came out of pity and gave my mom what she wanted, but didn't need. You paid for the habit that killed her."

"I paid child support, dammit!" His voice rises, surprising me so much I take a step back. "I didn't even know you existed until days before I showed up the first time. I came for you, Hayes. I wanted to know you, I wanted your brother to know you. But she wouldn't allow it."

No. He's lying. My mom told me he ran out on us when I was an infant. She said he didn't want the responsibility of a child. *He's lying.*

"The first day of every month I came back, asking to see my son, but each time she told me no. She was afraid I might take you away from her. And I didn't know until the end that your mom needed help. If I had, I would have helped her. I did what I could—what she would allow—and I'm sorry it wasn't enough."

I shake my head, not willing to believe anything he says. "You're lying."

He puts his hands in his pockets with a sigh. "Ask your aunt Kelly. She'll tell you everything I'm saying is the truth."

"I can't deal with this right now," I mutter as I spin around and head back to where my backpack is lying on the floor.

"Kamden wanted to press charges for his broken nose, but I was able to convince him not to."

I don't turn around as I say, "You expect me to thank you for that?"

"Not at all. I just wanted you to know."

Bending down, I snatch my backpack off the floor. "And now I know."

I'm walking away when his voice travels behind me. "When I first learned I had another son, I wanted more than anything to raise my boys together so they could grow up close, like I did with my brother—your uncle."

Shaking my head, I keep my gaze forward and away from him. "Never gonna happen, old man."

I keep walking, and he keeps talking.

"I've come to realize that may never happen with you and Kamden, and I can accept that. But I was hoping you and I—"

"Also not gonna happen." I turn around, cutting him off before he wastes his breath as I pin him with a glare. He nods, sorrow falling over his face, but I don't care. It's nothing compared to the hurt I felt every month he came to see my mom and made everything worse for us both. I spin away again, but before I can walk out, he's talking.

"Think about it. And talk to your aunt Kelly." His voice grows distant as I approach the door, but I can still hear him. "I'm at every home game if you ever want to talk."

I push open the doors and step out, leaving him somewhere behind me where he belongs.

I've gotta go get my girl back.

CHAPTER 26

BROGAN

"I miss him so much, Elodie." I swipe away the tears blurring my vision as I look at my sister on the screen of my phone.

"Then tell him, honey. Tell him how you feel. The good, the bad, and the ugly."

"I just don't know how I can ever get past him keeping that from me. He had countless opportunities to tell me. And while he didn't exactly betray me personally, he left me wondering what else I should know but don't."

I know he may not have been ready to talk about it, but it makes me feel dirty. Like I was just someone to use between the two of them.

"I've never seen you like this over a guy, Brogan. Which leads me to believe he isn't just *some* guy."

"He's not," I tell her truthfully, looking down into my lap. "He's so different from any other guys I've met."

"Babe," she says sternly, making my eyes find hers. "Then what the hell are you talking to me for? Go get him."

She's right. "You're right." For the first time in over a week, a smile grows on my face. "I'm gonna go get my man." I blow her a kiss then end the call.

I spring to my feet and shuffle around my room until I find

my slipper shoes. Not caring that I'm wearing a pair of sweatpants and a sweatshirt with no bra, I slide them on. Excitement ripples through me. I'm not sure why I waited so long to go to him—everyone close to me would say it's my stubbornness—but I'm going to him now.

I'm really doing this.

Just as I pull open my door to leave, I remember Hayes has a game tonight. It might be over, but there's a good chance he's at Legends. I could call him, or text him, but I need to do this in person.

Dammit.

I go to push the door closed, but it stops just shy of latching. In a swift motion, I rip it open and there he is.

"Hayes." Tears spring to my eyes. "You're here?"

"In the flesh." His thumb swipes under my eye, wiping away the dampness. "I've missed you, Legs."

"I've missed you, too." A surge of warmth rushes through me as I fall into him. My heart swells as he wraps his forgiving arms around me. "I'm so sorry I ignored you." I take a step back so I can see his gorgeous face. "I wasn't being fair and I know that now."

Hayes puts an arm around me, resting his hand on the small of my back as he leads me back into my room. "You don't have anything to apologize for. I'm the one who's sorry." He closes the door behind us. "I should have told you Kamden is my brother. My hatred toward him got the best of me and I guess I didn't want anyone to know I could be related to such a heartless prick. Let alone be the son of one."

I shake my head because I already understand that part. "What hurt me the most is that you didn't trust me enough to tell me in the first place. But now I know—it wasn't about me. It was about you. I don't care that Kamden is your brother—or who your father is." I grab his hand and stroke it gently.

"Of course you don't. You're the most understanding person I've ever met, Legs." His lips twitch with a smile. He knows damn well I'm the least understanding person he's ever met. I'm not even a little bit surprised that he's cracking a joke to lighten the mood right now. It's what he does.

I swat him playfully. "You're such a pain in the ass, Hayes."

His brow arches. "Wow. Thanks. I think."

I pace in front of him, saying everything I should have said a long time ago. "You really are, though. You say all the wrong things at all the wrong times. You put words in my mouth and you overanalyze *every. Single. Thing. I. Say.* You're crazy, and you make me crazy." My feet stop moving and I look at him watching my insanity unfold. "I mean, listen to me, I don't even know what I'm saying."

"You were in the middle of giving me an array of compliments." Stepping up to me, he puts his hands on my waist. "Just say what you're trying to say, Legs."

"Ugh," I grumble, knowing I'm screwing this up and nothing I want to say is coming out right. "I guess what I'm trying to say is, you keep me on my toes. You put me in my place and I need that. I don't think a day has gone by since you came back into my life that you haven't surprised me. The bad boy facade you put on for everyone else is lost when you're with me. You're sweet and considerate and not the arrogant asshole I thought you were."

"Stop." His hand sweeps through the air. "Now you're just making me blush."

"I'm serious, Hayes." I stand in front of him, mere inches from his face. "You're my balance and I don't want to ever be without you again." I gulp. "Now that I've gotten all that off my chest, is there anything you want to say?"

"I have a lot to say." He jerks my body flush with his. Our noses brush, and he whispers, "I don't like many people, Legs. But I'm sort of crazy about you."

I thought I needed to hear that I wasn't a game to him, but I think deep down I already knew. I know Hayes, and I think he might know me pretty well too. "You are?"

"So fucking crazy about you," he sings. "In fact, I think it's safe to say, I've fallen head over heels in love with you."

My heart expands inside my chest, filling me with a feeling of contentment. "I love you, too, Hayes." No truer words have been said. *I love him.*

The warmth of his breath hits my skin as he softly presses his lips against mine. A spark of electricity shoots through my body, making my heart race as I melt into him.

Nothing else matters. And the last week without him is a distant memory.

For the first time, it feels like all the pieces of my life have fallen into place and I know without a doubt that Hayes is my person.

When the kiss ends, Hayes's lips ghost my ear, and he whispers, "Do you still have that video?"

"Sure do." I nod with a grin.

"What do you say we delete it and create something even hotter?"

"Mmm," I hum. "I like the way you think."

EPILOGUE

BROGAN

"ALL RIGHT, BROGAN," Mrs. Daniels, my academic advisor, says as her long, manicured nails tap on her keyboard. "You are officially on track for a degree in fashion design. Congratulations."

A wave of relief washes over me, mixed with nervous excitement. "Thank you so much, Mrs. Daniels."

I walk out of her office feeling like I'm on top of the world.

Not only did I just take control of my future, I get to watch my man do his thing tonight on the ice.

It's still three hours before game time, but I know Hayes just got there to warm up, so I decide to go to the arena and wish him luck before the game.

A quick fifteen-minute bus ride later, and I'm texting him to let him know I'm walking through the doors.

> Hayes: Meet me in the food court.

Bypassing the ticket counters, I enter the food court in search of him. Suddenly, two hands grasp my hips from behind, telling me he found me first.

I spin around and crush my chest against his as my arms wrap around his neck. I'm surprised to find he's still in a pair of gym shorts and a t-shirt. I thought for sure he'd be all geared up by now.

"Hey, beautiful." He peers down at me. "You ready to watch us win?"

"Sure am." I waggle my brows before pressing my lips to his. "There's a little good luck kiss to seal the deal."

A groan climbs up his throat as he squeezes my ass. "Damn, Legs. Your mouth makes me hard. How about you give me something else for luck tonight."

"What exactly did you have in mind?" I bite my lip and he looks like he might lose control right here. *I love it.*

Without another word, he grabs my hand and walks steadfastly through the food court, bringing me with him. "Come with me."

"As if I have a choice," I tease.

It feels like we've walked a mile when Hayes comes to a sudden stop in front of a closed door. Glancing left, then right, he reaches back, turns the handle, and pushes the door open.

One long stride backward, and he pulls me into the room with him, closing the door immediately. "Where are we?" I giggle as I look around the dark room. The only light is a sliver of reflected fluorescents coming from under the crack of the door.

In the blink of an eye, the room is illuminated, and I see a string dangling from a light bulb above us. I look around to see that we're in some sort of storage closet. It's fairly empty, aside from a mop sitting in a dry yellow bucket, and a few random things on the shelves.

"Hayes!" I gasp. "You can't seriously expect us to get it on in here. What if someone comes in?"

He wastes no time pushing down his gym shorts and boxers. "Still too good to use the word fuck, Brogan?"

I glare at him and he laughs. "No one ever comes to this end of the arena. We're good."

That's all I needed to hear to kick out of my shoes. I'm not sure where they go, but I'll figure that out later.

Hayes grips me by the hips, spinning me around until I'm facing the shelf. His hands fumble with the waistband of my leggings and panties, and in a swift motion, he tugs them down. I step one foot out, leaving the other side bunched around my ankle.

He leans into me, his chest cloaking my back. The heat of him feels so good, and I push my ass into him. I've been wet since his hands grabbed me and I can't wait to feel his fingers opening me up for him.

The way he rubs them inside of me is addicting, as evidenced by the way I went along with this insane idea so easily.

"You want me, baby?" he asks gently, two fingers toying around my pussy as he finds me wet and waiting.

"You can feel how much I want you," I say, rocking my hips into him. Two fingers press inside my cunt and he swirls them around, making my head lean back.

"I'm gonna fuck you hard and fast, Legs. You ready for me?"

"Yes." I exhale a heady breath while tingles of desire shoot through me. "Just fuck me, Hayes."

Pulling his fingers out, he immediately fills me back up with his big cock. I gasp on impact as I lunge forward. Reaching out, I grasp one of the shelves, my nails engraving the wooden surface.

The scent of lemon floods my senses, a reminder of how spontaneous Hayes and I are, and I love every fucking second of it.

His cock glides in and out of me with intensity, the shelves threatening to give way under my hold. He wasn't lying when he said he was going to fuck me hard and fast.

Hayes moves his hips in a powerful rhythm, driving his length in and out of me while he grips my waist tightly. Every time his piercing slides out then goes back in, I think my eyes actually cross. I get lost in the sensation. Our heavy breathing tangles together while my back arches and I step my foot out, spreading wider for him.

Each thrust sends a wave of pleasure through my core, and

even in a public place, I can't control the moans that slip through my lips.

"Fuck, baby," He gasps and grunts as he slams into me, making sure I feel every single inch of him. His fingers tighten, no doubt leaving marks I will get to appreciate later. I love it when he loses control with me like this, as if I'm the only thing that matters.

It's an intoxicating feeling to have a strong, powerful man at your mercy. Which is why I want to test something. "Stop," I say, and he instantly does. I let him slip free from me as I turn around. His eyes track me carefully, but I grin. "I want to see your face when I come on your cock."

He groans, stepping forward to lift me in his arms. My legs go around him as he turns and places my back against the wall without shelves. Looking into his mystical eyes that held me in a trance the first time we met, that's what always feels right with him.

I claim his lips as he slides back into me and even though he is going fast, I can feel him savoring the moment with me. My nails find his back and I scratch him just the way he likes, marking him so that everyone in the locker room will see that Hayes Madden has a girl and she marks her territory.

He moans, moving one hand between us to rub circles on my clit. I cry out into his mouth and he swallows it down like he's greedy for every little sound.

Pressure builds inside me with an insatiable need to release. Every muscle tightens and I hold my breath as a wave of heat rushes through me. "Ahhh," I cry out. "Oh God, Hayes."

"That's right." He leans back to stare into my eyes. "Come around my cock, baby."

I do. My hips roll into him as I ride each wave. But he isn't done yet. He pinches my clit and I whimper while he thrusts frantically against me, pinching harder and harder, until...*oh, God*, I'm coming again.

I feel his head swell, his piercing pulsing against my G-spot as he pants heavily. He stills for a moment before giving one final thrust.

"Holy shit, Legs." He exhales heavily, giving me a long kiss while our sweaty heads press together. "We need to come to this closet before every game."

"I'm not opposed to that idea. Being sneaky is pretty hot." I straighten my back and he pulls out of me to set me down, our mixed arousals now dripping down my legs.

Hayes fidgets with his shorts on the floor before standing with his boxers in his hands. He runs them up and down my legs, cleaning me up. "I've got an extra pair in my locker."

"Thanks, baby." He does this every time we have sex and it makes my heart melt. Using his boxers is new, but our resources are limited right now.

Once we're decent, Hayes opens the door and pops his head out before gesturing for me to follow.

After a kiss goodbye, he heads to the locker room to gear up.

I'm waiting outside of the locker room for Hayes, texting my mom to tell her the Devils won tonight, when a soft hand lands on my waist. Warm fingers sweep my hair to one side and his hot breath fans the back of my neck, bringing a smile to my face. "Are you ready to admit it, Legs?"

I tuck my phone into the pocket of my hoodie, grinning. "Admit what, exactly?"

He walks around me, dragging his hand against my hip and sending shivers down my spine. "That hockey is more thrilling than football."

"This again?" I sigh. "Get off it already, babe."

"Come on. Just say it. You know it's the truth."

He's not lying. I love watching a good football game, but there's something so exhilarating about hockey, especially when Hayes is playing.

"Come on," he teases, tickling my side.

"Fine," I mumble, keeping my voice low so no one but Hayes hears my confession. "Hockey is more thrilling than football."

His fists fly in the air. "Hell yes it is."

I grab his arm, lowering it to his side, and he brings down the other. "Let's forget I ever said that and go. Thanksgiving break has officially started and I'm ready to get the hell out of here and spend some time with my man." I stretch my neck to meet his lips, giving him a soft peck as we walk out of the arena.

Shifting to a serious note, I tug his hand as we cross the parking lot to the bus stop. "Did you talk to your aunt Kelly?" I ask, hoping he did. He's been mentioning for days how he wants to ask her about his dad, but he hasn't done it yet.

He swallows and nods. "Talked to her this morning."

"That's great, Hayes. And what did she say?"

He lets out a breathy sigh. "He was telling the truth."

"Wow," I drawl, pleasantly surprised, but also a little worried that this has conflicted Hayes's feelings. He already knows I support whatever he does and I've told him he doesn't need to rush his decision, but I know this has been heavy on his mind. "What do you plan to do?"

"I dunno." He shrugs. "Maybe it's time to move on—time to let go. I'm not saying we'll ever be father and son, but there's no harm in starting small, right?"

I smile, so proud of him for this. Letting go of a grudge is not something to be taken lightly with Hayes, I should know. "Definitely not. Baby steps are still progress, and I'll be right beside you as you take them."

"I know you will." He flashes me a wink. "Fuck ever having a relationship with Kamden, though. He's said and done things that are unforgivable and I won't allow a shitty-ass person like that into my life or yours. But do I dare let in the man who raised him?"

"I can't answer that for you, baby." I squeeze his hand. "You have to do what feels right. I think it's fair to say that just because Kamden is an asshole, that doesn't mean his father is.

We all make our own choices and I think Kamden is the kind of guy who has made some shitty ones all on his own."

He nods in agreement and throws an arm across my shoulders. "He invited Aunt Kelly over for Thanksgiving dinner," he says with cautiousness in his tone. "And he asked her to extend the invitation to us."

My eyes widen. That was pretty bold of his dad to think Hayes is just going to jump right in and go to his house for dinner.

"And what did you tell her?"

"Fuck no." He squeezes me tight to him. "I'm not going anywhere near Kamden. I don't even wanna see him, let alone sit across from him at a dinner table."

I'm not surprised at his response. And I don't blame him one bit.

"But I haven't closed the door completely. He came to the game tonight and I waved. I know it's not much, but it felt like a start."

I grin, knowing that's more than a start. He agreed to let his dad in and that's a big deal. "That's huge, Hayes. Not long ago you were plotting his and Kamden's demise."

"Sometimes I still do." He grins. "Well, Kamden's demise anyways."

We reach the bus stop and stand under the flickering lamppost. I push myself up on my tiptoes and press my lips to his. "Well, I'm proud of you. Not for the murder plot, but for following your heart and taking the steps to heal."

His arms wrap around my waist and he pulls me close. "I couldn't have done it without you."

"Now just promise me you won't murder Kamden without me."

He laughs. "I don't ever want to do anything without you, Legs. Whether it's plotting someone's demise, making sex videos, decorating your dorm for Halloween, or bribing security to let us ice skate after hours."

"Good," I tell him as I peer up into the kaleidoscope that

holds my future. "I don't want to do those things with anyone else either. I especially loved when we put up the Christmas tree a week before Thanksgiving while singing Mariah Cary together."

The glare he gives me is icier than the rink he just skated on. "Yeah. Highlight of my year," he deadpans, and I can't help the laughter that bubbles out of me. Hayes was a grump that day, a real grinch, but I eventually got him with hot cocoa and a Santa Claus movie.

"Ya know," he begins, and I listen intently. "I always thought hockey was my ultimate adrenaline rush. Then I met you and I experienced the ultimate high. Even if you don't see me and I just see you, knowing you're there makes me feel like I can conquer the world."

"I feel the same way, baby." I kiss him again. "I love you so much, Hayes."

"I love you, too, Legs."

The End.

**Thank you so much for reading Beautiful Devil.
I hope you enjoyed Hayes and Brogan's love story. You can catch up now with the Astor girls in Brogan's sister, Elodie's, book, Heartless Monster!**

ALSO BY RACHEL LEIGH

Bastards of Boulder Cove

Book One: <u>Savage Games</u>

Book Two: <u>Vicious Lies</u>

Book Three: <u>Twisted Secrets</u>

Wicked Boys of BCU

Book One: <u>We Will Reign</u>

Book Two: <u>You Will Bow</u>

Book Three: <u>They Will Fall</u>

Misfits

Heartless Monster

Wicked Scandal

Beautiful Devil

Redwood Rebels Series

Book One: <u>Striker</u>

Book Two: <u>Heathen</u>

Book Three: <u>Vandal</u>

Book Four: <u>Reaper</u>

Redwood High Series

Book One: <u>Like Gravity</u>

Book Two: <u>Like You</u>

Book Three: <u>Like Hate</u>

Fallen Kingdom Duet

<u>His Hollow Heart</u> & <u>Her Broken Pieces</u>

Black Heart Duet

<u>Four</u> & <u>Five</u>

Standalones

Forget Me Not

Ruthless Rookie

Devil Heir

All The Little Things

Claim your FREE copy of Her Undoing!

ACKNOWLEDGMENTS

Thank you so much for reading Beautiful Devil I hope you enjoyed it!

A special thanks to my wonderful team for all the hard work you put into helping me create this book: My dedicated PA, Carolina Leon. Drita, my amazing ARC team manager. All my girls for your support, friendship, and advice. My Street Team, the Rebel Readers for your help in getting the word out.

A an extra special thanks to…

My amazing alpha reader, and friend, Taylor. I couldn't do this without you!

Lori Jackson for the stunning cover!

Fairest Reviews Editing Service for the beautiful edit!

Rumi Khan for proofreading and being so flexible!.

Valentine PR for spectacular PR Services.

XOXO Rachel

ABOUT THE AUTHOR

Rachel Leigh is a USA Today and International bestselling author of new adult and contemporary romances. She loves to write—and read—flawed bad-boys and strong heroines. You can expect dark elements, a dash of suspense, and a lot of steam.

Her goal is to take readers on an adventure with her words, while showing them that even on the darkest days, love conquers all.

Rachel lives in Michigan with her husband, three little monsters (who aren't so little anymore) and a couple of fur babies. When she's not writing or reading, she's likely lounging in leggings, with coffee in her hand, while binge watching her favorite reality tv shows.

Join My Reader's Group: Rachel's Ramblers

facebook.com/rachelleighauthor

instagram.com/rachelleighauthor

bookbub.com/profile/rachel-leigh

goodreads.com/rachelleigh

amazon.com/author/rachelleighauthor

pinterest.com/rachelleighauthor